D0408149

Sail

A complete list of James Patterson's books is on pages 393–394. For more information about James Patterson and his books, visit www.JamesPatterson.com.

Sail

A NOVEL BY

James Patterson

AND

Howard Roughan

Doubleday Large Print
Home Library Edition

LITTLE, BROWN AND COMPANY
NEW YORK BOSTON LONDON

This Large Print Edition, prepared especially for Doubleday Large Print Home Library, contains the complete, unabridged text of the original Publisher's Edition.

Little, Brown and Company
Hachette Book Group USA
237 Park Avenue, New York, NY 10017

Little, Brown and Company is a division of Hachette Book Group USA, Inc. The Little, Brown logo is a trademark of Hachette Book Group USA, Inc.

ISBN-13: 978-0-7394-9215-4

Printed in the United States of America

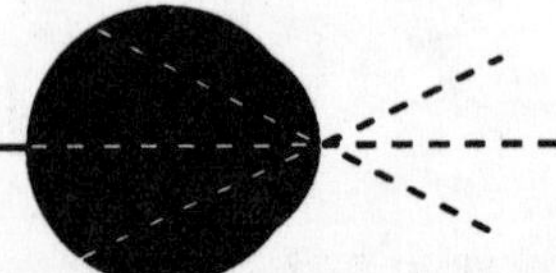

This Large Print Book carries the Seal of Approval of N.A.V.H.

For my sister, Shari—H.R.

For my sisters, Carole, Maryellen, and Terry—J.P.

Sail

The Crew

DR. KATHERINE DUNNE, forty-five, is a heart surgeon at Lexington Hospital in Manhattan. Four years ago she lost her husband, Stuart, in a scuba diving accident off their boat, *The Family Dunne*. As it turned out, Stuart was having an affair, and his mistress was there when he died. From that day on, Katherine's relationship with her three children has never been the same. Things have only gotten worse since she remarried, bringing the lawyer Peter Carlyle into the family. But Peter is bright, funny, and compassionate, and he won Katherine's heart.

CARRIE DUNNE, eighteen, is a freshman at Yale. That's the good news. The bad news is that Carrie is bulimic and has suffered from bouts of depression. She has always accused Katherine of being more devoted to being a doctor than to her kids. Carrie's best friend from New York recently told Katherine she was afraid that Carrie was capable of hurting herself.

MARK DUNNE, sixteen, is a sophomore at Deerfield Academy, where he's well liked but also the resident stoner. Zero ambition, zero enthusiasm. "Why should I bust my ass like Dad when at any moment, *poof!*—the Grim Reaper comes and takes it all away from you."

ERNIE DUNNE is ten—at least, that's what his birth certificate says. But in this family, where it's seemingly every Dunne for himself, he has grown up fast. And bewildered. "Mom, are you sure I'm not adopted?" Ernie asks Katherine at least once a day.

JAKE DUNNE, forty-four, is Katherine's former brother-in-law. A true nautical nomad, he dropped out of Dartmouth to sail the world. It was a path far different from that of his older brother, Stuart, who stayed ashore to chase, and catch, millions on Wall Street. But as different as the two brothers always were, Jake and Stuart Dunne did have one thing in common: they were both in love with Katherine.

Prologue

FAMILY DUNNE ALIVE

One

EASING THROUGH the marina's sapphire-blue water at a leisurely three-knot clip, Captain Stephen Preston took a long pull off his Marlboro Red, casually flicking the ash into the cool island breeze. Then, after waiting for just the perfect moment, he punched the horn of his forty-six-foot Bertram Sport Fisherman until everyone on the dock stopped to look.

Yeah, that's right, boys and girls, take a gander at what Captain Steve reeled in!

It was a quarter past eleven in the morning. His charter, the *Bahama Mama,* wasn't due back to shore until that afternoon at two, the same time as always.

But today was different.

Fuckin' A it's different, thought Captain Steve, hitting the horn another time. When you spear the biggest, baddest giant bluefin tuna ever seen around the Bahama Islands, you're done fishing for the day. Hell, you might as well be done fishing for the year!

"What do you think she's worth?" asked Jeffrey, the *Mama*'s first mate and Steve's brother. He'd been with the boat for eleven years. Never took a sick day. And rarely ever smiled, before that morning anyway.

"I dunno," replied Captain Steve, pulling on the rim of a Boston Red Sox cap. "I'd guess she's worth somewhere between a boatload of money and a *shit*load."

Jeffrey continued to smile widely beneath the brim of the tattered green visor he always wore. He knew a tuna this size could fetch upwards of $20,000, cash money, maybe even more if the sushi bidders at the Tsukiji fish market in Tokyo liked what they saw. And why wouldn't they?

Whatever the amount, he was in line to

get a very healthy cut. The captain was good that way, a fair man in every sense.

"Are you sure those bozos signed the contract, Jeff?" Captain Steve asked.

Jeffrey glanced toward the stern at the six-man bachelor party from the island of Manhattan. They'd been drinking since sunrise, when the trip began, and were already so stinking drunk they could barely high-five each other without falling overboard.

"Yeah, they signed the contract, all right," said Jeffrey with a slow nod. "Though I doubt they ever read the fine print."

If they had read the contract carefully, they'd have known that no binge-drinking, sunburned tourists would ever pocket a dime off a giant bluefin tuna. No way, not on the *Bahama Mama*. One hundred percent of the proceeds went directly to the captain and the crew. Period, end of Big Fish story.

"Well, then," said Captain Steve, cutting the boat's twin engines as they approached the dock, "let's go cause a scene."

Two

SURE ENOUGH, even in the ultra-laid-back Bahamas it took less than a New York minute for a large and curious throng to gather around the fishing boat, the buzz swelling as a forklift carried the humongous tuna toward the marina's official scale. *Christ, was that scale even big enough?*

Captain Preston beamed, giving a hearty slap to the back of the groom-to-be and announcing that he'd never met a finer bunch of anglers in all his life. "You guys are the best," he said. "And you proved it today."

"Rather be good than lucky!" one guy shouted back.

Of course, the truth would stay strictly between him and Jeff. These big-city misfits had no clue what they were doing. They couldn't catch a cold, let alone a fish.

Yet here they all were, basking in the relentless *click, click, click* of digital cameras—the crowd, the excitement, the anticipation of the weigh-in growing bigger by the second.

"Tie her up good!" urged Captain Steve as the tail of the tuna was wrapped with double-braided rope, the strongest on hand.

On the count of three, she was hoisted high into the air. The crowd oohed and aahed appreciatively. This was some fish.

Six hundred . . . seven hundred . . . eight hundred pounds!

The arm of the scale shot up like a rocket. When it finally settled at a record-busting 912 pounds, the entire marina let out a tremendous roar, the bachelor-party guys loudest of all.

And that's when it happened.

Plunk!

Something very strange fell out of the tuna's mouth.

Three

THE MYSTERIOUS STOWAWAY landed on the dock and rolled right up to Captain Stephen Preston's knee-high black rubber boots.

"What the hell is that?" someone asked from the back. "Let us in on the joke."

But everyone else could see plain as day what it was. A Coke bottle. The old-fashioned kind, real glass.

"That's some funny-lookin' bait you used, Steve," joked a captain from another boat.

The crowd laughed as Steve bent and scooped up the bottle. He held it up to the bright morning sun and immediately scratched his head of curly blond hair. There was something inside. *What the hell was it?*

Quickly he removed the makeshift seal of a small plastic bag held tight by a knot made of vines. This was getting stranger by the minute. With two shakes he was able to reach the edge of the contents with his pinkie.

He pulled it out.

It wasn't paper—more like some kind of fabric. And there was writing on it.

"What's it say?" asked Jeffrey.

The entire dock was silent as Steve Preston read the note to himself. The words were written in a deep crimson color, smudged but still legible. *Could that be blood?* he was wondering now. *And whose blood is it?*

"C'mon, what's it say?" asked Jeffrey again. "You're killin' us with suspense."

Captain Steve slowly turned the note so that those around him could see for themselves. The collective gasp that followed was instantaneous.

"That family—they're alive!" he managed. "The Dunne family."

In a flash, a vacationing reporter from the *Washington Post* reached for his cell phone to call his newsroom. He was back on the job.

Meanwhile, Captain Stephen Preston just stood before the crowd and smiled. All he could think about was how the note in the bottle ended, the part about the reward.

The dollar sign.

The number one.

And all those amazingly beautiful zeroes after it.

"Jeff," he said slowly, "this tuna's worth a hell of a lot more than we thought."

Part One

THE FAMILY (UN) DUNNE

Chapter 1

"I'M CRAZY, right? I mean, I have to be absolutely, certifiably mad to take this trip! This sailboat extravaganza with my family! And Jake!"

I've had this same thought for weeks, but today is the first time I'm saying it out loud. *Screaming* it, actually, at the top of my lungs. Thankfully, Mona's Upper West Side office used to be a recording studio for a talk-show host. The walls are sound-proof, or so Mona tells me.

The way I'm acting, they should also be padded.

"No, you're not crazy," says Mona, being

her usual calm self. "On the other hand, are you biting off more than you can chew? Perhaps?"

"But don't I always?"

"Yes," she says, "for as long as I've known you, anyway. *Don't* say the number."

Twenty-seven years, to be exact—ever since Mona and I met during our freshman orientation at Yale and discovered we were both closet *General Hospital* fans and harbored ridiculous crushes on Blackie, the character played by a very young—and incredibly cute—John Stamos.

Wow, did I just date myself, or what?

Anyway, for the past two months Mona has been more than my best friend and the sister I never had. She's also been Dr. Mona Elien, my psychiatrist.

Yes. I know. On paper, that arrangement might not be a good idea. But who lives on paper?

Not me.

I live on caffeine, adrenaline, and relentless sixteen-hour shifts at Lexington Hospital, where I'm a heart surgeon. I just didn't have the time or patience for the get-to-know-you phase of therapy. Besides, there's no one's opinion I trust more than Mona's. There's no one I trust more, period.

"It's not that I'm weighing in against the sailboat trip, Katherine. In fact, I think it's a great idea," she says. "My only concern is how much hope you're pinning on it, the pressure you seem to be putting on yourself and the kids. What if it doesn't work?"

"That's easy," I say. "I'll just kill them and myself and put us all out of our collective misery."

"Well," says Mona, straight-faced as always, "it's good to know you have a Plan B."

The two of us crack up. How many other shrinks could I do that with?

Mona's right, though. I *am* pinning a lot of hope on this sailing trip, maybe too much.

Only I can't help it.

That's what can happen when your family is falling to pieces before your eyes and you believe that it's all your fault.

Chapter 2

LONG STORY SHORT—boring personal story made palatable—the problems really kicked in four years ago when my husband, Stuart, suddenly died. It was a devastating shock. Even though Stuart had strayed on me, and more than once, I blamed my career and work schedule at least as much as I blamed him.

At any rate, Stuart's death was even worse for our three children. I just didn't realize it at first. Maybe I was too self-centered.

For some reason I thought our family would all rally around, that we'd pull through by pulling together.

I was fooling myself.

Stuart was the family's anchor; he was almost always there, while I was more often than not at the hospital, or at least on call. Without him around, the kids became their own little islands. They were angry, confused, and worse, they wanted little to do with me. Not that I could blame them. In all candor, I've never been in danger of winning any Mother of the Year award. I'm living proof—like so many other women, I suppose—of how hard it is to have both a successful career and time for a great relationship with your kids. Not impossible, just very hard.

But that's all about to change. At least I hope so. Desperately.

Starting this Friday, I'm taking a *two-month* leave of absence from Lexington Hospital. Dr. Katherine Dunne is officially checking out.

The kids and I are setting sail for the bulk of the summer on *The Family Dunne,* the boat that always used to bring us together when Stuart was alive. It was his pride and joy—and that's probably why I could never bring myself to sell it. I couldn't do that to the kids.

Of course, Carrie, Mark, and Ernie hate this whole idea, but I don't care. Even if I have to drag them kicking and screaming, they're getting on that boat!

"Oh, here's some good news," I tell Mona as we wrap up our session. "The kids have finally stopped referring to this as 'the dysfunctional Dunne family vacation.'"

"That *is* good news," says Mona with the tinkly laugh I love.

"Yeah," I say. "Now they're just calling it 'Mom's guilt trip from hell.'"

Mona laughs again and I join her this time. It's either that or start crying and maybe do a swan dive out her window.

What have I gotten myself into? And how can our family survive?

Two very good questions that I can't answer right now.

Chapter 3

AFTER A LIGHT DRIZZLE that persisted all through Friday morning, a noontime fog settled over the Labrador Island Marina in exclusive and very tony Newport, Rhode Island.

Fog.

How fitting, thought Jake Dunne, stretching his lean six-foot-one frame as he stood on the teakwood deck of his late brother's boat. Maybe that was because he still wasn't clear about this trip—what to expect, how it would play out. Would he live to regret it?

All he knew was how his former sister-in-law, Katherine, sounded on the phone when she called him a few weeks back. Desperate. Compelling. The way she talked about wanting—no, *needing*—to take this trip with the kids, you'd think it was her last hope in the world.

So how could he say no to her when she asked if he would be their captain? He couldn't, of course. He always said yes to Katherine.

Jake was about to resume his final inspection of the boat, admiring all the new lines and canvas, when he heard a familiar voice call out to him.

"How ya doin' there, J.D.? Good to see you." Jake turned to see Darcy Hammerman, the launch skipper for the marina. Darcy was standing directly below him on the dock. She was dressed in the same blue polo shirt with the Labrador Island logo that everyone on the staff was required to wear. Only Darcy's shirt was a lot more faded, a subtle sign of her seniority. And why not? She and her brother Robert owned the place.

"Hey, Darcy, what's happening?" said Jake in his usual laid-back tone.

"Not too much," Darcy answered, flashing an easy grin. She was in her late thirties, slender, attractive, and always very tan. "Just another day of shuttling rich people to boats that cost more than my house."

Jake chuckled, watching as Darcy turned her attention to *The Family Dunne.*

"So how's she looking to you?" Darcy asked. "Is she ready to set sail?"

"She was a little rusty, maybe, but she's definitely sea-worthy now," said Jake, who would know as well as anybody.

Growing up in Newport as the youngest in a family of devout sailors, Jake found boating a lot like breathing—it just came naturally. In fact, of all the Dunnes, Jake had become the most accomplished sailor. Twice he won the Cruising Division of the prestigious—and extremely arduous—Newport Bermuda sailing race.

Still, Darcy didn't look entirely convinced by his breezy appraisal. As she continued to eye the boat, she actually seemed a little concerned.

"What is it?" asked Jake. "You see something I didn't? Something come up in your overhaul?"

"Nothing—nothing at all."

"How long have I known you—about ten years? It's obviously *something.* So tell me."

Darcy's eyes narrowed into a squint. "No, it's just a stupid superstition, that's all."

Jake nodded and didn't press her on it. He didn't need to. He knew exactly what Darcy was talking about. Among sailors worth spit, the superstition was widely known. What's more, Jake believed in it. Sort of, anyway. It had been weighing on his mind as well. Like a two-ton anchor. *A boat that loses its captain at sea is forever a ghost ship.*

Stuart had died while scuba diving off *The Family Dunne.* His tank had malfunctioned, cutting off his air. Stuart went down and never came up—that is, until his body was recovered. So to Jake, superstition or not, his older brother's boat was a haunting reminder of a tragedy he'd just as soon forget. If only he could. Had it been up to him, he would've sold the damn thing before the dirt even settled on Stuart's grave.

But Katherine absolutely insisted on keeping it, presumably for sentimental reasons. Christ! A wedding band or a watch—those made for good keepsakes. Not a sixty-two-foot luxury Morris yacht!

Worse, the boat had done nothing but sit in some warehouse for the past four years. Katherine and the kids hadn't sailed it once. She hadn't even laid eyes on it.

Darcy grimaced. "I'm sorry, Jake. Stupid of me. I didn't mean to spook you with my typical bullshit. I'll shut my big mouth now. Better late than never."

"No worries, Darcy. Everything's going to be fine."

"Course it is. You're going to have an outstanding trip," said Darcy, smiling as best she could. "Do you need my help with anything before you head off?"

"I'm good. Give my best to Robert," said Jake, glancing at the Tag Heuer strapped to his wrist. The Manhattan Dunnes were late. *Of course.* "The only thing I need now is for my crew to show up."

Chapter 4

FORTY MINUTES LATER the Dunnes finally arrived. The junior contingent, at least. With the fog still hanging low around the marina, Jake heard his niece and two nephews before he actually saw them. Once again he thought, *How fitting.*

The mouths on these kids were something awful. Maybe this trip was just what they needed.

The last time Jake had had the ear-numbing pleasure of their company was when Katherine remarried, eleven months ago on Cape Cod, at the ritzy Chatham Bars Inn. At least she had looked happy with Peter Carlyle—radiant, actually—but for that entire weekend it seemed as if the only thing Carrie, Mark, and Ernie Dunne could do was argue with each other.

Wait, correction.

It didn't seem that way. It *was* that way.

And as Jake listened to their bickering voices getting closer, it was clear that nothing had changed with the Dunne crew—*his* crew now.

"See, I told you it was this way, you idiots. I'm always right. I can see the boat."

Jake nodded to himself. *That's definitely Mark, slacker par excellence. Holden Caulfield for the twenty-first century.*

"Who are you calling an idiot, you idiot? I'm not the one who got caught smoking weed in his dorm room last month. *That* was impressive."

And that's definitely Carrie, our Yalie—our troubled Yalie, from what I hear.

"Oh, yeah?" said Mark. "The only reason *you* stopped smoking weed is because the munchies were making you *fat!* Your ass is dragging, sister."

"Up yours!"

"Right back atcha!"

A third voice chimed in then—much higher-pitched; kind of sweet, really. "Sorry to interrupt this stimulating conversation between my chronologically older siblings, but I was wondering something."

"What is it, twerp?" asked Carrie.

"Why hasn't Uncle Jake ever gotten married? You don't think he's gay, do you? Not that it's a bad thing."

Jake started to laugh. *That's absolutely, positively Ernie! An inappropriate question for each and every situation.*

The three Dunne children finally appeared through the wisps of fog. They all smiled instantly at the sight of Jake. Whatever contempt they had for one another, they all loved their uncle. He was the "cool" relative. In fact, he was the only reason they had ultimately relented and agreed to the trip.

Not that they were about to admit it to Jake, though. That would be so *un*cool.

"How are you, Carrie?" asked Jake, giving her a hug. Everything about the poor girl looked thinner to him. *Too* thin. Well, hopefully they would remedy that soon.

Carrie plopped a hand on her bony hip. "I gave up an entire summer by the Seine in Paris for this family bonding nightmare. How do you think I'm doing?" she huffed. "Paris, the family Dunne. Paris, the family Dunne. Which would you pick, Uncle?"

"Good to see you too, sweetheart," said Jake, unfazed. "And I already picked the family Dunne for my summer."

Next he turned and banged fists with Mark. "What about you, good buddy? What did you give up for this trip?"

"Valerie D'Alexander," Mark answered, running a hand through his disheveled long brown hair, which hadn't seen a barber, or maybe even a comb, in months.

"Vaaaal-ler-rieeee!" squealed Ernie. "That's his hot and heavy girlfriend from Exeter. Well, actually, she's not heavy. They're having premarital sex!"

"Sorry I asked," said Jake. "Did I ask?"

Ernie shrugged his chubby shoulders. His baby fat continued to be a stubborn holdout on his body. "Actually, Uncle Jake, I think I'm the only Dunne kid who wants to be here," he said. "In fact, I know that's true."

"I suppose one's better than none."

"Yeah, I read in one of Mom's medical journals that a change of scenery is considered essential for kids who are raised in a predominantly urban environment."

Jake chuckled in disbelief. Whatever happened to kids reading comic books? "How old are you again, Ernie?" he asked. "Nineteen, right?"

"Ten. But in Manhattan years, that makes me about sixteen. Plus I have a twelfth-grade vocabulary."

"Duly noted. Now where's your mom?"

"Back with Mr. Hot-Shot Lawyer and the gear," answered Carrie.

"Mr. Hot-Shot Lawyer, huh? Do I still detect a touch of hostility toward your new stepfather?" asked Jake. "Never mind. What about the gear? Don't they at least need a hand?"

"*Duh.* What do you think the limo driver from the airport is for?" said Mark.

Jake blinked a couple of times in disbelief. Did the kid really just say that?

Yeah, he did.

As the fog around the marina began to lift, something clicked for Jake. He still wasn't totally clear on how this little boating adventure was going to play out, but one thing he was suddenly sure of. *Doesn't*

Katherine see what the problem is? The real problem? These brats are spoiled. Rotten. They're getting love all right, but the wrong kind.

It was nothing he couldn't fix, Jake figured. Two months on *The Family Dunne* would be ample time, he thought. Rigging, raising, trimming the sails. Cranking the jib. Scrubbing the deck. Come hell or high water, he was going to work these kids' spoiled asses right back to normal.

Chapter 5

"KAT, ARE YOU *SURE* you don't want me to come along?" asked Peter. "I will, you know."

"Hmmm, let's see," said Katherine, playfully scratching her chin. "You've got a big, important trial just about to start back in Manhattan, your plane is waiting for you at the airport with the engine practically still running, and you don't have a single change of clothes with you. Sure, honey, come aboard!"

The two stood in the parking lot of the Labrador Island Marina as the limo driver, a burly Italian man with thick arms and an even thicker accent, labored with the huge pile of luggage. Not that the limo guy minded. He knew a big tipper when he drove one, and this Peter Carlyle fellow fit the bill in every way, beginning with the fact that he owned and piloted his own Cessna Skyhawk. *We're talking serious denaro here!* Plus Mista Carlyle was polite and not the self-centered bossy type. A pleasure in every way.

Katherine reached for Peter's hand and played with his platinum wedding band, which still looked shiny and new. "I appreciate your flying us all up here," she said. "It means a lot to me—to all of us, sweetheart."

"Really, it's the least I could do. Oh jeez, I'm going to miss you so much, Kat. I'm already missing you."

She kissed him softly on the mouth, then gave him a second kiss. "I've got some nerve, huh? We're not even married for a year and here I go leaving for two months."

"It's okay, I understand. I really do. The kids caught a really bad break in life. This is a good thing you're doing. It's great."

"That's why I love you so much—you

do understand. This trip is so, so important to me, Peter."

"And I'm proud of you for making it happen. That's why I love *you* so much. You're a terrific person, Katherine Dunne." He leaned in, whispering in her ear. "And you happen to be damn sexy. Do we have time?" Peter winked at her. "The limo?"

Katherine blushed a little, something she rarely, if ever, did. *How did I get lucky enough to find him?* she had wondered. She had never thought she could be in love again after Stuart's death, and yet here he was, Peter Carlyle, the famous New York trial attorney.

Truly, the newspaper idiots had him all wrong, just as they got most things wrong. They called him "Gordon Gekko with a law degree" and the "love child of Genghis Khan and the Wicked Witch of the West." But Katherine knew it was all an act, a role he played to defend his clients.

The Peter she had come to know and love—the man outside the courtroom—was a kind and gentle soul and almost always considerate of her needs. Of course, it didn't hurt that he was also handsome and pretty sexy himself!

Best of all, though, Peter clearly didn't want anything from Katherine except her love in return. Any jerk who could read the gossip columns of those same newspapers knew that she'd been left a substantial fortune by Stuart—over $100 million—and yet it was *Peter*'s idea to sign a prenup. "I have money," he told her. "What I don't have is a whole lot of happiness. At least, I didn't until I met you, Kat."

Like two lovesick teenagers, Katherine and Peter kissed passionately in the middle of the marina's parking lot, blissfully oblivious of the passersby and their "Get a room!" looks, which Katherine equated with jealousy. And you know what, who wouldn't be jealous of her and Peter?

He suddenly stepped back as if remembering something. "Now, tell me, do I have anything to worry about with Jake?" he asked.

"No, he's an expert sailor," said Katherine. "He's first-rate all the way. Been sailing since he could walk."

"That's not exactly what I meant, Kat."

Katherine broke into a smile, giving Peter a quick poke in the stomach. "I *know* that's not what you meant, wise guy. And to answer your question, he was my *brother-in-law,* sweetheart."

"Still, I saw the way he looked at you at our wedding," said Peter, gazing at Katherine as if she were a reluctant witness in one of his trials.

"Don't even try to pretend you're jealous of Jake, or anybody else."

"Yeah, I guess not." Peter shrugged. "But I'd feel a little better if he didn't look like he walked out of some L.L. Bean catalog. Guys with permanent tans make me suspicious."

Katherine folded her arms. "What about you, stud? All alone in the big city for two whole months?"

"Alone? Aren't you forgetting about Angelica?"

"Our somewhat overweight and uncommunicative Guatemalan housekeeper notwithstanding, maybe I'm the one who should be worried."

Peter grabbed Katherine in his arms again and pulled her tight against his chest. "I don't think so, Kat. I waited half my life to find you. I think I can wait another two months to get you back. Especially since you're out here performing a mercy mission."

"Pretty good answer, Counselor. You are a slick one, aren't you?" said Katherine with a quick peek at her watch. "Now, c'mon, I've got a boat to catch."

Chapter 6

STANDING no more than a couple of hundred feet from *The Family Dunne,* dressed in a teal Brooks Brothers polo shirt and tan Tommy Bahama shorts, another Newport boat person was busy hosing down the deck of a sleek CatalinaMorgan 440.

Except this man wasn't actually from Newport.

In fact, this wasn't his boat.

Gerard Devoux was simply "borrowing" it for a while so he could blend into the Newport scene, as it were. To anyone who might look his way he was just another multimillionaire pampering his baby.

But no one *was* looking his way. So good was Devoux at not being noticed, it was almost as if he weren't there on the dock.

A trick of the mind, he knew.

An illusion that he was very good at creating.

No wonder his nickname for himself was the Magician.

Through dark Maui Jim sunglasses—another prop borrowed just for the occasion—Devoux watched as the Dunne crew prepared to set sail. One by one he checked them off in his head, a mental roll call to make sure all were present and accounted for. That was important, of course. Devoux was in complete control of every aspect of his working plan save for one thing: *attendance.*

But there they were—the pretty M.D. mother, the equally handsome but petulant kids, ranging from eighteen to ten, and the rebellious uncle who looked like George Clooney in docksiders.

Oh, and let's not forget the loving new husband, the fancy-pants Manhattan lawyer. What's the matter, Peter Carlyle—don't you like to sail? Afraid to get your hair messed?

Devoux smiled to himself. This was usually a part of his work he didn't care for—surveillance duty. Totally necessary, yes, but also boring to him; a waste of his impressive skill set, as far as he was concerned.

Only today was a little different. Devoux was actually having a decent time, reveling in the moment and, more important, in what was to come. And he knew exactly why.

This was no ordinary job; it was his biggest, boldest, most challenging undertaking yet. It brought all those impressive skills of his to bear, and then some. In short, this had the potential to be a masterpiece of planning and expectations fulfilled.

Devoux glanced down, checking the time on his brushed-steel Panerai watch. Submersible to a thousand meters, it fit right in with the rest of his nautical costume. However, it was the one thing he actually owned. Devoux loved watches but only the very best of the best. He bought them like Carrie Bradshaw bought shoes in *Sex and the City.* Ten thousand, twenty thousand, fifty thousand dollars—the cost didn't matter. What mattered was the precision, the perfect orchestration of many different complex movements resulting in unyielding accuracy. There was no greater beauty than that. None that he had discovered, anyway.

Two oh one, declared the Panerai. Precisely.

Soon Devoux would slip away from the marina, vanishing, not unlike the noontime fog. Until then he would stand his post and keep a watchful eye, waiting for *The Family Dunne* to head off over the horizon.

Never to be seen again.

Because Gerard Devoux, aka the Magician, specialized in one trick and one trick only.

He made people disappear.

Chapter 7

I STAND at the tip of the bow, like Kate minus Leo in *Titanic,* and take a deep breath, sucking in all the fresh air that my lungs will allow. Then, with my lips pursed, I let go of it gently, as if I'm blowing out a candle in slow motion.

I am getting thoroughly drenched, but that feels pretty damn good.

In fact, so far—amazingly—this entire trip feels pretty good. Who would've thunk it? Maybe I'm not so crazy after all. Or maybe I'm simply getting too much oxygen. An "ocean high," as the boating crowd calls it.

We've been at sea for only a little while,

but with the land fading away at our windblown backs, I'm filled for the first time with a very strange feeling about this trip.

I think it's called hope, and it's definitely a very positive vibe.

Jake's sense of humor has really taken the edge off the kids—well, at least off Mark and Ernie. Carrie continues to look beyond miserable, and I'm worried about her.

Jake's so good with them, though. Why can't I be better? I do love them more than anything.

Give it time, Katherine. Be patient.

I do notice something a little different about him, however. Jake, that is. Usually he's Mr. Laid-Back, and for the most part he's that way now. But there's something else thrown into the mix, although I can't quite put my finger on it. Maybe it has to do with this being Stuart's boat.

Whatever the reason, he does seem more focused. Or is it a different word I want? *Responsible,* perhaps?

Of course, he *does* have the responsibility of being our captain, something he made clear the moment we left the marina. He gave the kids some time to settle in, unpack their gear, and get their sea legs. "Then we'll go over the rules," he told them.

Rules?

I didn't think Jake Dunne knew the meaning of the word.

This is the guy who's never much followed anything except the wind. He's never actually owned a car or a home, never voted in his life, and as far as I know never paid a dime of income tax. He owns only two things in this world: a duffel bag full of clothes and a vintage 1968 Harley-Davidson. He bought the motorcycle the day he decided not to return for his sophomore year at Dartmouth. Instead he took a job crewing on some millionaire's sailboat.

An "extended semester at sea," he called it.

His father called it something else. *The biggest fucking mistake you'll ever make, Jake, mark my words. This is the beginning of the end for you.*

But Jake didn't care. His parents already had Stuart, the golden boy, the firstborn, the one walking the straight and narrow down at Wharton. As roads went, Jake much preferred, in the words of another

Dartmouth dropout, Robert Frost, the "one less traveled."

I allow myself a secret and forbidden thought: *No wonder I've always been attracted to him.*

"Hey, Katherine?" he calls out.

It's possible that he's psychic. Wouldn't surprise me one bit.

I walk back to Jake, who's at the wheel of the boat, his absolute favorite place on earth to stand. He told me that once, and only once, since Jake doesn't repeat himself.

"Can you gather up the kids?" he asks. "I want to go over those rules I mentioned. I know they don't want to hear them, but too bad."

"Sure thing." And then I mutter, "*Rules.* This should be interesting."

I duck belowdecks, where I immediately see Carrie and Ernie in the galley. Ernie's snacking on double-center Oreos—no surprise—and Carrie's looking at him as if he's a big fat pig. Also no surprise.

While Carrie's still too thin, at least she's not in the bathroom throwing up lunch—purging, as it's called. I've noticed that her teeth aren't stained and her hair is regaining its fullness—good signs. Both the school psychologist and her nutrition counselor at Yale said she's making progress, so I shouldn't nudge her about her eating.

I won't go there.

But would it kill her to cheer up a bit? *Snap out of it, kid! You're stuck on this beautiful boat with all of us, so get used to it! And I'm here for you, Carrie. I am.*

"Uncle Jake wants to have that talk now," I announce. "Where's Mark?"

Carrie and Ernie both point toward the sleeping quarters. I head in that direction while the two of them climb up on deck, as if they're about to be drawn and quartered by good old Uncle Jake.

"Mark?" I call out.

He doesn't answer, which is his usual response. So I check each cabin and he's nowhere to be found.

"Mark?" I call again.

And finally he answers. "Busy here. I'm in the head," he says. "One minute."

I'm about to tell him to come up and join us when he's done. Then I hear it, that incriminating sound. *Sssssst.*

And I completely go apeshit.

Chapter 8

I BANG ON THE DOOR so hard I think I'm going to break the lock. "Open up this instant!" I yell. "Mark, open the door *now!* I'm not kidding, buster."

I hear the porthole window snapping shut and that telltale sound again. *Sssssst.* Now all I can smell is the air freshener. It reeks of potpourri.

Or should I say *pot-be-gone.*

Mark finally opens the door and tries to look innocent as a newborn, which is pretty hard to do with glazed-over eyes. I lay into him so hard and fast he doesn't know what hit him. He's just lucky it's not my fist. That's how pissed off I am at my oldest and most immature son.

And when he tries to deny he was smoking, I yell even louder. I've taken way too much of his crap lately.

"Whoa, whoa, whoa," I hear over my shoulder. "What's going on?" asks Jake, who has Ernie in tow.

I fold my arms and take a deep breath, trying mightily to reel in my anger. It's a losing battle, though. "Why don't you ask the little stoner here," I say. "We're barely under way and he gets high!"

This finally brings a little half-smile from him. "Gee, I'm sorry, Mom. Should I have waited a whole day?"

"Don't be a wiseass, Mark. It doesn't become you. You're in enough trouble already," warns Jake.

"What, like you never smoked pot when you were younger?"

There it is, the quintessential teenage gotcha question. As Mark lobs it into Jake's court, he looks like the smuggest sixteen-year-old living on the planet.

But Jake doesn't buy any of it.

"Yeah, I smoked weed, buddy, and you

know what it did? It helped turn me into a huge asshole and idiot for a while, kind of like the one you're being right now."

Game. Set. Match.

Mark has no comeback, no return. He's not used to Jake's being angry at him and he's speechless. The only sound is a stifled giggle from Ernie.

"Rule number one of the boat," says Jake. *"No getting stoned."* He sticks out his palm, practically in Mark's face. "Now hand it over. All of it."

With a defeated sigh Mark reaches into his pocket and surrenders a tin of Altoids. Needless to say, it's no longer housing curiously strong mints.

"Here," Mark snarls. "Don't smoke it all in one place."

Jake cracks the slightest of smiles as he stuffs the tin into his back pocket. Meanwhile, I can't help thinking how lucky I am that he agreed to come with us.

Then something dawns on me. "Who's steering the boat?" I ask.

"I gave the wheel to Carrie," says Jake. "She's fine. It's like driving a car in an empty parking lot."

No sooner do the words leave his lips than the boat suddenly swerves hard right, tossing us like a salad!

I go down, and my head hits the floor—*smack!* I nearly black out. My brain flickers on, off, on.

"Carrie!" yells Jake, scrambling to his feet. "What are you doing up there?"

She doesn't answer.

The boat rolls violently again, upending Jake for the second time. He falls hard on Mark, knocking the wind out of him.

"Carrie!" yells Jake again.

No answer.

The boat finally steadies and we quickly rise to our feet. What the hell's going on? Jake leads the mad dash up to the deck.

Frantically, we look around. Carrie's not at the wheel.

Carrie's not anywhere.

Chapter 9

NEXT JAKE POINTS out to sea and screams at the top of his lungs, *"Man overboard!"*

My heart plummets as I turn and track his finger off the starboard side, where I see Carrie's blond head bob, then slip beneath the water.

For a split second of panic I lock eyes with Jake before his instincts take over. "Grab the wheel and come about!" he tells me.

Then he grabs a life preserver and dives headlong off the boat.

I watch him surface and begin to swim until Ernie reminds me, "The wheel, Mom!"

Finally *my* instincts kick in, those gained from two summers of sailing Sunfish boats at the YWCA camp in Larchmont, New York, as a teenager, combined with whatever I gleaned from being Stuart's first mate on this boat when he was alive and we sailed together every other weekend. It isn't much practical experience, but it's enough to tack the sixty-two-foot *Family Dunne.* I yell at Mark and Ernie to watch for the swinging boom as I furiously spin the wheel. I can't see Carrie anywhere. I keep checking on Jake's progress, his powerful arms ripping through the water in pursuit of my daughter.

Oh, God, please don't let her drown!

She must be hurt — it has to be that, I'm thinking. She was a superb swimmer at her prep school, Choate, first team, all this and that, trophy after trophy. She could tread water for hours if she had to. Now she can't even stay afloat.

"Hurry, Jake!" I yell, not that he can hear me out there.

Mark and Ernie edge over to the side of the boat. All they can do is watch helplessly, same as me. None of us are particularly strong swimmers, and suddenly

I'm incredibly guilty about that, and everything else.

Jake reaches the spot where Carrie went under, although it's hard to know for sure with the shifting waves. I see him take a deep breath and disappear, leaving the life preserver behind. Why did he do that?

But then I figure it out—it's for me to have a target.

I steer for it as the boat does a full one-eighty, cutting back through the wind. There's still no sign of Jake or Carrie, though, and all I can do is think about that feeling of hope I had just a short time ago. It's slipping away, so fast I can't stand it!

I strip off my sweater, yanking it up over my head. "I'm going in after them!" I tell the boys.

"No!" says Mark. "You'll only make it worse!"

What's worse than losing Carrie?

I know Mark's probably right, but I don't care. I step up on the edge of the boat, about to dive, when Ernie shouts, "Look! Mom, look!"

It's Jake!

And, in his arms, Carrie!

They're both gasping for air as he grabs the life preserver and pulls it in close.

"All right!" exclaims Ernie, raising his hand for a high five from Mark. But Mark leaves him hanging. He's too busy watching something else.

That's when I see it too. I was so relieved I almost didn't.

Something's not right. In fact, something is very, very wrong.

Chapter 10

JAKE JUST COULDN'T BELIEVE the pain shooting all through his body. His heart was pounding in his chest like a jackhammer. His arms, his legs, his lungs—everything ached.

From the boat, Carrie had looked so close—a good dive and a couple dozen strong strokes to reach her, that's it. But in the water she felt much farther away. A million miles!

No matter.

He got there somehow. He had her now! This wouldn't be a repeat of his brother— no, Carrie wouldn't be another Dunne claimed by the sea. She was alive.

Only now she was maybe too much alive.

As Jake struggled to hold her nose and mouth above water, Carrie kicked and screamed wildly in his arms. What was wrong with her?

"Carrie, I've got you. Just relax," urged Jake, trying to sound calm against her panic.

That's what this is, isn't it? he thought. Carrie was still panicked from almost drowning. She was scared to death— literally. That's why she was fighting him.

He tried again, louder. "Carrie, it's me. It's Uncle Jake! Stop fighting me."

He was sure she'd snap out of it any second. She'd realize she was safe and calm down.

But she didn't. If anything, she was getting worse, twisting and thrashing around like a tornado in his arms. A ninety-eight-pound killer tornado! Where was she getting so much strength?

Meanwhile, Jake had none to spare. His muscles were spent, his thighs and calves beginning to seize up and cramp. For the first time in his forty-four years he actually felt his age.

Forget the calm voice. Jake yelled at her. "CARRIE! STOP IT NOW!"

Her name and a couple of other words were all he could get out of his mouth before it was filled by a swell of salt water burning the back of his throat.

He managed to hold on to her with one arm; with the other he clung to the life preserver. Carrie was splashing so wildly now he could barely see her or anything else. Certainly not the boat. *Do I scream for help?* he wondered, thinking it might be his only choice.

The thought had barely crossed his mind when he felt Carrie slip out of his grasp. She immediately sank beneath the surface without so much as a struggle. *What the hell's going on?*

Jake sucked in a quick lungful of air and went after her headfirst. Damn it! The water was too murky to see through. The best he could do was feel around for her. She was going to drown, wasn't she—just like Stuart.

Ten seconds . . . twenty seconds . . . thirty seconds . . .

He felt nothing!

Except his lungs about to explode.

Then, a few more feet down, as his head began to ache from the pressure, he felt something, the soft, slippery feel of flesh. Carrie's arm!

Jake pulled on it fast and hard, as if he were starting a lawn mower and had only one try. *Hang on, girl.* Up they went, breaking through the surface without a moment to spare. They both gasped. Air had never felt so precious to him.

Jake even found the life preserver again. For a second time he'd saved Carrie. And for the second time it seemed as if—

No, he thought. *This can't be happening.*

But as he continued to struggle with her, what else could he think? She was no longer just kicking and screaming, she was violently pushing him away!

Carrie knew exactly what she was doing. She had known all along.

Jake was certain of it now.

His niece didn't want to be saved. *Carrie was trying to drown herself.*

Chapter 11

MARK THROWS UP HIS HANDS in disgust. He can't believe this, and neither can I. "What the hell's Carrie trying to do, *drown* him?"

"Shut up!" I say. "Please, Mark. Not now."

That's only because I know it's a good question, one that's too painful to answer. It certainly does look that way, though. Worse, Carrie seems to have the upper hand. Jake outweighs her by eighty or ninety pounds, easy, but it doesn't seem to matter. The way she's fighting him, he can barely stay afloat, let alone hold on to her.

"Carrie, it's going to be all right!" I yell. "Let Uncle Jake help you! Carrie!"

That's when the awful truth comes blaring out of her mouth. "Let me be!" she screams back. "I don't want anybody's help! Let me go!"

Let me go?

My knees suddenly go weak. *Oh, dear God.* Carrie didn't fall overboard, she jumped. She tried to kill herself!

And she's still trying.

Again I'm about to dive in the water to help if I possibly can. I can't stand here and watch this—I have to do something! But again I stop at the last second.

The sound of Jake screaming in pain freezes me. There's blood streaked on his forehead. Carrie must have scratched him with her fingernails.

As the blood trickles down his face, Jake's expression immediately changes. *That does it! No more Mr. Nice Uncle!* He's had enough of this.

With a thunderous grunt he swings his arm around Carrie's neck, taking her in a tight chokehold I've seen cops use in the emergency room at the hospital.

I never thought I'd be so happy to see someone do that to one of my children.

Carrie's still kicking, but with her arms restrained against her chest, Jake can now drag her over to the side of the swimming platform at the stern. Mark, Ernie, and I reach out and grab her by her wrists and ankles. We pull her onto the platform, landing her like a fish.

"Stop it!" she wails. "Leave me alone! Just leave me alone!"

My heart is breaking into a million little pieces.

We walk her up to the deck, where she flops around, throwing a tantrum. Finally she curls up in the fetal position, crying pitifully. It's contagious, and I start crying too. I'm at a loss. I don't know what to say to her. What can I do for Carrie?

"A little help here, guys," comes Jake's out-of-breath voice from behind us. We turn to see him treading water—waiting—next to the platform. He's a lot harder to pull up than Carrie, but we finally get him onboard too.

"Thank you, Jake," I tell him. *"Thank you."*

For a few very strange moments all we can do is exchange confused looks, saying nothing. Eventually Jake speaks up. "Boat rule number two," he says between heavy breaths. "No trying to kill yourself."

The line doesn't lighten anyone's mood, but as I catch Jake's eye I realize that that wasn't his intention. He's serious, and so is what just happened.

First things first, though.

Carrie's freezing, shivering from head to toe.

"Mark, go grab some towels," I say.

He nods, taking off belowdecks. Within seconds, however, he's standing at the top step to the main cabin, a panicked look etched across his face. He doesn't have the towels.

"We're in deep shit," he says. "I'm not kidding either."

Chapter 12

WHAT NOW? That's the exhausted look I give Jake, and he gives it right back to me. I have no idea what Mark has discovered, but I know from his tone, the quiver in his voice, that it's definitely something.

And it's definitely very bad.

"Ernie, stay right here with your sister," I say, falling in line behind the still dripping Jake, who looks as if he's answering the bell for about the fiftieth round in a prizefight. The two of us head belowdecks so Mark can fill us in on the latest crisis.

But he doesn't have to say a word to either of us. It's obvious, it's right there at our feet. Water! Everywhere I look. It's covering the entire cabin, four to five inches deep and rising quickly.

"Where's it coming from?"

"The only place it can," answers Jake. "Down below. Has to be, Kat. I'm going."

He pushes past Mark, trudging over to the galley and the small, square hatch in the floor that leads to the engine room. The Atlantic Ocean is literally forcing its way up through the hinges as Jake reaches down and pops the handle. He's about to open the hatch, and God only knows what he'll find when he does. My heart is in my throat again.

"Are you sure you want to do that?" asks Mark.

"It's either that or we sink, buddy," says Jake matter-of-factly. "I choose taking a look."

Mark's Adam's apple literally disappears beneath the collar of his Abercrombie & Fitch T-shirt. "What can I do?" he asks quickly.

"I'll tell you in a minute."

It's more like a split second. Pulling up the hatch door, he takes one look at the situation beneath our feet and starts giving emergency orders.

Chapter 13

"KATHERINE, I need a mask and a snorkel from the Hail Mary box!"

"The *what?*" I ask.

"It's a red box under the boom with anything and everything for emergency situations," he explains quickly. "Like now."

Oh, I get it—unfortunately. The Hail Mary box.

Jake turns to Mark, pointing at him. "And Mark, you go grab anything and everything that looks like a bucket."

Mark nods hesitantly but doesn't move. I haven't moved either. What are we waiting for?

"GO!" shouts Jake. "GO!"

That does the trick pretty well. Mark and I bolt from the main cabin as if we're on fire.

"What's going on down there?" asks Ernie.

Mark beats me to the punch. "The boat's gonna fuckin' sink!" he blurts out.

While it's not exactly the way I would've phrased it, I'm not about to quibble. Not right now. "Ernie, help your brother find some buckets," I say. "We're not going to sink." *Please, God, don't let us go down.*

"What about Carrie?" Ernie asks.

We all look at her at once. She's curled up on the deck, her head buried in her hands.

Again Mark beats me to the punch. "Don't worry—we *all* may be jumping ship soon!"

Ernie stares at me, his eyes wide as Frisbees with stress and fear. The little boy who's always acted older than his age is suddenly like any other ten-year-old. He can barely get the next couple of words out. "Is . . . that . . . really true, Mom?"

"It's going to be okay," I tell him. *I hope.* "Just help your brother, okay? No, no. You keep an eye on Carrie."

I'm about to turn around to dash for the snorkel gear when I catch a glimpse of the only good thing to come out of this latest drama.

Carrie.

Slowly she's climbing to her feet, wiping away her tears. "I'll help," she says softly.

Maybe she doesn't want to die today after all. So this flood down below is a good thing?

I take one step to hug her—to be the mother to her that I so desperately want to be—when I hear Jake's voice from below. What he yells puts all hugs on hold.

"Let's hurry, folks! In ten minutes or less, *The Family Dunne* is going down!"

Chapter 14

I FEEL LIKE I'm back in the hospital emergency room, or a badly equipped operating theater. I raid the Hail Mary box, rifling past a first-aid kit, an inflatable raft, and God knows what else until I come upon the desperately needed snorkel and mask. Racing back belowdecks, I toss them over to Jake.

He's already assembled the hand pump and is feeding a hose down the hatch. The electric pump in the engine room, he tells me, will be too flooded to work.

I look down at my bare legs. The water level's really climbing. The four inches in the cabin are now at least six. It's cold, too. My ankles feel as if they're frozen in blocks of ice.

"You think the boat hit something?" I ask.

"I certainly didn't feel anything if we did," answers Jake, quickly slipping the mask over his head.

It dawns on me. "Maybe when you were in the water with Carrie. Maybe we were all so caught up in watching you that we didn't feel it."

"I doubt it," says Jake, straddling the hatch. "If something ripped this hull, you'd feel it, all right. We didn't hit anything."

"Then what do you think it is?"

"I'm about to find out," he says. "Just in case, though, do you remember how to work the radio, the emergency channel?"

"I remember," I answer. "In case of *what,* though?"

"Nothing. I'm just making sure," he says with an unconvincing smile. "You never know. Here goes nothing."

Jake shoves the mouthpiece of the snorkel between his teeth and eases into the flooded engine room. As he disappears like some kind of Navy SEAL, I stand almost comatose for a moment before realizing I've got work to do. I grab the hand pump and get busy pumping, even though I sense it's a losing battle.

The only way we stay afloat is if Jake finds the leak in an awful hurry.

And can fix it.

Otherwise the Dunnes will officially be listed in the *Guinness Book of Records*: "The World's Shortest Family Vacation."

Chapter 15

"WHERE'S UNCLE JAKE?" asks Carrie, the first of the bucket brigade to descend the stairs into the main cabin. Mark and Ernie follow right behind her. I haven't seen this kind of togetherness among them in a long while.

"He's down there, hopefully saving us," I say, pointing at the hatch. "In the meantime, you need to start bailing while I pump."

I get the kids to form a line heading up to the deck. It's the best way, I explain. Carrie will scoop the water, hand a bucket off to Ernie, who'll hand it off to Mark, who'll dump it over the side.

Simple as that. A definite NB, as I like to say in the operating room. *No-brainer.*

Ha!

We've barely started before the complaining begins. So much for family harmony.

"Ernie, hold the bucket steady when you pass it! Can you concentrate on one single thought? You keep spilling the water!" gripes Carrie.

"Yeah, well, Carrie, you've got to move faster!" says Mark. "Get with the game."

"Look who's talking, Stoner Boy!" she counters.

"At least I don't have a death wish!"

"Hey, why don't you shut up, Mark?" says Ernie.

"Make me, you little shit!"

The next thing I know, Ernie flings a full bucket of freezing water right into Mark's face. "Whoops, there I go spilling the water again," cracks Ernie.

He starts to laugh at his own joke when *wham!*

Mark leaps from the steps of the cabin, his body slamming Ernie and his arms grabbing him in a headlock. As Ernie tries to break free, the two spin around and around, officially turning my no-brainer assembly line into a free-for-all wrestling match.

"Stop it!" I yell, moving in to break them up. "Stop it right now!" But all I do is get knocked down for my efforts. The boys are too rough for me—they're really fighting.

Where's Jake now?

Wait a second!

Where's Jake, *period*?

Chapter 16

I TURN BACK TO THE HATCH, staring at nothing but rising cold water. I've lost track of the time, but he's been down there for at least a few minutes. How long can he hold his breath with just a snorkel? I don't really know the answer to that.

Not *this* long, I'm thinking.

I grab a mop from the storage closet by the refrigerator and start jabbing the end of the handle through the water, banging hard on the floor of the galley. The noise immediately gets Mark and Ernie's attention and they both stop to see what I'm doing.

What about Jake? Did I get *his* attention?

"He's been down there a long time, hasn't he?" says Carrie. At least her head is clear now.

I nod as we all stare at the open hatch. There's no sign of Jake coming up for air. Meanwhile, for the first time I feel the weight of the gathering water's drag on the boat. It's as if the ocean is slowly but surely sucking us down.

From the corner of my eye I glimpse the radio and remember Jake's words about using the emergency channel. *You never know,* he said.

And I don't want to.

C'mon, Jake, where are you? Come up for some air. Please.

Suddenly we see a rush of water surging up from the hatch. A hand appears and then a head.

Jake hoists himself up to the galley and stands before us in his mask and snorkel. And nothing else.

"What happened? Where are your clothes?" I ask.

"Plugging the through-hull fitting," he answers.

I shake my head. The what?

"It's the hose that takes on water from the outside to cool the engine," he explains. "Don't ask me how it ruptured, but it did, and it took everything I had on to plug the leak. As soon as we bail ourselves out I'll rig a more permanent fix."

It's good news. No, it's *great* news. Still, all I can say is one thing. "Uh, Jake . . ."

"Yeah?"

"You're naked."

He looks down. "Oh, yeah, you're right," he says with a sheepish grin. "Then again, it's nothing a doctor hasn't seen before, right?"

"I was thinking about the kids."

"Nothing I haven't seen before either," says Carrie with her first half-smile of the trip.

"Oh, really?" I say back with a half-smile of my own. "Then there's no reason you should be *staring* at it so much!"

Carries blushes a healthy red, Ernie and Mark start cracking up, and Jake grabs the bucket out of my hands and covers himself.

"On that note, I think I'll go put some clothes on," he announces.

Chapter 17

IT TURNS OUT there's no quick way to rid a boat of more than a thousand gallons of freezing cold, sloshing seawater. Nor, for that matter, is there a pain-free way.

For the remainder of the afternoon and deep into the evening, Jake and the rest of us unload bucketful after bucketful back into the ocean. We keep waiting for the electric bilge pump to kick in and help us, but it never does. Jake's guess is that the motor's too flooded to recover. We discuss returning to Newport or calling SeaTow to pull us back to shore but agree to keep on.

If the boat has more problems after we've pumped it out, we'll reconsider.

Head to toe and all parts in between, we're completely exhausted. So much so that by the time *The Family Dunne* is finally dry again, Carrie, Mark, and Ernie have only one word for me: goodnight.

Too tired even to eat dinner, they trudge to their bunks and probably conk out before their heads ever hit the pillow.

I'd be doing the same if not for the fact that Jake is still slaving away down in the engine room. There's got to be a better fix for a ruptured cooling hose than stuffing it with clothes, right? I hope so.

We've all had an impossible day, but with Jake's having to save Carrie and then the boat, he is definitely our hero. The least I can do is stay up until he finishes.

Besides, it's an absolutely beautiful night out on the deck. So many stars. The heavens peaceful and calm. I'm reminded of my days as a churchgoer, and I say a few prayers of thanks.

Then I lean back on the cushioned bench behind the helm, wrapped warmly in a fleece blanket, my eyes tracing one constellation after another. Orion, Lyra, Cassiopeia. When I come across the Big Dipper, I can't help a bittersweet smile. "You know, sweetheart, technically the Big Dipper is not a constellation," my father told me over and over when I was around eight or nine. He either didn't know he was repeating himself or was worried that I'd forget. "It's an *asterism,*" he'd explain, practically sounding out the word for me every time. "That means it's only part of a larger constellation."

My father was the consummate backyard astronomer, and also a great talker and storyteller, and he was the one who took us to church every Sunday, not my mom, who was an ER nurse. On summer nights, with the cool grass beneath my bare feet, I would stand with him for hours as we took turns looking through his telescope. One of the legs on the tripod was broken at the hinge, and I remember how my father held it together with thick black tape from his basement workroom.

"In a way," he'd continue, "we're all Big Dippers, part of something much bigger than ourselves. At least I hope that's how you come to see yourself."

I think that's why he liked looking at the stars so much. My father believed there was something out there, a higher power. Something much bigger than we are. Maybe I'm starting to believe that again myself.

To this day, I still miss him so much, all the time. When people ask me why I became a cardiac surgeon, a field dominated by men, I always give the same answer. It's one sentence that never needs further explanation.

When I was sixteen, my father died of a heart attack.

Chapter 18

"THERE YOU ARE," Jake says, almost sounding as if he's back to normal.

I'm so wrapped up in my father and the stars that I don't hear his footsteps coming up from belowdecks. He's standing behind the railing of the helm, smiling at me.

"How's it going?" I ask. "Any luck?"

"Yes, finally. I was able to trim some of the hose from the fuel line and insert it where the cooling hose had ruptured. It was kind of like one of your bypass surgeries."

"A sailor *and* a surgeon. I'm impressed."

"Don't be, Kat. At least, not yet. We'll have

to see if it holds. They're radically different sizes."

"And if it doesn't?"

"Plan B."

"What's that?"

"SeaTow, Coast Guard, chopper? I was hoping you knew. You usually have a backup for everything."

"In the operating room, yes. Out here in the real world, sometimes no."

We both laugh as he walks around the helm to join me. In his hands are two glasses and a bottle of white wine. What a good idea that is.

"I thought we could both use some of this," he says. "For medicinal purposes."

"That's the understatement of the year."

Jake sits on the bench opposite mine and removes a corkscrew from his pocket. He's changed into some warmer clothes, a red crewneck sweater and a pair of faded jeans with some rips and a splattering of white paint that remind me of the kind you see back in Manhattan selling at some SoHo boutique for five hundred bucks.

Of course, his pair is the real deal. Authentic. Just like Jake.

As he opens the bottle and pours I catch

a glimpse of the all-black label and immediately recognize the wine. It's a La Scolca Gavi di Gavi, one of our favorites.

"I haven't had that in a while," I say. "In fact, the last time was probably with you."

The words leave my mouth and are followed by an awkward silence. It's as if we both remembered at exactly the same moment, which is probably true.

The last time we shared a bottle of La Scolca Gavi di Gavi was the last time we made love.

Chapter 19

JAKE CHANGES THE SUBJECT, or should I say ignores it. He hands me my glass, proposing a toast. "Here's to smoother sailing ahead, and to a really good vacation. This is going to work out, Kat."

"I'll drink to that," I say.

We clink glasses and sip, the wine tasting crisp and delicious as it rolls over my tongue. I've never been much of a wine aficionado and probably wouldn't know a Bordeaux from a Burgundy, but I think I know good when I taste it. And this is good. Very, very good.

"Hey, do you hear that?" asks Jake.

I sit perfectly still and listen. "No, I don't hear anything."

He grins. "That's just it. Not anything. *Nothing.* Just peace and quiet."

He's right and it's wonderful. Only instead of enjoying it, all I can think about is how it won't last. The minute the kids wake up tomorrow morning, it's over. Or rather, it all starts again. The insanity that has taken over my family.

Mark's serial pot-smoking is one thing. But a suicidal daughter?

"Jake, what am I going to do about Carrie? There were signs, but I didn't believe she was this bad."

He thinks for a moment before letting go with a slight shrug of his broad shoulders.

"One of two things," he says. "We can turn the boat around and drag her to a psychiatric hospital, where they'll observe her for a few days while making sure to keep her away from all sharp objects and any clothing that can be turned into a noose. After that, they'll either dope her up and commit her or dope her up and send her home to you. Either way, you'll never really know if she'll try to kill herself again.

Or if she would have gone all the way through with it. Remember, Carrie is a terrific swimmer."

"Gee, you make it sound so appealing," I say.

"That's because it isn't."

"What's the other option?" I ask. It can't be any worse!

He leans toward me, his voice dropping to a near whisper. "We keep sailing for the summer and show her that her life is worth living."

"Do you think we can do that?"

"Honestly, I can't say for sure. The only thing I know is that if we don't try—if you don't give it everything you've got—you'll regret it for the rest of your life. As for Carrie, I think she'll come around. Right at the end out there, she stopped fighting me. She saved herself."

Jake takes another sip of his Gavi di Gavi as his words settle into my head and take root there. It's amazing, really. I know a lot of men who have more money, more possessions, certainly more prestigious jobs than Jake, but none who have more of his good old-fashioned common sense.

It's a comfortable silence that ensures

for the first time that I can truly appreciate the peace and quiet. *Of course* it won't last. But maybe that's what makes it so enjoyable—how fleeting it is. Like life itself.

It figures, what happens next. I can't help it. I start thinking about Stuart's death on this very boat. The complications of our marriage, the mistakes we both made. Turns out I'm not alone.

"You want to hear something crazy?" asks Jake.

"Crazier than the day we've had?"

"Yes, if you can believe it." He pauses to refill our glasses. "About a half hour ago, when I was alone in the engine room, I thought I heard someone laughing. It was a guy's voice, very familiar. I assumed it was Mark, maybe even Ernie. But when I poked my head up through the hatch to listen for them, I couldn't hear anything. Then suddenly there it was again."

I'm confused. "So it was one of the boys after all?"

"No. The laugh was coming from inside the engine room, and I realized why it sounded so familiar. It was Stuart. It was his laugh. And when I turned around to get back to fixing the cooling hose, I—"

He stops, not wanting to finish the sentence.

I press him. "What? What happened?"

"For a brief second," says Jake, "I could swear I saw him. I know I didn't, but I felt like I did. It was scary, Kat, especially because it seemed so real. *As if he* was *really with us.*"

Chapter 20

I'M NOT SURE how to respond to this. Is Jake wigging out on me? Did he smoke some of the pot he confiscated from Mark? Maybe he hit his head earlier?

"I told you it was crazy," he says.

"No, it's not so crazy," I try to assure him. "There are times when I'm out at a restaurant or walking down the street back in New York and I think I see Stuart."

"You're talking about seeing people who look like him. I'm talking about seeing . . ."

Again he can't finish the sentence. So I do it for him.

"A ghost?"

I'm no psychiatrist, but I can't help strapping on the shoes of my best friend, Mona. If Jake were telling her this while sitting in her Manhattan office, what would Mona say? Honestly, I'm not sure. I guess it would be something better than the obvious "There are no such things as ghosts, Jake."

That's when it occurs to me. The two of us have never really talked about it.

"Do you think it's the guilt?" I ask.

He looks at me as if I just pulled back a giant curtain on his innermost thoughts.

"I was Stuart's *brother.*"

"Yes, and I was his *wife.* I was going through a really rough time in our marriage, and you were there for me. Neither of us expected it to happen. It wasn't the right thing to do, and after a while we both realized that."

"You sooner than me."

"I had to think about the kids, Jake. And Stuart, even though he was no angel."

He nods ruefully. "I know you did. You were right."

"The thing is, we'll never be able to change what happened. And honestly, I wouldn't want to."

"No. Neither would I." He reaches over and touches my hand, then takes his away.

Jake forces a smile, and the subject is dropped for now. We finish off the wine and even manage a few laughs about our first day at sea, unmitigated disaster that it was.

But as I say goodnight and settle into bed, my conversation with Jake begins to echo in my mind. I know all too well about the guilt our affair caused. It wreaked havoc on my conscience and still does to this very day.

Especially because even Jake doesn't know the whole truth.

If there's any silver lining, though, it's this: I learned my lesson. I've been given a second chance at love and he's waiting for me back in Manhattan.

No matter what, I could never cheat on Peter. I love him more than life itself.

Chapter 21

BAILEY TODD SLOWLY, teasingly opened the door to her one-bedroom Greenwich Village apartment. She was wearing a devilish smile and not too much else. Only a black bra and panties, to be precise.

Exactly what Peter Carlyle was hoping she might pick out for tonight.

Sometimes Bailey wore fire red, other times it was lily white. But nothing got Peter's blood pumping to all the right places more than black. Jet black was dirty, and Peter liked that the best.

"Hello, handsome," she purred, putting it on a little, but not too much, he hoped.

Peter remained in the hallway for a few moments, eyeing Bailey up and down as he would a spectacular and very expensive work of art. The thick auburn hair, the smoky eyes, the twenty-five-year-old killer body, still tight as a drum. And the sweet face, the look of an angel, what made her the masterpiece that she was. There was a rule about women, and a very good one: half your age plus seven. Bailey was close enough.

"I couldn't stop thinking about you all day," he gushed, and that wasn't far from the truth.

Bailey tilted her head. "Even when you were kissing your wife goodbye on her sailing trip?"

"Especially then," answered Peter without any hesitation. Bailey at twenty-five, Katherine at forty-five. There was no contest in his mind; it wasn't even close—although Kat did look pretty good for her age. Which just happened to be *his* age as well.

He stepped inside the apartment, blindly closing the door behind him with his heel.

Bailey edged up against him, whispering in his ear. "I want to fuck you so bad. I want to suck, then fuck you."

The feeling was way beyond mutual. Peter was so unbelievably turned on he was nearly dizzy. He leaned in to kiss her, her thick lips only inches away. Before he could reach them, Bailey stepped back with a giggle. She motioned with her index finger. "Follow me. This is *my* house."

She led him to the bedroom but not to the bed. Instead she sat him down in a brown leather chair by a window that looked out on her quaint, attractive neighborhood.

What was she up to? he wondered. So many dirty, hedonistic, illegal-in-seventeen-states kinds of thoughts crossed through Peter's mind. Then came another idea, this one comical. *God bless NYU Law School!*

That was where Peter had met Bailey only a few short and deliriously thrilling months ago, when he was a guest speaker at a class symposium on the role of Miranda rights in the criminal justice system. Bailey approached him afterward and tentatively, most respectfully, asked if she could pick his brain for a paper she was writing.

Maybe she was hitting on him, maybe

she wasn't. All Peter knew for sure was that she was double drop-dead gorgeous. Within a week the two of them were between the sheets.

And in the backseat of his limo.

And in the men's room of the Guggenheim.

And in the elevator of the Crowne Plaza overlooking Times Square.

But as the third-year law student lit a few candles on her dresser and slowly closed the curtains on the downtown world, Bailey Todd was beginning to make a strong case for there being no place like home.

Chapter 22

"DO YOU LIKE the Supreme Beings of Leisure?" asked Bailey, pressing Play on her iPod Nano. "Do you even know who or what they are, old man?"

Peter assumed that was the group whose music was beginning to fill the room from her small Bose speakers. True, he'd never heard of them, but they sounded decent enough. Hypnotic. As for their name, well, what could be more perfect?

"They're my new favorite band," announced Peter. "And don't call me old man, little girl."

Bailey smiled, showing off her perfect teeth.

Then she danced, just for fun.

To the sultry beat of the Supreme Beings of Leisure, she began to gently sway her hips and arms, her smooth skin glistening in the low candlelight.

Peter gripped the arms of the leather chair, his eyes refusing to blink. He didn't want to miss even a millisecond of this performance.

"You dance beautifully," he finally said.

"For a lawyer, I guess."

And she was just warming up to the music.

Slowly she lifted her index finger to her lips, slid it in her mouth, and sucked on it.

What Peter wouldn't give to be that finger.

Soon enough, soon enough!

Then out it came.

Bailey removed her finger and began to work it south. She traced a line down her neck. She lingered on the curve of her breasts jutting up perfectly from her bra.

Down across her ribs, counting them, it seemed to Peter.

Her navel.

The line of her panties, over a tiny bow on the left side.

Until the finger disappeared behind the black lace as she spread her long legs very, very wide.

Bailey closed her eyes and threw her head back, her hand working up and down as she moaned softly. *A Supreme Being of Leisure indeed,* thought Peter.

What he wanted most in the world at that moment, more than anything, was to jump up from the chair and throw Bailey onto the bed. Or take her right there on the hardwood floor.

But as he leaned forward, ready to pounce, Bailey raised her other hand, motioning for him to stay right where he was. He'd have to wait a little while longer.

Peter edged back into his seat and grinned. Oh, how cruel! She was just perfect, wasn't she? Bailey was like the master who trains the dog to sit with a treat perched on its nose. The longer he couldn't have her, the more he absolutely had to. And that was the whole point of her little show now, wasn't it?

Clever girl, thought Peter.

And one very lucky dog, he had to admit.

Chapter 23

A MERE TWENTY BLOCKS south of Greenwich Village, the Magician, Gerard Devoux, stood at the wet bar in his SoHo penthouse loft pouring two knuckles of 1964 Glenlivet. The rare single malt, which sold for over $2,000—assuming you could find a bottle for sale—was a gift from a former client. A very satisfied client.

Just as all the others had been.

Glass in hand, Devoux strolled over to a built-in bookcase along an interior wall that separated the living room from his bedroom. On every shelf was a signed first-edition novel. In total, the collection numbered over three hundred and included Joseph Heller's *Catch-22* and Steinbeck's *The Grapes of Wrath.* There was also a leather-bound *For Whom the Bell Tolls,* although the signature on it suggested that Papa Hemingway had indulged in a fair share of good scotch himself before picking up the pen to inscribe the book.

But as valuable as these first editions were, what was behind them was even more so. With his right hand, Devoux reached for the spine of E. M. Forster's *A Room with a View.* Instead of pulling it out, though, he gave the valuable book a push—all the way back, until it seemed to disappear into the wall behind it. *Like magic.*

Patiently Devoux waited for the sound, that soft hydraulic hiss of the pressure seal being released. Then, slowly, the bookcase slid four feet to the left. As in a James Bond film, perhaps, but this was very real.

His office was now open for business.

The room itself was only ten by ten, but it was spaghetti-wired with enough sophisticated computer and surveillance equipment to tap into almost any cell phone conversation, hack almost any secure website, or jam trading on the New York, NASDAQ, Nikkei, and Hong Kong stock exchanges.

All in a day's work for a highly disgruntled former CIA man, an "asset" who had once been at the top of his craft.

Tonight, however, there was only one thing on the agenda: to chart the progress of a certain sailboat out at sea.

How was your first day, my dysfunctional family and friends? Anything interesting happen? Perhaps a ruptured cooling hose?

Devoux made a few keystrokes, chuckling as he pictured poor Uncle Jake going to the rescue.

There's no way you turned back to shore for repairs—not you, sailor boy. Not your style. You cut a piece from the fuel line to fix it, didn't you? Of course you did.

After a few more keystrokes, Devoux's monitor glowed brightly with the exact coordinates of *The Family Dunne.* The homing beacon he'd planted on the boat the night before was working nicely.

Like magic.

Part Two

MAYDAY

Chapter 24

RICARDO SANZ alias Hector Ensuego alias any number of false or stolen identities sat alone watching a Spanish-dubbed rerun of *Friends* on the huge plasma TV in the presidential suite of the Bellagio hotel in Las Vegas. The sun had just set. He hadn't slept for two days and was working on the third. *That's what you get for sampling your own product.*

Suddenly there was a knock on the door.

Sanz reached for his gun. He wasn't expecting anybody. Even if he had been, he'd still be reaching for his gun.

Occupational hazard.

"Who is it?" he called out, rising quickly from the couch. He was dressed in the official outfit of drug traffickers, made famous by Alfred Molina in the movie *Boogie Nights*—skintight skivvies, an open robe, lots of jangling gold.

"Housekeeping," came the faint voice of a woman behind the door.

He edged closer. "What do you want? I don't need nothing in here."

"Turn-down service," she answered.

He peeked through the peephole. Hotel staff uniform? Check. A maid's cart loaded with towels and toiletries? Check.

Still. He didn't need no turn-down service.

Then again, he really did like those little chocolates that had been on his bed when he checked in. They were shaped like seashells and were laced with some kind of liquor. Rum, maybe? All he knew for sure was that they were addictive.

He peeked again through the door. *Hmmm.* Maybe she would give him a box of chocolates. He could probably work out something with her.

This hotel maid was actually cute. Young,

too. If she ditched that ugly gray uniform and let her hair down, she'd probably be quite the hot little number.

"One second," he told her.

Sanz tucked the gun down the back of his skivvies and tied up his terrycloth hotel robe. He opened the door and let the pretty maid come in.

In walked Agent Ellen Pierce of the DEA.

"I brought you some extra towels, too," she said.

Chapter 25

THE FLOOR PLAN of the suite's layout fresh in her mind and her arms piled high with fluffy white towels, Ellen made an immediate left turn and headed straight for the master bedroom. The real chambermaid would know exactly where she was going, right?

It was details like that—or rather, overlooking such details—that could blow an agent's cover. Worse, get an agent shot, especially when a scummy dealer like Ricardo Sanz was involved.

Not Ellen, though. She'd been on this case far too long to let a stupid mistake bring it all crashing down. Not today, and not ever. And she knew how dangerous Sanz could be.

Sanz called after her, "Hey, lady, you got those chocolates you put on the bed, right?"

"Yes, they're on my cart," answered Ellen over her shoulder.

Satisfied, the drug dealer returned to the television show. It was the *Friends* episode in which Phoebe sings the "Smelly Cat" song. Only in Spanish it was "Un gato que huele mal."

He stood watching it for a bit before sitting down again. At the last second he remembered the gun tucked above his backside. Pulling it out, he gently placed it in the right front pocket of his robe. *Hey, is that a gun, or are you just glad to see me*?

Meanwhile, in the master bedroom, Ellen was getting down to work.

She and her team had been charting Sanz and all his aliases for the better part of a year. They almost had him back in New York, where he had operated out of Spanish Harlem. It was assumed he felt the heat, because one day he just disappeared.

Now he was back—in Las Vegas—with two black Samsonite suitcases filled with what they suspected was uncut Colombian cocaine. The street value was $4 million, which the agency would probably announce to the press as $10 million. Ellen hated the bullshit lying and the politics, but there wasn't anything she could do about it right now.

But before the DEA could bust down any doors, they had to be sure. Enter Agent Ellen Pierce, who had a reputation for doing her own dirty work.

She placed the towels on the edge of the bed and began her search with the closets. Damn it. Nothing except a couple of tacky silk shirts and a pair of puke-gold trousers. Next she checked the lower drawers of the armoire that housed another large plasma television. Nothing worthwhile there either. No coke.

Where was Diablo when you needed him? He was the agency's best drug-sniffing German shepherd. Unfortunately, letting him tag along with her would've been just a tad obvious.

That's when Ellen caught a faint reflection from under the bed.

It turned out to be the metal handle of a suitcase. A black Samsonite suitcase.

She immediately dropped to her knees and dragged it out. *Please don't be locked.*

It wasn't. As silently as she could, Agent Pierce popped open the case. The first *click* was nearly silent. So was the second.

But as she opened the case and found it stuffed with bag after bag of snow-white powder, the third *click* scared the living shit out of her.

That *click* was Sanz cocking his gun.

Ellen quickly straightened up.

"What the fuck are you doing?" Sanz demanded, standing in the doorway. His gun was aimed squarely at Ellen's head.

"I need more towels," she said.

"You *what?*"

The answer made no sense to Sanz, but to the DEA guys stationed in the hallway, the message was loud and clear. Ellen was wired, and she needed help.

Mayday! Mayday!

Within seconds the front door to the room burst open and a horde of agents stormed in. As Sanz turned to fire at them, Ellen reached between the towels she'd placed on the bed. She grabbed her .40-caliber Glock and pumped two rounds into Sanz. He collapsed to the floor with a heavy thud.

Ellen stared for a moment, frozen, as the drug dealer's robe soaked up his bright red blood. She was known for her droll sense of humor, but there were no quips to be made as her fellow agents spilled into the bedroom. No one-liners right now. This wasn't the movies or some bullshit TV cop show.

This was Ellen's real-life job, and it had almost got her shot today. Not just that, she had killed another human being.

Lowering her gun, she took a deep breath.

And let it all out.

Chapter 26

BEFORE I LEFT on my so-called sailing sabbatical, there must have been at least ten people at the hospital who told me I should keep a diary while I was out at sea. Do my own *Two Years Before the Mast* kind of thing, give Sebastian Junger a run for his money. A fellow surgeon, two nurses, one of the night janitors, even a candy striper flashing braces on her teeth—they all thought it would be a great idea for me to record my thoughts about our trip on paper.

To think I almost took their advice and started my own little record of our journey.

Good thing I didn't. I surely would've thrown the damn diary away by now. That, or burned it. After all, how many entries in a row can begin with *I want to kill my kids!*

We've been out to sea for six days now, our first port in the Bahamas is only a couple of days away, and it's been nothing but SOS for the Dunne family.

Same. Old. Shit.

Carrie hasn't tried to kill herself again, but she's a long way from becoming Miss Sunshine. I suppose we're not helping the situation, as we're constantly watching over her. It's no surprise she's getting paranoid. Worse, she's starting not to eat again, though she swears she's okay.

Mark, meanwhile, is his own brand of miserable. Clearly he misses his pot and is coming down from some kind of dependence. He hasn't said anything—not that he ever would—but I can tell. Getting high was his only escape from this boat—and life itself—and now he just has this bug-eyed expression on his face day and night, as if he's trapped. When he bothers to talk, it's usually to lash out at either Carrie or me. I am well aware of the possible withdrawal symptoms—aggression, anxiety, stomach pain, decreased appetite. I'm watching Mark closely.

As for Ernie, he seems caught in the middle of everything, poor kid. One minute he's trying to play peacemaker, the next he's whining like the little guy he is. Unfortunately, every minute he seems to be eating. He knows it, too. "I'm suffering from stress-related obesity," he claims, his chubby index finger pointed up as if he's some Ivy League professor. Sadly, he's probably right. Maybe he'll become a doctor when he grows up.

Which leaves Jake.

The poor man, he's trying his best. He's given all the kids chores to do, in an effort to instill some sense of responsibility in them—or at least some peace and quiet on the boat. I can only imagine how much he regrets saying yes to being our captain. If it's not Carrie jumping ship again, I'm afraid it might be him.

It's enough to make me reach for the satellite phone. The thing is, I told Peter I wouldn't call him during the first two weeks. Don't ask me why I said it, I just did. I guess I wanted to look strong, show him I wouldn't come crying at the first sign of trouble. Of course, that's all I've wanted to do these past six days. I'm running out of willpower. I've never been a wuss, but I'm getting close now.

Six days is practically two weeks, right? Plus I really miss Peter.

I close the door to my cabin and dial our home number. It's about nine o'clock at night and he should be there. But he isn't. After five rings the answering machine picks up. At least I get to hear his voice on the tape—briefly.

I dial his office next, thinking he's working late. He must be extremely busy with his big trial about to start, and Peter is maniacal about preparation. I've never seen anyone who hates to lose so much. That's why he works a lot of late nights.

Bummer—there's no answer at his office either. Where is Peter? Out to dinner?

Finally I try his cell phone. It's the fail-safe. The thing is practically glued to his ear when he's out and about. Sometimes he answers before it even rings on my end.

Not this time, though.

I listen to one ring and then another . . .

Where are you, honey? I really need to talk to you. I really need your support.

Chapter 27

IN THE THREE-PLUS MONTHS since Peter had begun his affair with Bailey Todd, not once had she asked him about his marriage, and until the sailing trip she hadn't even mentioned Katherine. In fact, the only time his being married had ever come up was that very first night they met on the NYU School of Law campus. That's when Peter told her flat out, "You know I'm married, right?"

"Yes, the ring on your left ring finger sort of gives it away," answered Bailey. "Of course, what your wife doesn't know won't hurt her, will it?" she added, with a carefree laugh reserved for the young.

It wasn't so much the words themselves as how she said them. He knew right then and there that he was smitten.

It was her confidence that got him, the way that she was able to will the situation to her advantage. Unabashed. Unashamed. It happened to remind Peter of someone very near and dear to his heart: himself.

So that's why now, as the two of them lay in her bed after some spectacular, sweaty, someone-ought-to-pull-a-muscle-type sex, he was all the more surprised by the question Bailey asked him out of the blue.

"Would you ever leave your wife for me? Just . . . theoretically, of course."

Peter was speechless, no small feat for a defense attorney of his caliber. As he scrambled in his brain for a response, though, Bailey let him off the hook.

"It's okay, you can plead the Fifth, Peter," she said. "I know she's worth, like, a gazillion and a half dollars. Your silence is answer enough. Also, it's not a problem for me."

Yeah, right, Bailey. Peter wondered—worried, actually—whether maybe the affair had already "jumped the shark."

Bailey was too young and too beautiful; she had her whole amazing life ahead of her. It was a good bet she wouldn't waste any more time with him if the relationship had nowhere to go.

But there it was again: that confidence of hers, a rare thing of beauty—from where he was lying, anyway.

She rolled onto her side and gave Peter a playful jab to the ribs. "Then again," she said, "if I really tried, something tells me I could probably change your mind. Theoretically."

Peter grabbed her and pulled her naked body close, nibbling on a breast. "You might be right," he said. "You just might be right."

He was about to kiss her when his cell phone rang on the nightstand. It could've been anyone calling, and yet Peter immediately knew otherwise. He just had a hunch.

So did Bailey.

Chapter 28

"IT'S HER, isn't it?" she asked. "The missus is thinking nice things about you. How sweet. I'm so glad I could be a part of this."

Peter leaned over, glancing at the caller ID on his Motorola 1000. Sure enough. "Yeah," he said. "That's her satellite phone from the boat."

The second ring filled the bedroom. Then the third. An annoyance, to put it mildly.

"Aren't you going to answer it?" asked Bailey. "C'mon, Peter. Be nice. Show me how sweet you can be."

"Not now," he said. "Not *here.*"

She smiled. "What, are you afraid I might giggle while you're talking to her? Or moan?"

"No, of course not. You wouldn't do that."

A fourth ring. A fifth.

"Go ahead, then," said Bailey, and it was clearly a dare. "You never know, she might get suspicious. You don't want that, do you?"

No, Peter didn't. Especially because he *always* answered his cell when Katherine called. The only exception was when he was in court. And court was definitely not in session at this time of night.

Ah, what the fuck...

Peter scooped up the phone, flipping it open with a flick of his thumb. "Hi, sweetheart," he began, making the seamless switch to his loving-and-faithful-husband routine. Damn, he was good. No wonder Katherine adored him.

Bailey lit a cigarette, inhaled slowly, and listened as Peter asked how things were going on the boat.

Clearly not well. Bailey could hear Katherine crying. That satellite phone provided an amazingly clear connection. Word for word. "I don't think I can do this," Katherine was saying. "I'm blowing it with the kids again."

"Listen, honey," replied Peter, "you said yourself that the trip wouldn't be easy. But you *can* do this. You're so strong. That's why I love you so much."

Finishing the sentence, he shot Bailey a wink. He was handling this a little too easily and he knew it. Hell, he was proud of himself.

So Bailey had an idea.

With a devilish wink right back at him, she began to kiss his chest softly, her thick auburn hair caressing his skin as she slowly moved south beneath the covers. Peter squirmed, trying to shoo her away, but she didn't stop. She kept going and he let her, mainly because he assumed she was kidding around. She wouldn't dare follow through with her tease.

Would she? And what would it say about her if she went all the way?

As Bailey began to lick tiny circles along his stomach, her last words about his not leaving Katherine echoed in his head. *If I really tried, something tells me I could change your mind.*

She was trying, all right.

Her lips, her tongue, her entire mouth moved down past his belly button. This was no tease. And any thoughts of stopping her gave way quickly to the sheer pleasure she was providing.

Peter could barely concentrate on the conversation. But he had to. The boat, the trip, everything . . . he had to listen to Katherine, give her the pep talk she so desperately needed.

"It's just so hard," Katherine was saying.

"I know what you mean, honey," he replied, and he was actually being honest for a change. "It's *very* hard."

Clearly Bailey wasn't giving up without a fight.

And clearly she was a ballbuster, just the way Peter liked his women.

Chapter 29

JAKE *FELT* IT FIRST.

For the past twenty years or so, he'd spent more nights at sea than on land. Even in his sleep he could detect the slightest shifts in the wind and the waves.

But there was nothing slight about this, and given recent events aboard *The Family Dunne,* he couldn't believe it was happening.

The second his eyes popped open, at a little past four in the morning, he knew this was a possible monster in the making. How, though? He had checked the weather before going to bed. The only storm on the radar was far off and heading *away* from them.

But there was no denying what was happening now.

He rose quickly and hurried on deck, where Katherine had the watch. Sure enough, she was asleep, despite the rising seas. "Wake up," he told her. "Wake the kids too. Make sure they're all up, Kat. Life jackets on. And ready to help."

Before she could ask why, she felt a swell lift the boat, pushing it around like a bath toy that somehow, impossibly, she and her children were passengers on.

"Yeah," said Jake, responding to the sudden fear in her eyes. "And it's coming fast!"

"All right, tell me what I have to do. I'll do it."

On cue, the first crack of thunder shook the one-inch glass of the porthole window. A few seconds later, it was as if a dam had burst in the sky. Down teemed the rain, hard and mean and unrelenting.

Katherine gathered the kids and brought them up to speed while Jake ran and checked the emergency weather band in the main cabin.

"Son of a bitch," he muttered under his breath as the latest report came in. By now all the Dunnes had gathered around the radio.

The storm was as big as he thought—even bigger—and *The Family Dunne* was right at its doorstep. This might not be the "perfect storm," but it was serious.

"What do we do?" the kids asked all at once.

"The only thing we can," said Jake. "We haul ass and try to get out of the way."

That was the game plan, pure and simple and most of all *quick.* If they were going to outrun this storm, they'd have to move faster than fast.

But first things first.

"We need to lift the sea anchor at the bow," said Jake.

Katherine volunteered. "I'll do it."

"No, it's too heavy and too dangerous," Jake came back. "Besides, I need you at the wheel, keeping the bow pointed into the wind. Mark, you'll help your mother."

"What about me?" asked Ernie.

"I need you and Carrie to stay here below. I want you to secure everything that's not already tied down. And I mean *secure.*

What you're feeling now is nothing compared to what's coming at us."

Ernie groaned. "I want to be up on deck."

"Trust me, little man. *You don't.*"

Chapter 30

JAKE PAUSED, steeling himself before he ascended the top step to the deck. He had every right to feel sorry for himself, Katherine, and the kids, but he refused to go there. The hatch door to the cabin, closed, was rattling so hard from the storm's fury it could've been a prop in *The Exorcist.*

He turned back to Katherine and Mark, who were still tightening the straps on their life jackets.

"Wait a sec, okay? Nobody goes up on deck, got it? I need to get the jackline harnesses."

"The what?" asked Mark.

But Jake had already rushed past them, dashing below. This was no time for a boating lesson.

Twenty seconds, thirty max, he was back. "*Here,*" he yelled over the howling wind, "put these on."

Katherine and Mark quickly stepped into the nylon harnesses, which looked like string bikinis on steroids. Meanwhile Jake fastened the ends of two ropes to the metal rings at their waists. *Click! Click!*

With two more clicks he hooked the other ends onto the rope that ran along the entire perimeter of the boat, otherwise known as the jackline.

Quickly he did the same thing for himself.

"There," said Jake once he was done. "The jackline harnesses—just in case any of us go for an unintended swim."

Mark nodded fearfully, but his eyes stayed unusually intent. He was getting his boat lesson after all. Even better, he was growing up fast.

Jake continued: "Now try to keep the wheel as steady as possible as I pull up that sea anchor, okay?"

The words had barely left his mouth when *wham,* the boat was pummeled by a huge wave, sending all three of them reeling. Katherine grunted in pain as she fell hard to the deck and struck the side of her face.

Jake scooped her up. "Are you all right?" he asked. "Kat?"

No, she wanted to say. But as the next wave spilled over the railing, delivering an ice-cold jolt to her face, she shook it off. There were more important matters to deal with.

"I've really got to get that anchor up!" said Jake. "And I need to do it *now.*"

He took off for the bow as Katherine and Mark positioned themselves at the helm, fighting the wheel as best they could. Through the sheets of rain, the deck light was all but useless. They could barely see Jake as he leaned like a phantom over the side of the boat.

Still, they could tell something was wrong already. He was having trouble. Was it his footing? Was the anchor line caught?

Jake's voice shot back to the helm. "Mark, I need you up here now! Hurry!"

Mark scurried away in a flash, too fast

for Katherine to stop him. Not that she could. His face showed fear, but there was something else there. Purpose.

The only thrill-seeking he'd ever done until now was through drugs. But here was this dangerous storm, a new and entirely different kind of experience.

As scared as Mark was, dodging up to the bow with the boat violently tossing, a part of him seemed to be enjoying the hell out of all this.

At least for the first five steps.

Then came the sixth.

Chapter 31

THIS WAS the biggest wave yet, hurtling fast at *The Family Dunne* with a white-capped curl that wasn't going to miss. Crashing high above the boom, it practically swallowed Mark whole.

As he disappeared from sight, Katherine involuntarily let go of the wheel. It was a natural impulse but potentially devastating, as she realized right away.

The boat angled sharply to port, knocking her flat on the deck again.

When she finally staggered back to her feet, she still couldn't see Mark. He'd gone overboard! She was almost sure of it.

"Jake!" she bellowed. "Mark is gone!"

There was no response. *There was no Jake!* The giant wave had apparently flushed him over the railing too.

Katherine didn't know what to do next. She had no answer. Who would? That's when she heard a gurgled yell from the ocean.

Mark!

She was only twenty or so feet from his voice, but as another wave slammed the boat, it might as well have been a mile. She could barely stand up, let alone get to Mark.

Getting onto her knees, she began to crawl. It was the only way. "I'm coming!" she yelled. She grabbed anything and everything along the deck, pulling herself forward as fast as she possibly could. Finally she reached the side and looked over.

My God, there he was!

Tethered to the boat by his line, Mark was bobbing amid the enormous swells, struggling just to stay afloat. Even with his life jacket, the force of the waves was way too much. *He was being sucked underwater again and again.*

"Mark, hold on!" screamed Katherine. "We'll get you up." Somehow.

Katherine knew there was no way Mark could pull himself back to the boat. She'd have to do it for him. But how? And where was Jake?

With both hands she grabbed hold of the line and pulled as hard as she could, using every ounce of her strength. But the line wouldn't budge more than a couple of feet.

The more she tried, the more it felt like her muscles were going to rip from her bones. It was no use. She couldn't do it herself. *She needed help.*

Chapter 32

I'M DEAD MEAT, thought Jake as he dangled from the side of the bow. *I'm through.*

With one hand he'd barely managed to hold on when the wave flipped him over the railing. Now that one hand—four fingers, to be exact—was slipping from the edge.

Portside, stern, starboard—anywhere else and his harness could save him. Not at the bow, though. Not in this kind of storm. Not with the boat seesawing so violently. He'd be drawn under the waves the second he dropped. And then crushed by the weight of the hull.

If only he could reach up with his other hand.

But he couldn't. The reason was simple: he had no leverage. The side of the boat was too slick for his feet to grip, and he couldn't push himself up.

"Mark!" he screamed futilely. "Katherine!" Where were they? Had they gone overboard? Had they noticed he was missing?

His throat burned as he desperately called out their names. He couldn't possibly scream any louder, but he was afraid they couldn't hear him against the crashing waves and thunder. Hell, he could barely hear himself.

Then, like a sick, cruel joke, there *was* something he could hear. As the wind whipped against his cheeks, whistling fiercely in his ears, there came a familiar sound.

His brother, Stuart, laughing again.

"Shut up!" Jake screamed in vain. "I know what I did! That's why I'm here—trying to put your family back together again."

Another wave slammed his back and knocked some sense into him. He could feel the boat slipping farther away from his fingers. The pain was shooting down his arm like fire. How crazy was that? Drenched in water, and all he could feel was heat.

Then, out of nowhere, it came to him.

Literally.

There was a momentary break in the crashing waves—the break he was looking for.

Dropping from the last crest, the boat suddenly plunged deep into a swell—so deep that the bow and Jake were submerged completely.

If he could just hold on for a few more seconds, maybe Sir Isaac Newton would save the day.

For every action there was a reaction, equal and opposite.

Hell, yeah!

Like a slingshot, the bow of the boat soared back into the air, giving Jake the momentum he needed. Timing it right, he swung his other hand as high as he could, barely catching the edge but doing it.

Now he had the leverage. Tapping his last bit of strength, Jake pulled himself up and dragged his body onto the deck.

He was safe!

But as he spotted Katherine hanging perilously over the rail portside, he knew right away.

Mark wasn't.

Chapter 33

JAKE SCRAMBLED ACROSS THE DECK, every step treacherously off-balance, the storm threatening to toss him right back into the sea. If that happened, he was finished for sure.

As he ducked under the boom, the force of another wave finally took out his feet. He was about to be swept overboard again when he grabbed a cleat at the last second and hung on, gritting his teeth until his jaw ached.

Sprawled on his stomach, he looked up at Katherine struggling to pull Mark from the water somehow. The line wasn't budging, but she kept pulling and pulling. Her slender frame was contorted, and she looked like a hunchback. She was something else, wasn't she? The Dunnes were all turning out to be fighters.

Christ! thought Jake. He was so spent himself, could he even make a difference? Could the two of them do anything for Mark?

"I'm coming!" he yelled. "Hold on, Katherine!"

He lifted himself off the deck and covered the last ten feet to reach her. Immediately grabbing Mark's line, he looked out to see him swallowing a wave of water, his head barely staying above the surface.

"Please, Jake," said Katherine. It was all she could manage.

Jake looked down at her hands, the blood dripping from her palms. They had been shredded by the rope, but she wasn't about to let go.

Well, neither was he. With everything he had left, he started to pull. Slowly the line moved, inches at a time.

It wasn't enough, though, not nearly enough to get Mark back. Jake turned around to scan the deck, his vision one big blur through the sheets of rain. Then he saw something that might help.

"The winch!" said Jake. "The electric winch!"

Only it was too far away.

Unless . . .

Jake bolted toward the helm, using the rail to keep himself from falling. When he came back to Katherine, he had a coil of thick rope in his hands. Quickly he tied a knot around Mark's line and pushed the knot as far as he could from the edge of the boat.

Next he grabbed Katherine's hands.

"As I crank in the line, keep pushing the knot toward Mark. Push it out."

She nodded as he fired up the winch.

It creaked. It moaned.

Slowly but surely, it began to pull Mark up from the storm. Then he was on the deck. He was shivering. But he was alive—and he looked a lot like the little boy he had once been.

Katherine hugged him, holding him as tightly as she did the rope. She wouldn't let go of her boy, and tears came to Jake's eyes.

"Catch of the day!" exclaimed Jake, overcome with relief now. “Now let’s get below!”

“What about the anchor?” Katherine asked.

“Forget it—it won’t be any help to us in this weather. We have to ride it out.”

Chapter 34

JAKE SETTLED THE LAST PIECE of important business on deck—reefing the mainsail. With it trimmed more than halfway, the winds wouldn't be able to capsize the boat. At least he hoped not.

The waves, however, were a whole other story. Beyond crossing his fingers, there wasn't much he could do about the power of the sea.

"Okay, let's go!" he shouted. "Get behind me and grab the waist in front of you!"

Katherine and Mark nodded agreement, no questions asked, no more arguments.

The three of them navigated their way back to the main cabin looking like a slow-motion conga line—a drunk one, at that. But at least it got the job done. When they reached the safety of the steps, they finally unhooked their harness lines.

"What took you so long?" asked Ernie the second they descended into the galley. He was pale as a ghost, obviously scared out of his mind. But at least he'd had the good sense to stay down here. "We thought we heard somebody screaming," he continued.

Jake couldn't help his gallows sense of humor. "Your brother decided to go for a swim."

"Funny," replied Mark, removing his life jacket, but even he could smile a little now.

"Whoa," said Jake. "You've got to keep that thing on, even down here." He looked at Carrie and Ernie. "You too, guys."

"Are we going to sink, Uncle Jake?" asked Ernie, his voice trembling with little-boy fear.

"No way, sport. We're all going to be fine. This is the end of the Indiana Jones adventure part of our trip."

Deep down, though, Jake wasn't sure. *The Family Dunne* was a big, strong boat, but she'd never really been tested.

And this storm was proving to be the mother of all tests. All the more reason why his next step was toward the radio. He wanted to establish contact with the Coast Guard, give them the boat's coordinates. It wasn't a Mayday call, at least not yet. Not that the Coast Guard, or for that matter the Navy, could actually do anything for them at the moment. The Dunnes were on their own.

"Pan-pan, Pan-pan, Pan-pan," began Jake into the radio. "This is the sailing vessel *The Family Dunne.*"

As he waited for a response, Mark asked him where some extra blankets were. He was still shivering, and he looked a little blue. A blue Popsicle!

Jake pointed to the bin above the galley seating, and the radio crackled with static. The Coast Guard was responding.

"Yes, *Family Dunne*, we copy," came a voice.

Except Jake didn't hear it. Instead all his attention had turned to Katherine, who had just finished bandaging her hands and was now helping Mark find a blanket. She was opening the wrong bin, the one with the scuba tanks. *Had Ernie and Carrie checked to see that they were secure?*

Just then another wave pummeled the boat, tipping it deep onto its side. Suddenly Jake had visions of heavy metal canisters flying through the air.

"No, Katherine, don't!" he yelled.

It was too late. The bin door swung open and the two tanks went flying. The first projectile missed Ernie's head by a couple of inches.

The second, however, found a target, smashing it to bits.

Mayday! Mayday!

The radio was dead.

Chapter 35

PETER CARLYLE approached the jury box as humbly as a man wearing a $6,000 custom-made Brioni suit and a hand-folded silk Hermès necktie could.

"What do you call a bus full of lawyers that drives off a cliff?" he asked the prospective jurors right off the bat. As they all stared at him blankly, he broke into a huge, contagious smile. "A good start, that's what!"

Everyone laughed—even the old, curmudgeonly guy seated at the end of the first row, who looked as if he'd rather be having a double root canal than serving on a jury.

Peter continued: "You hear the one about the lawyer who broke his nose? No? Turns out the ambulance he was chasing stopped short."

Even more laughter filled the stale air of what was reputedly the oldest and largest courtroom at 100 Centre Street, otherwise known as the Manhattan Criminal Courthouse.

Of course Peter's self-deprecating warm-up act was just that—an act. He called it the Carlyle Zigzag. *Just when they think you're going one way, make 'em believe it's the other.*

Beginning with their feelings about him.

His reputation, sealed by numerous newspaper articles and television appearances, was that of a cutthroat defense lawyer who made Attila the Hun look like a big cuddly teddy bear. But if Peter could turn that unflattering reputation on its head, showing these prospective jurors that in person he was really not what they expected, there was no limit to what else he could change their minds about.

Including his client's guilt or innocence.

This one was a real beaut, too. Candace Kincade, the well-known socialite and former *Vogue* fashion editor, was charged with trying to kill her husband, the real estate magnate Arthur Kincade. Forgoing the usual weapons of choice—a gun, a knife, a hit man, or poison in his scrambled eggs—Candace had opted for a $140,000 Mercedes SL600 Roadster.

All along, though, she'd been willing to swear on a stack of *W* magazines that she hadn't really intended to run over her husband. She had merely wanted to scare him, to give Arthur a little rise. No more or less than a practical joke. Only when she tried to hit the brakes, she accidentally gunned the accelerator. As Johnny Carson used to say on late-night TV, "That's some weird, wild stuff."

Speaking of opening monologues...

Peter was about to hit the jury pool with another lawyer joke when the opposing counsel, a supposedly up-and-coming prosecutor whose silver wire-rimmed glasses and cement-gray three-piece suit made him look as if he belonged in a Cleveland courtroom, not here in New York, stood up and objected.

"Your Honor, is this a courtroom or an

evening at the Improv?" he asked, arms in the air.

Peter suppressed a smile. *What a rookie! This guy is greener than the back nine at Augusta!*

More experienced lawyers never took the bait. They simply let Peter finish his comedy set, as it were. To do otherwise was to draw the ire of the jury pool. They were being mildly entertained, after all, following hours of being bored, bored, bored. Robbing them of a few harmless laughs could only cast the prosecutor as a major stick-in-the-mud, or possibly a loser.

Sure enough, a few of the prospective jurors frowned at the moke and his off-the-rack three-piece suit.

Peter quickly interceded, sparing the judge from having to rule on the objection. "I'm sorry, Your Honor, and I apologize to the prosecution for my attempt at levity. I just figured these people have been waiting around a lot and deserve a laugh. I guess we should get down to work."

With that, Peter turned his attention to the first potential juror, a young Japanese woman wearing a floral print dress and running shoes. She promptly sat up in her chair, straightening her small shoulders.

Before Peter could even ask her name, though, he was interrupted again. This time by Angelica, his Guatemalan housekeeper.

Huh?

What was Angelica doing here in the courtroom?

Peter did a double take as he heard her high-pitched voice from the back of the courtroom. "Excuse me, excuse me," she was saying. "I have very urgent message for Mr. Carlyle."

She hurried down the aisle, making a beeline for Peter.

"I apologize, Your Honor," said Peter smoothly, backing it up with a quick smile. "Obviously this has something to do with my *American Idol* submission tape."

That got his biggest laugh yet from the would-be jurors. Even the judge smirked.

But as Peter met Angelica halfway, with the eyes of the entire courtroom fixed upon them, it became clear there was nothing funny about what she was whispering into his ear.

Chapter 36

ANGELICA'S ENGLISH was spotty and at times nonexistent, but she managed to convey enough key words and phrases to get her message across. Or rather, the message she'd overheard being left by the Coast Guard on Peter and Katherine's home answering machine less than half an hour ago.

Storm.

Boat missing.

No hear from Missus Katherine or Mister Jake.

She'd also managed to write down a phone number that Peter could call for more information. Before he could dash off and do that, there was this little matter of jury selection in one of the highest-profile trials the city had seen in years. Peter approached the judge.

Naturally, everyone in the gallery—especially those sporting shiny press badges—was extremely curious to find out what this impromptu sideshow was all about. The murmuring was contagious. This murder trial was certainly buzzworthy enough. Now would this added twist put it over the top?

Also extremely curious was the young gun of a prosecutor. He wondered—no, *feared* that Carlyle was reaching into his renowned bag of tricks to gain the upper hand in choosing just the right jury. As fast as someone could say "Marcia Clark," he hurried over to join the hushed conversation going on between Peter and the judge.

Now even the court reporter and clerk were exchanging raised eyebrows. What the hell was going on here? What was Peter Carlyle up to this time?

That's when the judge picked up his oak gavel and banged it hard three times. Quiet quickly fell over the courtroom. But what the judge had to say did absolutely nothing to enlighten anyone. All he offered, in a gravelly voice reminiscent of Tom Carvel's, was that voir dire in the Kincade trial would be postponed "until further notice."

Again he went to his gavel, wielding it like a sledgehammer.

Bang! Bang! Bang!

And off Peter dashed, leaving everyone in the courtroom, including Angelica, in his pin-striped, wingtipped wake.

Chapter 37

PETER DUCKED INTO the privacy of an empty office near the courtroom and whipped out his cell phone. His thumb was a blur as he dialed. The number for the Coast Guard had a 305 area code. Courtesy of a couple of drug-smuggling cases he had worked as outside counsel over the years, Peter knew that code was Miami.

Angelica had scribbled the name of the Coast Guard lieutenant who had called. Andrew Toten, it read. Or was it Tatem? Peter squinted at the piece of paper in his hand. Angelica wrote English only slightly better than she spoke it.

No matter, he would get the correct information from this Toten/Tatem.

After three rings, a woman answered. "Lieutenant Tatem's office," she said curtly.

Tatem. There was one question answered. That left only about a hundred others.

"Yes, this is Peter Carlyle calling from New York City. Lieutenant Tatem left a message at my home earlier this morning. I understand there's an urgent situation."

"I'm not sure if he's available, Mr. Carlyle—let me check, please. One moment."

Peter blinked hard in disbelief. *She's not sure if he's available? How urgent does the situation have to be?*

Before he could respond, "He damn well better be available!" Peter was put on hold. Actually, his first thought was that he'd been disconnected. The Coast Guard apparently eschewed Muzak, preferring stone-cold silence instead.

Finally a man's voice came on the line. He sounded official enough, although younger than Peter expected. "This is Lieutenant Tatem," the man said.

Peter hurriedly identified himself and

asked what had happened to *The Family Dunne.*

"That's part of the problem. We're not quite sure," replied Tatem. "We know the boat's been caught in a severe storm that boomeranged out over the Atlantic last night. We lost radio contact with it sometime after four-thirty this morning, Eastern Standard Time. It could be something with their radio."

"Oh . . . my . . . God," said Peter softly.

"There is every reason to be optimistic, Mr. Carlyle. About two hours ago we received an EPIRB signal."

"What exactly is that?" asked Peter.

"Emergency Position Indicating Radio Beacon," answered Tatem. "It's a tracking device, kind of like LoJack for boats. That's how we found you, in fact. The boat's owner, Dr. Katherine Dunne, listed Peter T. Carlyle, Esquire, as the emergency contact. Are you her attorney?"

"No, I'm Katherine's *husband.* Wait, I'm confused—is my family okay or not?"

"I can't say for certain, Mr. Carlyle. But the device *is* manually activated. Somebody set it off. We'll be sending out a search-and-rescue mission as soon as we can."

Peter's voice sharpened to an edge. "What do you mean, *as soon as you can*? What the hell are you waiting for?"

"The storm, Mr. Carlyle," said Tatem, unruffled. "It hasn't fully passed through the area the signal is coming from. I can't send out a search-and-rescue effort unless I know the team can actually make a rescue—or for that matter won't end up needing to be rescued itself."

"So when will that be?" Peter asked, sounding desperate. "What's your estimate?"

"As I said, it should be very soon."

"What am I supposed to do in the meantime? I mean, what can I do?"

"I'm afraid there's not much more you can do besides wait. I'll call you as soon as the situation changes and we know more."

This struck Peter as wholly inadequate. As far as he was concerned, telling people to wait was tantamount to blowing them off. He felt like he was being handled. He hated being handled.

Still, there was no sense showing this Tatem character the full force of his trip-wire temper. Peter knew he could ill afford to piss off the Coast Guard. He definitely needed them on his side.

"Lieutenant, there must be something more that can be done," he pressed gently.

Tatem exhaled a prolonged and heavy sigh. "Well, I don't know if you're a religious man, Mr. Carlyle, but if I could suggest one thing, it would be prayer."

"Thank you, Lieutenant, that's good advice," said Peter, who didn't think he'd said a prayer in the last twenty years.

Chapter 38

"HOLY MOTHER OF GOD," muttered Jake, emerging from belowdecks as soon as the storm had passed. "That was something else."

Katherine and the kids, still wearing their life jackets, were right behind him. Their reactions echoed his as they gazed around. All in all, the Third Commandment never stood much of a chance. Mark in particular sounded like a broken record. "Jesus H. Christ," he kept repeating. And for good reason, too.

The deck looked like a war zone in the middle of Iraq. There was splintered wood at nearly every step, shattered nautical instruments along the helm, and a veritable obstacle course of strewn ropes and seat cushions everywhere else.

And it only got worse when they all peered upward.

"Jesus H. Christ!" said Mark again. "I don't believe it."

"If you don't believe, then stop calling on poor Jesus," Jake finally said, but then he patted Mark's shoulder.

The tremendous jolt they had all felt while riding out the storm the night before was exactly what Jake had said it was. Lightning. The mainmast must have been hit dead on—which pretty much explained the second jolt, which immediately followed.

The top of the mast had been completely sheared off! Cut in two.

It had plummeted eighty feet, smashing into the deck. Or rather, what was left of the deck.

The new developments were what had prompted Jake to activate the EPIRB. Even if they were lucky enough to survive the storm, he knew that without a workable mast, their sailing days on *The Family Dunne* would be absolutely, positively . . . *done.* This vacation was over, and given the circumstances, none too soon.

Now, standing on the deck in daylight, he could see that his decision was the right one.

"Uncle Jake, when will the rescue people get here?" asked Ernie. "How soon?"

"I imagine the Coast Guard has to wait a bit for the storm to pass the area," he answered. "As soon as they can come, though, they will."

"Are you sure?" asked Carrie, less than convinced and looking a little paler than usual.

"Yes, I'm sure they'll be here. They know there's a problem. They're good at what they do."

"They better be!" said Mark, still staring at what remained of the mast. Scorched black where the top had broken off, it looked like a big burnt match.

Jake reassured the kids for a second time while stealing a couple of concerned glances at Katherine. They all had been holding on for dear life during the storm, but it was Katherine who appeared the most shaken up right now.

"You okay?" he said to her.

She nodded—and to almost anyone else that's all it would've been. A simple nod. To Jake, though, it was more. He could read between the lines. Katherine had been dealing with more than just her fear; she was also dealing with the guilt. This trip had been her idea. The trip was her fault.

That's when it clicked for him.

His eyes darted from Katherine to the kids, each one looking more dour than the next.

I'm not doing my job, he suddenly realized.

He was still captain, responsible for their well-being, and as such he was setting the wrong example right now. After the eight-hour, white-knuckled ride of their lives, this was no time for doom and gloom. They should all be happy. No—on second thought, they should be celebrating.

They were alive!

Who cared if the boat was basically destroyed? They weren't. None of them was even hurt. Soon, thanks to the EPIRB, help would be on its way and they'd boogie out of here.

"So what do we do now?" asked Ernie.

Jake flashed a grin.

He knew just the thing.

Chapter 39

JAKE LUNGED FORWARD with a mischievous laugh, grabbed Ernie by his life jacket, and swooped him high into the air.

"What do we do now, little man?" he said. "We go swimming, that's what we do!"

With a heave-ho, Jake launched Ernie over the railing. "Noooooooo!" Ernie screamed all the way down to the water, which he hit with an impressive splash.

Mark and Carrie broke into spontaneous laughter while Katherine dashed to the edge of the boat. She was sure Ernie would be in tears, or worse, thanks to Jake's practical joke, or whatever it was he thought he was doing.

But Ernie was just fine. Actually, he was better than fine. Against the neon-bright orange of his life jacket, his smiling teeth looked whiter than white. He looked up at the boat and shook a playful fist at Jake. Then he began splashing around, having an absolute ball.

Jake spun on his heels, casting a devilish eye on Katherine, Mark, and Carrie. "Who's next?" he asked. "It's one of you for sure. Who can I catch the easiest?"

Like bugs under a lifted rock, they all scattered across the deck. One by one Jake hunted them down, singing blissfully off-key the entire time. It was a favorite Blondie song. "One way or another, I'm gonna getcha, I'll getcha, I'll getcha, getcha, getcha!"

He gotchaed Carrie first. She wriggled in his arms hopelessly, trying to break free. "I don't understand," joked Jake as he lifted her over the edge. "I thought you liked going overboard!"

Carrie laughed uncontrollably; she couldn't help it. The first day of the trip and her suicide attempt seemed like a long, long time ago.

"Geronimo!" yelled Jake as he tossed her over the side.

That's when Mark tried to turn the tables on his fun-loving uncle. At least he was finally taking some initiative. He snuck up behind Jake and grabbed him around the waist. "I say *you're* next!" he shouted.

But Mark could barely lift his much bigger uncle, let alone send him for a swim.

"Nice try, hotshot," said Jake before applying a wrestling spin move on Mark that would've made Dusty Rhodes proud.

In two seconds flat, Mark was hoisted over the side.

"And then there was one!" declared Jake, eyeing Katherine, who was trying to hide out at the bow.

"Okay, that's enough. I'm good," she said. "I'm the mom. I say game over!"

"Game over?"

Jake began slowly angling toward her, cutting off escape routes. She was cornered and she knew it.

"No, really, c'mon," she said. "I give up . . . Uncle! *Uncle, Jake!*"

He shook his head. "Do you really think

you're going to talk your way out of this one, Doc?"

"But my hands . . . ," she said, holding them up, her bandages looking like mittens.

"The water will be good for them."

The kids had gleefully paddled toward the bow, making no secret of what they wanted to see. A grand finale.

"C'mon, Uncle Jake, send her over!" yelled Ernie. "I'll catch her."

"Yeah," shouted Mark. *"Katherine Dunne — c'mon down!"*

Jake laughed and then shrugged. "Sorry, Kat, but you heard the boys."

He rushed in, lifting her up in his arms and spinning her around. For a quick but unmistakable moment their eyes met, the memories of their secret flooding to the surface — only to disappear as fast as the kids screamed for Jake to hurry.

Which he did.

With everyone laughing and having the time of their lives — lives that had seemed in doubt only a short time ago — Jake stood at the bow, triumphant.

"I'm king of the boat!" he yelled as he

released Katherine into the air. "King of the—"

BOOM!

In the blink of an eye *The Family Dunne* exploded, the entire boat disappearing within a massive orange fireball.

Chapter 40

"THERE HE IS! There's Carlyle," shouted a reporter, wielding his arm like a jousting stick as he pointed down the long, echoing hallway of the courthouse. Off they all raced, a pack of hyenas with roughly the same manners as hyenas.

In some ways it was like a scene out of an old movie, the intrepid reporters milling around until the man of the moment showed his face. Within seconds of stepping out of the office where he'd called the Coast Guard, Peter was surrounded.

Every reporter, from the *Post* to the *News* to the *Times* to the *Journal*, was utterly convinced that the message Peter had received in the courtroom had something to do with the Kincade case. Something very juicy and rewarding! That had to be it. What else could it be to pull him out of voir dire?

They weren't about to get an answer, though. Not yet, at least. Not until Peter knew more about the mystery himself. The reporters clung to him like paper clips to a magnet, but Peter didn't let out a peep to their onslaught of questions. Not even a "No comment."

What a tease he was. Years and years of practice.

The renowned attorney Peter Carlyle—the man who loved trying his cases in a packed courtroom and always managed to have a few words, if not an entire monologue, for the press—remained absolutely buttoned-lipped this time.

Instead he silently pushed his way through the wall of handheld recorders and ducked through a nearby door that guaranteed his escape thanks to a sign on the frosted glass that featured five magical words, words that all of this society sorely needed.

No Press Beyond This Point.

The door led to the administrative lounge, and from there it was a mere two flights down a secluded staircase to reach an exit at the back of the building.

Walking through a narrow alleyway, Peter did a quick check around the corner of the soot-laced brick building, his eyes carefully taking in the sidewalk before him.

Hmmm. It looked reasonably good. No reporters to the left, no reporters to the right.

In the clear.

Peter eased his way into the crowded foot traffic of lower Manhattan, blending in as best he could. He didn't know yet where he was going. Wherever it was, he could at least get there in peace and then try to respond to the disturbing news he'd just gotten.

But then, two blocks farther, a newsstand caught his eye. While those bloodthirsty reporters back at the courthouse were busy searching for tomorrow's headlines, Peter had yet to read today's. Screw the war on terror, world hunger, and the latest celebrity adoption—*what were the pundits saying about him and the Kincade trial?*

Or really, just him? Strangely, he felt a need for self-justification right now.

Peter snatched up a few local papers before pointing at a small refrigerator with a sliding glass door directly behind the turbaned guy manning the stand.

"And a Red Bull," said Peter.

What happened next was unbelievable, but pure Peter Carlyle. The moment the guy turned around to open the refrigerator, Peter reached into the tip jar on the counter, pulled out a handful of singles, and stuffed them in his pocket. Never mind that he was carrying over six hundred bucks in his wallet.

The counterman turned back around with a cold Red Bull in hand. He quickly added up the total, including all the papers. "Five twenty-five," he muttered, sounding vaguely Pakistani.

Peter reached into his pocket and counted out six of the stolen dollars. "Here," he said. "Keep the change."

Chapter 41

SO YES, I'm a bastard, he was thinking. *Worse even than some people think.* Spotting an empty bench at a playground up the block, Peter sat down and sifted through the newspapers while enjoying his Red Bull, but also the daring petty theft he'd pulled off so beautifully.

The papers were full of him. Sure enough, the start of jury selection in the Kincade trial was getting a lot of ink. That meant so was Peter.

Shark.

Pit bull.

Eight-hundred-pound gorilla.

Only the *New York Times* managed to steer clear of the proverbial zoo and the rather biased comments on his courtroom reputation. In a brief story in the Metro section, it opted for "Peter Carlyle, a prosecutor's worst nightmare."

That had a nice ring to it, didn't it? God bless the *Times* and Mr. Sulzberger.

Peter read the printed phrase over and over, the words dancing in his head. The rumba. The tango. The cha-cha!

That's when a soft, cultivated male voice cut in. "Fancy meeting you here, Counselor."

Peter lowered the paper to see his surprise visitor sitting on the bench right next to him. It was as if he had appeared out of thin air.

How'd he do that?

"Shouldn't you be in court?" asked Devoux.

"Shouldn't you be anywhere but here?" Peter spoke angrily.

There was a fine line between mutual respect and contempt, and the two men were sitting right on top of it. In Peter's mind, what happened next would be crucial.

"There's no reason that you and I can't

be seen together," said Devoux. "It's not like we've done anything wrong."

"You're right," agreed Peter. "In fact, *we* haven't done anything at all, have we?"

Devoux smiled behind black Armani sunglasses that matched his black Armani three-button suit. "Spoken like a true lawyer."

"The same one who once saved your ass, if I'm not mistaken. Am I mistaken?"

"Am I not returning the favor?"

"For a damn good price you are."

"I gave you a terrific discount off my usual fee. How quickly they forget."

"I'm touched," said Peter.

"Of course, if you had only known Mother Nature might be willing to do the job for free."

"So you heard..."

"Yes," said Devoux. "I assume you've already heard from the Coast Guard?"

"Just minutes ago, in fact. The officer I spoke to said they lost radio contact with the boat. But he also said they were receiving some kind of signal."

"An EPIRB."

"Yeah, that was it," said Peter. "The officer told me it's manually activated."

"Indeed it is."

"That means Katherine and the brats are still alive?"

"Not necessarily. I would expect a little more logic out of you."

"The Coast Guard at least knows where to look for them, though, right?"

Devoux smiled again, this time as wide as the Atlantic. "So they think."

"What's that supposed to mean?"

"It means . . . they received the wrong coordinates. It means I'm very good at this."

"How?" asked Peter.

"Presto, that's how."

Fair enough. Peter didn't need to know Devoux's dark secrets. Better if he didn't. Besides, he could give a shit how he had rigged the EPIRB. Just so long as he had done it.

"Good," said Peter. "So the Coast Guard *won't* be able to find them. Is that what you're telling me?"

"No, I didn't say that. Eventually they would, if not for one thing."

Peter knew exactly what that thing was. It went without saying, but Devoux said it anyway—clearly just to amuse himself.

"Trust me, if the storm didn't kill your loved ones—*ka-blam, ka-blooey*—my bomb sure as hell will. It's a done deal. The family Dunne is history."

Devoux was a sick fuck all right.

Precisely why Peter Carlyle had hired him to murder his family.

Part Three

KA-BLAM, KA-BLOOEY

Chapter 42

THE FIRST THING I'm aware of is the intense heat, red-hot. It scalds my hair and skin as I tumble through the air. Everything about this is unreal. I'm on fire!

And it only gets worse when I hit the water.

Because I don't hit the water.

Instead I come crashing down on a jagged piece of the hull that, like everything else, has been sent hurtling from the boat, or what used to be known as the boat.

Snap! goes my right shinbone. I know exactly what's happened. I can literally feel it burst through my skin.

As I roll off the piece of the hull and into the water, my body immediately goes into shock. My arms, my hands, my one good leg—they're useless. I can't move a muscle. If not for my life jacket, I'd be drowning.

This is unbelievable! What the hell just happened? I can't begin to imagine an answer.

I look back at the boat—except it's not there. It's not anywhere. It's gone!

As if in a magic trick, *The Family Dunne* has disappeared from sight.

That's when the terrifying, gut-wrenching thought travels down from my brain and tears through my heart at warp speed.

My family!

All I can see is thick black smoke rising from the water's surface. Bits and pieces of the boat are in raging flames. Each second that passes without my seeing Carrie, Mark, or Ernie makes the fear and panic grow. Oh, God, where are the kids? Where's Jake?

I'm bobbing helplessly in the water as I call out their names between painful, racking coughs. The billowing smoke fills my lungs, and I feel myself getting weaker by the second. I'm losing too much blood from my leg. I'm on the verge of passing out.

Still, all I can think about is the kids.

"Carrie! Mark! Ernie!"

I keep screaming their names, but I don't hear them call back. I don't hear *anything* around me. No one calls out to me. The only sound is a muffled, hollow ringing in my head. It's aftershock from the blast, I know. Blunt trauma to the ears.

The black smoke surrounds me like a wall now, and I can barely breathe. Every attempt to scream for the kids turns into another cough as blood begins to spray from my lips. I cover my mouth, only to watch my hand turn bright red. Where is the blood coming from? I wonder. Did I fracture a rib? Is it poking a lung? Or did I just bite my tongue when I crashed into the water?

And what about Jake?

He was on the boat when it exploded. Now he's nowhere.

Are they all gone?

Am I the only one who survived?

No! No! No! PLEASE, NO! I can't even fathom the thought—insidious, horrible.

My entire family is dead.

Chapter 43

I CONTINUE TO CALL their names.

Then I hear a voice cut through the wall of smoke, filling me with hope, thanks to one small word, the most beautiful word in the English language right now.

"Mom!"

It's Ernie, and he's alive.

My hearing snaps back and I twist my body around to see him swimming toward me. His face is seared black from the blast and he looks absolutely petrified, but he's alive. Oh, but he's so scared, poor guy.

I forget about my leg at the sight of him and try to meet him halfway. That's when a violent rush of pain reminds me that I'm in no condition to swim. Tears are all I can manage as I wait for him to reach me.

I immediately throw my arms around his life jacket and hug him as hard as I dare.

"Are you okay?" I ask.

"I think so," he says. "Are you, Mom?"

I'm about to lie—I don't want to scare him any worse—when he sees the blood around my mouth.

"I'll be fine," I say.

He doesn't quite believe me. "What is it? What can I do?" he pleads.

"Nothing," I assure him as my field of vision begins to narrow. I can feel my eyes rolling back now. Not good—really not good. I might pass out, and then Ernie will be all alone out here. Next I start to shiver, and my teeth are chattering. Not good.

"Mom!" he yells. *"Mom!"*

I blink hard, forcing myself to stay conscious. I need to think in straight lines, like a doctor, like myself. I need to stop the bleeding in my leg.

What I need is a tourniquet.

The M.D. in me takes over and I quickly remove one of the straps from my life jacket. Reaching down in the water, I fasten it as tight as I can above my knee. Within seconds I can feel it helping, if only a little.

"There, that's better," I tell Ernie. "Are you in any pain? Tell me if you are."

"No, I'm okay."

"You sure?"

"I'm sure."

He nods, and I ask him about his brother and sister, whether he's seen them or not. I almost don't want to hear the answer.

"No. Not so far," he says, shaking his head. "What about Uncle Jake?"

"I don't know, honey. I haven't seen anybody but you yet."

Again I'm about to lie. I want to tell Ernie that everything and everyone is going to be okay. I want him to believe me, and I want to believe it myself. But I can't do it. It's not the way I was trained, and it's not who I am.

He reaches out and puts his hand on my shoulder. He looks so small draped in that big orange life jacket. "Don't worry, Mom," he assures me. "It's going to be okay. I promise you."

I want to cry.

It's the sweetest lie I've ever been told.

Chapter 44

HOLY SHIT—what was that?

Carrie's eyes fluttered open, only to be met by the cold, salty sting of the ocean. Her head snapped back, and immediately she began to cough her lungs clean of the smoke that was everywhere.

She didn't feel particularly lucky, but that's what she was. *Unbelievably* lucky. She'd been lying with her face on the side of her life jacket, unconscious. Another minute or two and she could have been dead. For sure, if her face had been in the water.

At first she didn't know where she was.

Even when she saw Mark ten feet away, she still didn't know. The only thing clear was that her brother needed help.

Like her, he'd been knocked unconscious by the blast on board *The Family Dunne.* Unlike her, he'd yet to come out of it.

As fast as she could, Carrie swam toward him. With each labored stroke she began to remember. Jake chasing them all around the boat . . . their getting thrown in one by one . . . her mother being the last to go overboard. *But wait – did Mom get off?*

Then everything had gone black on her. She still didn't know what had happened. Like, where was the boat? Where was the rest of the family?

"Mark!" she said, reaching her brother. "Wake up! *Wake up!*"

He wouldn't, though. She grabbed him by his life jacket and slapped his cheeks. *C'mon, Mark* . . . "I said c'mon, Mark. This is important—*wake the hell up.*"

Finally his lids peeled back and his pupils shrank into focus. "What happened?" he asked woozily. "What's going on?"

Carrie still wasn't sure herself. "There might have been an explosion," she said.

Mark glanced around at what little remained of the boat, bits and pieces still in flames. His hair was singed, and a nasty gash on his forehead was bleeding freely, but his sarcasm remained unscathed. "Gee, you think so?" he quipped.

"I should've left you unconscious," Carrie was about to say when they both turned their heads.

"Do you hear that?" asked Mark.

Carrie nodded. "It's Mom!"

There was another voice too. Thank God, it was Ernie! She had never been so happy to hear her loquacious little brother.

Mark and Carrie called out to them and began making their way through the wafting smoke and wreckage.

"Here!" their mother shouted. "We're over here!"

A hurried minute later, all the Dunnes were united in the water.

All of them except Jake.

Chapter 45

"LOOK!" said Ernie, pointing. "Over there! Will you all look!"

The smoke still hovered everywhere like a dense fog. It was impossible to see anything clearly. But as the wind shifted slightly, they all caught a glimpse of what Ernie saw.

Jake.

He was forty, maybe fifty yards away.

"Uncle Jake!" called out Carrie.

It quickly became obvious—painfully obvious—that he wasn't about to respond. Jake was facedown in the water with his arms out, motionless. Otherwise known as the dead man's float. Katherine gasped. "Oh, God, no!"

Mark immediately commandeered Carrie and Ernie. "You two stay here with Mom," he said. "I'll go get Uncle Jake."

He pushed away from the tight square their family had formed in the water.

"No, wait, I'll come too," said Carrie. All she could think about was how Jake had come to her rescue on the first day of the trip.

"Fine," said Mark. "Let's move it, though."

They both took off. Mark was fast, but Carrie was even faster. Of the two swimming records she still held at her prep school, one was the fifty-meter freestyle. It was no surprise she reached Jake first.

Right away she almost wished she hadn't. His arms and legs—what she could see of them, at least—were severely burned. Blood was seeping out of the burns. His skin, raw and blistering red, had bubbled like paint under a heat gun. Carrie suddenly felt sick to her stomach.

Fighting back her urge to throw up, she tried to flip Jake over. He was too heavy. Fortunately, that's when Mark caught up and gave her a hand. Together, they turned him on his back. It had to be done.

"He's not breathing, is he?" asked Carrie, her voice trembling. "He's dead, Mark."

Mark unhooked Jake's life jacket, then dropped his head onto his uncle's chest. "I can't hear a heartbeat," he said. "Maybe there's a faint one?"

Carrie froze. She felt paralyzed, and scared to death. Then she heard a voice from her past: her CPR instructor. Everyone on the Choate swim team had to be certified.

It was a long time ago, but it came back to her.

"Hold his head up!" she told her brother. "I know mouth-to-mouth, Mark. We have to try."

Mark propped Jake up by the neck as Carrie tilted his head back to open his airway. She pinched his nostrils together and covered his mouth with hers. Then she started breathing into Jake's mouth.

"C'mon, Uncle Jake!" she pleaded between breaths. *"C'mon!"*

Thirty seconds passed—at least that long. Carrie was exhausted, her lungs pushed past their limit. Still, she wasn't going to give up.

"Damn it, Uncle Jake! *Breathe!*" she yelled.

That's when he did.

A small breath gave way to a bigger one.

And an even bigger one.

Until he was breathing on his own.

His eyes were closed and he was still out of it. But he was back from the dead.

Mark listened again to his heart, just to make sure. When he heard it beating harder and more regularly, he pumped his fist in the air. "Jesus, you did it, Carrie! You really did it!"

The two looped their arms around Jake and slowly dragged him back to their mother and Ernie.

The crew of *The Family Dunne* was together again. Just the way it ought to be.

"So what do we do now?" asked Ernie. "Who has an idea?"

"We wait," answered Mark. "As Jake said, the Coast Guard should be here soon."

He looked up at the huge cloud of smoke hovering over their heads. "We shouldn't be too hard to find."

Chapter 46

LIEUTENANT ANDREW TATEM stood on the edge of the giant indoor simulation pool at the U.S. Coast Guard base in Miami. With a slow, emotionless stare he surveyed the six rescue swimmers in training as they treaded water in their wetsuits.

They were a young, strong, and pretty bright bunch of kids who were also green as a plate of snow peas.

That would soon change, though. It was Tatem's job to make it change.

These days, at least.

Two years ago he had been one of the

guard's best rescue men. He still would be if he hadn't shattered his right leg during a mission off the Grenadan coast. Thanks to a dozen metal screws, the leg had healed. He could walk fine, in fact. Running, however, was a different story. And as for jumping out of helicopters in the middle of the ocean, those days were definitely over for him.

Now he was spending half his days behind a desk; the other half he was trying to clone himself at the Guard's rescue-swimmer training school. He wasn't bitter. He just really, really missed the action.

"Anytime you're ready, sir!" joked one of the trainees in the pool. He and the rest of the group had been treading water for over twenty minutes.

Tatem checked his watch: twenty-three minutes, to be exact.

They were good and tired, which was exactly the point of this grueling exercise.

Because now they were good and ready as well.

"Let 'er rip!" he called to the control booth.

His top lieutenant, Stan Millcrest, gave a thumbs-up to Tatem. Then, with a flip of a switch, he turned on the world's largest ceiling fan. The twenty-foot blades began circling above the pool. Within seconds they had reached their top speed, 3,000 rpm. Or, as Tatem affectionately called it, "Apocalypse Now."

"I love the smell of chlorine in the morning!" he yelled to the trainees. "Don't you all agree?"

The purpose of the exercise was to simulate the gale-force winds of a storm out at sea so the trainees would know what to expect once they were in the water trying to save lives. Safe to say, this exercise was no day at the beach.

Tatem looked on as the young men and two women struggled to stay afloat, their arms and legs shifting from tiredness to utter exhaustion. At the first sign that any trainee couldn't hack it he would signal to Millcrest to cut the rotor engine on the blades, and the trainee might be excused from the program.

Tatem glanced at his watch again. "Two more minutes!" he yelled.

While keeping a close eye on the fake storm in the pool, he couldn't help thinking about the real storm that had raged during the night a few hundred miles offshore. All in all, the base's search-and-rescue teams (SARs) had been fortunate—which was to say that almost every vessel in the area had been lucky enough to steer clear of the storm's hull-battering grip.

The one exception was a sailboat called *The Family Dunne.* That one was still missing.

But there was every reason to be somewhat optimistic. The boat's EPIRB had signaled its coordinates, and his very best SAR team was already on its way. In fact, Tatem was scheduled to get an update from the team at the top of the hour. By then they should just be arriving on the scene. They would know what had happened.

Suddenly the rotor engine stopped.

Shit!

Had his lieutenant seen something he hadn't? Had one of the trainees gone under?

Tatem did a quick head count. No, they were all there. And according to his watch there were still thirty-five seconds left in the exercise.

What gives?

He looked up at Millcrest in the control booth for an answer. Only he wasn't there. Instead he was walking straight toward Tatem on the pool deck with a look on his face that Tatem had seen before.

Something was wrong in paradise.

Chapter 47

"WHAT DO YOU MEAN, it just disappeared?" asked Tatem. "I'm not following you."

He and Stan Millcrest had stepped into the pool's locker room after telling the class to take five. The trainees were more than happy to oblige.

"All I know is that the radio room just buzzed me to say they lost the EPIRB on the Dunne boat," said Millcrest. "One minute it was loud and clear, the next it was gone."

"Are they sure?"

"Positive."

"It's not equipment failure on our part? Wouldn't be the first time. One of our dishes malfunctioning?"

"That's the first thing I asked," said Millcrest. "They told me they checked everything on our end twice. No glitches, no anything."

Tatem lit up a Camel. Smoking and poker were his only vices, and he usually didn't do one without the other. The only exception was when things went wrong at work. Like right now.

"I'm thinking it's one of two scenarios," continued Millcrest, displaying the trait that Tatem liked about him: he wasn't afraid to give his opinion to his commanding officer. "Either the battery went dead on the *Dunne*'s EPIRB, or they turned it off for some reason."

Tatem took a long drag and let it out slowly as he thought. Both scenarios were plausible—more than plausible, in truth. *But were they probable*?

That was the thing. In all his years with the Coast Guard, he'd never encountered an EPIRB that had stopped working once it had been activated. Of course, there was always a first time for everything.

"Either way," said Tatem, "it's not as if the initial coordinates changed. We'll just have to expand the search area a bit to allow for the prevailing currents."

"That shouldn't be much," said Millcrest. "The storm's past now. It's pretty calm."

"Exactly. But do me a favor, will you? Get on the radio with the SAR team and tell them to kick it into high gear. Call it a hunch, but the faster they can get to that boat, the better."

Millcrest nodded before spinning on his heels. "I'll keep you posted," he said, walking away.

Tatem hung in the locker room for another minute, guiltily finishing his smoke. For some odd reason the voice of Peter Carlyle, the lawyer from New York who had called earlier that morning, was still lodged in his head. Something about the call was troubling him.

Over the past ten years Tatem had dealt with countless people who were anxiously waiting to hear something— *anything*— about their loved ones stranded out at sea. On the surface, Carlyle seemed no different. He was impatient, somewhat emotional, and most definitely concerned. So what was the problem?

Again, Tatem wasn't sure.

Maybe he just didn't trust lawyers.

Chapter 48

"I'M FR-FR-FREEZING," says Ernie, his teeth chattering behind puffy purplish-blue lips.

We're all freezing. We've been waiting like this for hours, our life jackets truly saving our lives this time. There's no more dog paddle in any of us. We're on empty, physically exhausted.

Emotionally, too. A creeping horrible feeling is beginning to take hold of me. Then Carrie puts it into words that none of us want to hear.

"They're not coming for us, are they?"

"Of course they are," I assure everybody.

There's obviously been a delay. "The Coast Guard probably had lots of boats to rescue because of the storm. We just have to wait our turn."

I only half believe that myself. But to say anything less hopeful to the kids would only scare them, especially Ernie.

"Come here," I say, pulling him tight against my chest. This is a good idea for all of us, to form a tight circle holding each other and Jake, trying to prevent hypothermia. That's what we'll do next.

"How's your leg?" Ernie whispers in my ear.

"Fine," I whisper back. "No problem, bud."

I know it's not, though. I'm just not up to dealing with it right now. It's numb as rubber and I'm trying not to think about it. *Classic case of denial,* says the doctor in me. Now I know what so many of my patients must be thinking when I bust their humps about taking better care of their hearts. *Can it, Doc!*

Amen.

Besides, I'm far more concerned about Jake.

Although his breathing is holding steady, he's barely conscious. Worse, his burns need to be dressed—I'm afraid he's losing too much blood. And plasma. And he is dehydrating fast, too. If that happens, Jake will go into shock and we'll lose him. Ironically, being submersed in the cold water helps with the plasma.

One way or another we've got to get out of this water, though. Even in the heat of the afternoon sun the temperature's too low. Come sunset, I'm afraid it won't matter how tightly we're hugging each other—we'll suffer hypothermia.

"Maybe we can string together a makeshift raft," says Ernie, looking around us. There are still bits and pieces of the boat floating within sight. Not for long, though, given the wind and strong currents.

"Maybe," I say.

Mark chimes in, his voice so raspy I can barely hear him. He echoes me. "Maybe."

Wait a minute! That wasn't Mark talking!

All at once we turn to Jake, whose head is barely clearing the surface of the water.

"He's awake!" says Carrie.

She's right—and he didn't say *maybe.* It sounded more like *Mary.*

"Jake, it's me, Katherine," I say. "Can you hear me? Jake?"

His lips tremble, struggling to form words. All he can manage is the same one.

"Mary," he says again.

"No, Jake, it's me . . . Katherine."

His eyes are closed, his face lifeless. Still, the lips are moving. He struggles with a second word.

"Hail," he mumbles. "Hail . . . Mary."

It suddenly clicks and I turn to Mark. "The Hail Mary box!" I say.

It's got things we need. The answers to at least some of our prayers.

So long as it survived the blast.

"What color is it?" asks Carrie.

"Red," I answer.

"Oh, I think I remember seeing it on the boat," says Ernie.

Mark and Carrie immediately decide to go looking for it. They break away in opposite directions, agreeing to swim clockwise.

Mark spins his finger. "We'll cover the area in circles, okay?"

"Got it," says Carrie.

"Stay close to each other. Please," I call to them.

Meanwhile, I try to keep Jake talking.

Maybe there's something I can do to ease the pain. It's no use. His lips fall still again.

"It's okay," I tell him.

He's barely conscious, and yet all he needed to help us was two words. *Hail Mary.*

He's still our captain.

Chapter 49

TEN OR SO MINUTES LATER, Carrie's voice cuts through the air. Her jubilation is tempered by sheer exhaustion.

"I found it!" she yells.

I can hardly believe it. Hell, I can hardly see Carrie. She's got to be over two hundred yards away, and she looks like a black dot out there.

"I found it!" she yells again. "The Hail Mary box!"

Hallelujah! It's a miracle!

I call out to Mark, who's about as far away from us as Carrie, only in the opposite direction. He's still searching for the box.

"Come back," I say. "Carrie found it!"

He hears me and begins swimming back, taking his time. Who can blame him? I'm amazed he and his sister can swim even a single stroke at this point. They're both in better physical shape than I'd have thought.

"Do you think there's any food in that box?" asks Ernie. "Because I'm starving."

I think back to when I was searching through it for that mask and snorkel Jake needed. I can't remember seeing anything edible.

"Let's hope so," I tell him. "We'll be okay, Ernie."

We watch as Carrie slowly gets closer. *Very* slowly. She's dragging the box as best she can, and it can't be easy. As she gets closer, I can see the fatigue etched all over her face. The poor girl, she's absolutely pooped!

"Carrie, take a break," I yell.

Of course she doesn't.

I turn to Ernie, kidding. "Typical Carrie. I say one thing, she does the other."

Only Ernie's not listening to me either. He's not even looking in my direction. I can't see what he's staring at, but my ears immediately tell me there's a problem.

When he was a toddler he used to make this strange clicking noise from the side of his mouth whenever he was scared, only it wasn't loud. The only way anyone else could hear it was if they were really close to him. *As I am now.*

"What is it, Ernie? What do you see?"

"I'm not sure yet," he answers. "It's something, though."

He points and I squint. I still can't see it. If Mark is at three o'clock and Carrie at nine, whatever it is—or isn't—is directly at six.

"Ernie, I don't—"

My mouth suddenly freezes. I *do* see it now. "*Omigod.* Is that what I think it is?"

Ernie's clicking faster and louder than he ever has.

"Yes," he says. "Carrie, look out! *Carrie! CARRIE!*"

Chapter 50

IT'S NOT THE COAST GUARD here to rescue us, that's for sure.

It's a shape, a triangle. Two feet high, darkish gray, and slicing through the water.

One terrible word is on my tongue. *Shark!*

"It's coming right for us," says Ernie. "What do we do?"

Every muscle in my body, every bone—broken or otherwise—is screaming panic. Panic like there's no tomorrow!

But I don't allow this to happen. I have my operating room calm on now.

"Mom," repeats Ernie. *"What do we do?"*

"It's what we don't do," I say. "We don't move. Maybe it won't find us."

"I think it already has. I'm pretty sure. Look."

I glance at Ernie, who's staring down at the water. It's red. Between the blood from my leg and Jake's seeping burns, we've all but set the table for this creature.

Great.

We both look out again at the fin coming toward us. Actually, make that two fins! There's a smaller one directly behind it, about fifteen feet back. Immediately I think it's a second shark, maybe a baby. But then I realize something worse, even more terrifying. That's no baby—*that's the tail fin of the same shark.*

This mother's a monster!

"Mark? Carrie?" I call out.

Mark answers first, and there's no need for me to bring him up to speed. He sees exactly what we see. "Holy shit!" he yells. "I'm coming back!"

"NO!" I yell back. "Stay right there!"

"But—"

"No buts! You don't move, do you hear me? You stay where you are."

If we're about to be shark lunch, Mark doesn't need to be the dessert.

"That goes for you too," I yell to Carrie.

She's close enough that I can see the fear in her eyes as she stares at the fin. I'm sure her eyes look like mine right now. Small, dark pinpoints.

I grab Ernie by his life jacket and pull him so close we're practically touching noses. My broken leg is pulsing with pain, but I don't care. "Okay, here's what we're going to do," I say. "You're going to take Uncle Jake and get behind me."

I have to stop talking for a second. Tears are pouring down Ernie's chubby little cheeks.

"Mom..." is all he can say. *"Mom..."*

"Shhhh, it's going to be okay," I whisper. "You have to listen to me now—this is important." I take a breath, and then I go on. "If that shark attacks me, you don't try to help. Do you understand?"

I know he doesn't. How could a child comprehend that? He stares at me blankly.

"Listen to me, Ernie. *You don't try to help.* You swim away to your brother as fast as you can. All right?"

"What about Uncle Jake?" he asks, his voice a shiver.

I was afraid of that question.

"You leave him here with me," I answer. "You just focus on swimming away as fast as you can. Now tell me you understand."

He doesn't want to answer.

"TELL ME!" I finally have to yell. I can't help it, I love him too much. I can't let him die with me—no way.

He finally nods and I help him grab Jake so they both can get behind me. Ernie's too scared even to cry anymore. He falls silent. We all do. All I can hear is the slap of the water around us.

Slish-slosh, ripple-ripple.

Slish-slosh, ripple-ripple.

I stare at the large fin slicing toward me and I take the deepest breath of my life.

I'm hoping against hope it won't be my last.

Chapter 51

CARRIE'S BLUE GAZE ricocheted all around the water. The shark. Her mother. Her brothers. Uncle Jake.

The damn shark again. *Why won't it just go away? Does it sense how defenseless we are? Of course it does, it's a predator.*

She felt helpless, stuck in limbo. There had to be something she could do, though. What?

That's when it hit her—literally.

The Hail Mary box.

She didn't even realize she'd let go of it until a small swell sent it smack against her head.

There would definitely be a bump later. If there was a later.

What mattered was now. Was there something in the box that could help? Maybe?

With a frantic burst of energy, Carrie grabbed the latch and snapped it open. Flipping back the lid, she quickly tried to push herself up from the water to look inside.

It only half worked. She caught some glimpses—a first-aid kit, some blankets, an inflatable raft—but even tilting the box to her eye level, she couldn't see what was buried underneath.

Screw it, just dump everything out! she thought.

She thought again. What if some of the stuff didn't float? What if the one thing she could use sank to the bottom before she could grab it?

She had no idea what that might be, but the thought was enough to make her try to reach deep into the box instead. She felt around.

C'mon! There's got to be something . . .

Her hand desperately moved from one

item to another. Was that a bottle of water? A flashlight?

She glanced over her shoulder as she continued to search. The shark was no more than a hundred yards from her mom and Ernie. Probably less than that.

Hurry!

Carrie's hand kept blindly jumping from one item to another. Then, with a depressing thud, her fingertips hit the bottom of the box. Damn!

Nothing.

Her eyes welled up, the frustration pushing out the tears, when all of a sudden she felt something tucked tight against the rear corner. It was cold. It was metal.

It was a gun!

She was pretty sure of it. The smooth curve of the trigger gave it away.

She yanked as hard as she could. Out came the gun. Only it looked like no gun she'd ever seen. There were large casings attached behind the grip—were those bullets? No, she realized. They were flares. It was a flare gun.

Who cares? As long as it fires!

She turned back to the shark. Her hand was shaking. So was the rest of her. With her left hand, she tried to steady herself against the Hail Mary box. She'd never pulled the trigger of any gun in her life.

She started yelling at the top of her voice and splashing. Sure enough, the shark turned her way. Was that really such a good idea?

I can do this! Just aim it and shoot . . . Just aim and shoot . . .

Carrie lined the sight up against the shark, counting back from three...

Two...

One...

She squeezed the trigger.

The flare fired, amid a barrage of smoke and sparks so thick she couldn't see a thing. *Including the gun dropping from her hand, sinking.*

She couldn't help it—the sparks had scalded her knuckles. Had the gun malfunctioned? How old were those flares? All she knew was that her hand was practically on fire. "Son of a bitch!" she yelled.

And for a couple of seconds her voice was the only sound she heard.

Then came another sound.

Cheering!

All at once Ernie, Mark, and Katherine

screamed for joy. As the smoke finally cleared, Carrie saw why.

The flare gun had worked, at least well enough. The shark had turned around. It was swimming away. She'd scared the dumb beast.

Lunch wouldn't be served after all.

At least not here.

At least not the Dunnes!

Chapter 52

DEVOUX SAID GOODBYE to Peter Carlyle from the bench near the Manhattan Criminal Courthouse. He walked down the block until he had completely disappeared from Peter's view.

Then he turned around.

Where to next, Peter? Pray tell.

Clients were more than just clients to Devoux. They were an investment. Or, if you really wanted to get down to it, a high-stakes gamble. Big risk, even bigger reward. So naturally one had to keep an eye on them.

Carlyle especially.

He represented the largest payday yet

for Devoux. But it was hardly money for nothing.

All things considered, the dirty work was the easy part. Devoux excelled at killing. He was trained for it, had a real knack. Up close, far away, and everywhere in between. The CIA for sure had hated losing him, but there had simply been no alternative. Once you go off the reservation, you can't come back.

That's what had led Devoux to Peter in the first place. He wasn't the first covert agent to freelance on the side, nor was he the first to get caught.

He was, however, the first to hire a hot-shit attorney who marched straight down to Langley to negotiate a highly classified severance package: his client's life in exchange for his silence.

It was a deal both sides could live with, because they had no choice.

Just to make sure, though, there was a sealed envelope in escrow, hanging in the balance.

"You hold a lot of my dark secrets," Devoux had told Peter. "Let me know if you'd ever like me to hold on to one of yours. Be my pleasure."

Yeah, the dirty work was the easy part for Devoux. It was what came after, post-op, which caused concern in his newly found career. *Hoping a client wouldn't fuck things up, and consequently fuck him over.*

In Carlyle's case, the key question was whether he could withstand the media glare, and for how long? Sure, the über-attorney was a cool customer who was used to intense pressure. But the stakes in a courtroom were one thing. In this game there was a lot more on the line.

So for the next twenty minutes Devoux followed Peter as he continued on foot, heading uptown.

The guy wasn't really going to walk all the way home to the Upper East Side, was he?

No, he wasn't.

Near the NYU School of Law, Peter stopped in front of a prewar brownstone with narrow windows. Before climbing up the steep stone steps he glanced to his left and right.

Watching from the end of the block, Devoux chuckled. *Peter, Peter, Peter . . . are you doing something you shouldn't be? Or someone?*

Of course he was.

Devoux had known it the first time they met and discussed his own case. Peter Carlyle wasn't addicted to money, or sex, or anything of the kind.

He was addicted to risk.

Chapter 53

PETER KNOCKED on Bailey's apartment door, all too aware that this would be his first visit that didn't involve their having sex. It certainly wouldn't be for a lack of wanting on his part. It's just that he wanted something else even more.

Katherine's estate. The ultimate score. Over $100 million if he survived both her and her obnoxious kids.

If that was to happen, he needed to start playing the role of the distressed husband right away. Even with Bailey.

Especially with Bailey.

She was a bit of a wild card—suddenly

part of his life but certainly not part of the plan. Hell, he hadn't even known her when he concocted this whole thing and made his pact with Devoux.

Now that he did know her—and wanted to keep on knowing her—he had to make sure that she saw no connection between him and *The Family Dunne*'s disappearance. Like everyone else, she couldn't suspect what a cold-blooded bastard he was.

Peter was about to knock on her door again when he heard that unmistakable New York sound of multiple turning locks. As Bailey opened the door, he prayed that she wouldn't be wearing anything too sexy. *A man can possess only so much willpower.*

"Peter, what a wonderful surprise," she said. "I couldn't believe it when you called. I only got back from my last class twenty minutes ago."

The good news was that she had considerably more clothes on than just her bra and panties. A pair of sweatpants and a Fit T-shirt, in fact. The bad news was that she immediately leaned in to kiss him with those beautiful bee-stung lips. He would have to pull back from her. *Just do it, Peter. This isn't the time for screwing.*

"What's wrong?" she asked. "Hey, wait," she said, a slightly confused look overtaking her face. "Today was your jury selection—shouldn't you still be in court?"

"Something happened," said Peter.

"That Kincade woman didn't try to run you over too, did she?" she joked, grinning.

Peter didn't laugh. As much as he wanted to, he couldn't. *What a shame,* he thought, because that was actually a pretty funny line. Gorgeous, smart, and a great sense of humor to boot. Bailey Todd had the whole package.

After stepping into her apartment, Peter first grabbed a Diet Coke from her fridge. Then he took her through the events of the morning, from Angelica charging into the courtroom to his call with the Coast Guard lieutenant. The conversation with Devoux, of course, was conveniently omitted from his already far too melodramatic storyline.

Bailey was stunned, to say the least. She couldn't believe it, had to sit down.

She also felt incredibly guilty, and told Peter as much.

"Why?" he asked.

"No, forget it. I'm too ashamed."

"It's okay, you can tell me anything."

She hemmed and hawed and started to blush. Finally: "When you told me your wife's boat was missing, my first thought was that maybe I could have you all to myself. Isn't that horrible? It is. I feel like such a dick."

"No, it's just very human," he said, reaching out to caress her cheek. "That doesn't make you a bad person."

"Really? You don't think so?"

"No, I don't. You didn't do anything wrong. You're definitely not a dick. Besides, I'm sure the Coast Guard will be calling me any minute to tell me they found my family and they're all okay."

Peter had barely finished the sentence when his cell phone rang. They both had to smile at the timing.

"Is it the Coast Guard?" asked Bailey as Peter dug into his suit pocket and took out his phone.

He glanced at the caller ID and shook

his head. Then he did something odd, at least as far as Bailey was concerned. As the phone continued to ring in his hand, he simply stared at it.

"Who is it, Peter?" she asked. "You look surprised."

He definitely was.

Chapter 54

HOW DID SHE find out so fast?

Peter knew he would eventually have to meet the press, as it were, regarding the disappearance of *The Family Dunne.* It was only a matter of time.

He just didn't think it would be quite so soon.

After listening to one more ring, he finally answered. "What took you so long?" he said sarcastically into the phone.

If he had let the call go to his voice mail, he knew she wouldn't be content to leave a message. Instead she'd have one of her attack-dog production assistants track him down in person. That's how she worked.

"Peter, I'm so, so sorry," said Judith Fox, host of the number-one daytime cable talk show. "You must be worried sick about your family. I know family comes first for you."

"Thank you, Judy. Yes, it's been a very hard day so far."

Peter mouthed who it was to Bailey, who immediately looked impressed. Indeed, Judith Fox was a household name, even giving the queen herself, Oprah, a run for her money lately in the ratings.

One reason was Judith's uncanny ability to break stories. She was a dogged reporter first and foremost, with a genuine sixth sense for the news. Plus she had the mother of all Rolodexes. She knew *everybody,* including Peter.

They had first met at an American Bar Association party in the ballroom of the Waldorf-Astoria while Judith was still a beat reporter for WNBC. Peter had just successfully defended a big-time rap star on an attempted murder charge and was enjoying his first bite-sized taste of national publicity.

Naturally Judith sought him out at the party, and in turn Peter managed to charm the pants off her that night.

Panties, too. Which was why she allowed him to call her Judy. For the next year, right up until she launched her cable show from Times Square, the two became what Page Six of the *New York Post* referred to as "best friends with benefits." Of course, the merciless bloggers who covered the media had another term for it: "fuck buddies."

Put simply, he and Judith Fox had history. And now she had his ear, and dibs on the story.

Counting the seconds in his head, Peter waited for her pitch. For sure, it was coming.

"You absolutely, positively have to do my show this afternoon," she pleaded. "You must."

Peter was about to say no, that it was too soon, when she beat him to the punch.

"Peter, before you decline and tell me you're still digesting the news, consider this," she continued. "By getting this story out there right away, you ensure that the

Coast Guard spares no effort or expense in finding your family. You want that, don't you? Of course you do."

The irony was so thick Peter could've choked on it. *No, he didn't want that!*

But the game now was all about appearances, wasn't it? And like it or not, that would mean doing his best acting job on *The Judith Fox Show.*

Hell, maybe it was a blessing. The sooner he could expand his role as the worried, emotionally distressed, *innocent* husband to a wider audience, the better.

"Sure, Judy, I'll do it," he said. "Anything to help save my family."

Chapter 55

WHAT WAS THAT AD SLOGAN you saw all over? Ellen Pierce wondered. *What happens in Vegas stays in Vegas?* Ha! Not if you're an agent with the DEA.

What happens in Vegas becomes a nightmare of paperwork back in Manhattan.

For the third straight day since returning home from Vegas, Ellen was stuck behind the desk of her small office at the DEA's New York Division on the Lower West Side.

This part of the job never made an iota of sense to her. Screw up and lose your bad guy, and you only had to file one report. Actually bring him down and you had to file three. It was almost as bad as being a doctor and dealing with insurance companies. The thought had probably come into her head because Ellen had once considered pre-med rather than pre-law at Wake Forest.

No wonder she was procrastinating so much today. Her latest diversion was the *New York Times* crossword puzzle, and she was stuck on seven across, a six-letter word for *nonringer.*

"Single!" she finally shouted out, a quick smile pushing up her cheeks. She was surprised she hadn't figured out the answer sooner. After all, that was all her mother talked about. "Why on God's green earth is my beautiful daughter still single?"

Because she's married to her job, Mom, that's why. And maybe she's not all that beautiful anymore.

Getting back to her busywork, Ellen began organizing the receipts for yet another report. Expenses. In the middle of checking her math, she stopped cold at the sound of a familiar voice in the room, one that turned her stomach.

Ellen looked up at the small television she always kept on in the office. It generally served as background noise, and she'd barely paid any attention to it all day. A couple of minutes of *The View.* An occasional look in at *SportsCenter.*

Until now.

On the screen was none other than the defense lawyer Peter Carlyle. *Ugh! Double ugh!*

Ellen gnashed her teeth. How could she forget that arrogant prick of a lawyer's voice? To this day it was like nails on a blackboard to her. She had spent two long years of her life gathering cold, hard evidence against a known Mob boss for bribery and racketeering charges, only to have Carlyle prevail in the trial, thanks to his relentless grandstanding and, worse, outright lies on behalf of his scumbag client.

Turn the channel, she told herself. *Get rid of this piece of crap.*

She couldn't, though. It was like watching a car wreck, and she had to know what had happened.

Ellen reached for the remote control on her desk and turned up the TV's volume. Carlyle was being interviewed by Judith Fox. Didn't they once date or something?

Ellen listened. What was he promoting

now? she wondered. A racy new book? A recent verdict? It didn't matter. What Peter Carlyle promoted above all else was himself.

But that thought quickly gave way to a twinge of guilt. The interview was about his missing family. Hell, even a jerk like him didn't deserve to lose his wife and stepchildren out at sea.

He was pretty shaken up, too. His signature voice was actually trembling a bit as he recounted the way in which he had heard the news. "I have every faith that the Coast Guard will find them," he said with a stiff upper lip. "I've got to stay positive, and I certainly will."

"I think that's the only thing you can do," said Fox, turning to her live studio audience with a slow nod. "The Coast Guard is renowned for its search-and-rescue missions, and I'm sure its teams are doing everything in their power to find your family safe and alive, Peter."

Without even knowing it, Ellen was nodding along with Judith Fox, completely wrapped up in the story already. It certainly made for compelling television. There was drama, suspense, and just enough hope in the face of severe sorrow. Suddenly Ellen couldn't wait to find out how it would end.

That's when she got a strange feeling.

She didn't know why she had it, only that she felt it strongly in her gut. The more she listened, the more she felt it. She stood up and got even closer to the TV.

There was something in the way Peter Carlyle was telling his story. Past tense, almost.

As if he already knew how it ended.

Chapter 56

WITH A QUICK PULL on a black strap, the life raft from the Hail Mary box inflates before our weary eyes. *Thank God we're getting out of this water, at least. No more dog-paddling. No more sharks.*

Mark and Carrie climb aboard first and then help Ernie on. I'm next. When they see my leg—or should I say, the white of my shinbone jutting out from my leg—the kids all fall deathly silent. It just about takes something like this to shut them all up, especially Ernie.

"Is there a doctor on the boat?" I joke, trying to lighten the mood.

The bad joke doesn't work very well. In fact, the raft only becomes more silent—if there is such a thing—after they struggle to pull Jake aboard.

He's in even worse shape than I thought. Almost his entire body is covered with second- and even some third-degree burns. His skin is like Bubble Wrap with every bubble popped.

Carrie can't bear to look, and obviously she's feeling extra guilt because of what happened earlier, when she tried to drown herself and possibly Jake.

Back on land, in the burn unit of Lexington Hospital, there would be a host of available treatments. Out here in the middle of nowhere is a different story. There's virtually nothing I can do for him.

"Hand me that first-aid kit," I say to Mark, gritting my teeth over the effort to speak.

The rest of what was packed in the Hail Mary box is scattered about the raft. In addition to the first-aid kit, there is a surprisingly large amount of bottled water and food, though the food is mostly dried fruit, crackers, and nuts, all vacuum-packed in plastic.

In total, it's not a lot, but it's certainly

better than nothing. And nothing is something we've got covered in spades.

We have no motor, no shade, no sunblock, no radio, and no satellite phone.

No fair!

We also no longer have a flare gun, but no one's about to get on Carrie's case for that after she saved our butts, and every other edible part of us, with one very timely shark-skedaddling shot.

"Here," says Mark.

He hands me the first-aid kit. I find some antibiotic ointment and gently dab it over the areas on Jake that run the highest risk of infection. Then I slowly pour as much water as I can into his mouth, until he can't swallow any more. With his head resting on the side of the raft, he doesn't move or say anything. I think he's drifted back to being unconscious, or just doesn't have the strength to talk.

"There," I say after applying a thin layer of gauze around his arms and legs, which will still allow his skin to breathe. "That will have to do until help arrives."

"What about you?" asks Ernie. "Your leg."

"For now it's okay. It needs to be set, but

there's about a twenty-four-hour window before there might be any permanent damage," I explain. "By then I'll be safely in a hospital bed having you all sign my cast."

"You really think they're still coming for us?" asks Carrie.

"Of course I do. Why wouldn't they be?"

Chapter 57

LIEUTENANT ANDREW TATEM slammed down the phone in his small office at the Coast Guard base in Miami. His lieutenant had just given him the latest update on *The Family Dunne.* The news wasn't good. In fact, it made no sense at all.

Bolting out into the hallway, Tatem made a beeline for the Sit, short for Situation Room. Millcrest had just called him from there.

"What the hell's going on?" Tatem demanded, pushing through the Sit's double doors. "This isn't tracking for me. Not one bit."

No one in the room said a word. Not the land-based mission supervisor. Not the radio specialist. Not the petty officer whose sole responsibility was charting the location of the SAR helicopter searching for the boat.

Instead they all turned to Millcrest.

It was one of those rare moments when the lieutenant wished he didn't have such a good relationship with his commanding officer. It was just assumed he'd do the talking to Tatem.

"Well, it's like I said," began Millcrest slowly. "The chopper reached the coordinates of the *Dunne*'s EPIRB, only there was nothing there. Not even the EPIRB itself."

Tatem immediately wanted a cigarette. *Badly.*

"Give me the SAR team," he ordered. "I want to hear exactly what they *didn't* find."

Millcrest turned to the radio technician, who nodded with a crisp snap of the head and quickly announced the helicopter's call signs into a microphone. The entire wall where he sat was lined with monitors and maps.

Within seconds the head pilot responded over an annoying burst of static.

"This is Rescue WOLF, one-niner-one, we copy," he said, his voice filling the room. The technician had put him on the loud-speaker.

Tatem walked over and grabbed the microphone. His voice was booming. He didn't ask, he demanded: "What's the story out there, John? This isn't making a whole lot of sense yet."

The pilot explained that he'd done three fly-bys over the given coordinates and there was absolutely no boat, no crew, no sign of anything in the water. They were beginning to search the immediate area, but their fuel level would limit how much surface they could cover before they had to head back to base.

"Any chance your coordinate readings are off?" Tatem asked.

"No, sir," came back the pilot. "We double- and triple-checked already."

Millcrest shrugged again. "Perhaps it was the EPIRB, Andy. Maybe it malfunctioned before it went dead, broadcast the wrong coordinates."

"Maybe," said Tatem. "If that's the case,

we'd better hope the numbers are off by only a little. Otherwise, our search area is as big as that storm and then some."

"Even with multiple SARs, that could take us over a week," said Millcrest.

"Exactly. Which means we'd better get started." Tatem folded his arms, half talking to himself as he turned to walk out. "Let's hope this Dunne family has some fight in them."

Chapter 58

IT'S A BEAUTIFUL SUNSET. How ironic is that?

If only we could enjoy this incredible orange glow dipping toward the horizon, the blue of the ocean seemingly melting into the purple clouds fanning across the sky. Instead, rocking endlessly back and forth on this raft, all we can see is the darkness that awaits us. Nightfall. And the numbing chill that's coming with it.

Never will a couple of blankets have to work so hard.

"I think Carrie was right," says Mark, his

voice sullen. "They're not coming for us. No one is."

"We can't think like that," I say. "We have to stay positive, and that's not a cliché, guys."

It's as if Mark doesn't hear me. "If the Coast Guard has our coordinates, don't you think they would've been here by now?"

"Yeah, something's wrong," says Carrie.

Ernie nods in agreement, sage little Buddha that he is.

"Listen, all we can do right now is stay here and wait for them to come," I say.

It's not exactly the most persuasive argument I've ever made, but it succeeds for a reason I didn't intend. All because I said the word *wait.*

It makes Mark stare down at my leg. As he looks back at me, his eyes do all the talking. There's one thing that *can't* wait. At least, not much longer.

Nothing like an open grade-IIIB tibia fracture to change the subject.

"It's time to do something about that, isn't it?" he finally asks me.

He glances at my leg again, and I do the same.

"Yeah," I say, nodding. "I'm going to need some help with it, though."

"Count me out," says Carrie immediately. "I'm sorry, Mom. I told you I couldn't do pre-med."

Mark shoots her a look. "C'mon. After all you've been through today, you're telling me you're afraid of a little broken bone?"

"When it's a bone I can *see?* Yeah, that's what I'm telling you."

Alas, my superhero daughter has met her kryptonite. Squeamishness.

"It's okay, Mom, I'll help," offers Ernie.

Wow. He says it in a way so incredibly sweet I want to cry. Still, cramming a bone back into my exposed flesh and setting it isn't something for a ten-year-old to experience, no matter how mature he is.

Hell, it's not something for this forty-five-year-old either, but I don't have much of a choice now, do I?

"Thanks, sweetheart, but I only need your brother for this," I explain.

Your brother and a whole bunch of morphine, I should add.

That's when I watch Mark dig into his shorts. Our clothes have been dry for hours, although I'm thinking that whatever he's got in his pocket must still be a wet mess.

That is, until I see the plastic bag and the Bic lighter.

He dangles the bag from his fingertips, giving it a shake before smiling. "Hey, what do you know, dry as a bone."

I suddenly don't know whether to hug him or hit him. Either way, "You were supposed to give *all* of it to Jake."

"I know. What can I tell you? I always carry a spare doobie," he says. He removes the already rolled joint and hands it to me. "Think of it as medical marijuana. Perfectly legal, right?"

A few seconds pass as all I can do is stare at the joint. *Am I really about to smoke my son's pot?*

That's when I gaze down at my leg again and consider the godawful pain that awaits me. It's amazing how much your world can change in one day.

"Hand me the lighter," I tell Mark.

Chapter 59

THE POT WORKS. Kind of, sort of.

It does reduce the pain a little. Instead of sheer agony, it's more like a mild form of torture.

All I know is that when I get off this raft and back to the hospital, I'm going to hug all the anesthesiologists. It's not that I ever took them for granted. I just never gave them enough credit for what they do.

Anyway, as far as I can tell, the "operation" was a success. Mark was a real trouper, never once flinching as we reconstructed my snapped shinbone. *You see a lot worse in those stupid chainsaw movies,* he told me.

Now I have to keep my fingers crossed that the wound doesn't become infected.

In the meantime, I'm dealing with a side effect that I never anticipated. The munchies.

Here I am, four hours post-op, with the kids all huddled together asleep, and I'm wide awake, doing everything in my power not to eat every last calorie of our rations.

Oh, and did I mention how damn cold it is? And windy?

I can't help wondering what's taking the Coast Guard so long. Is it the storm? Has it reached land, wreaking havoc with their rescue missions?

Or what about the EPIRB? It was working, wasn't it?

Yes, it was. I'm sure of it.

I'm also sure we haven't drifted that far from the wreckage of the boat. All afternoon we've been paddling back against the current, trying to hold our coordinates. Even if we're off by a mile or two, we're still well within sight of any plane or helicopter.

At least, that's what I keep telling myself.

I lean back against the edge of the raft, lcoking up at the stars. Millions of them, it seems. I think of my father again and his telescope in the backyard. I even hear his voice, so calming. *We're all Big Dippers, part of something much bigger than ourselves.*

Suddenly there's another voice I'm hearing. It's faint, barely audible, and I think it's one of the kids talking in his sleep.

Then I realize—*it's Jake.*

I quickly scoot over to his side. I see his eyelids flutter—he's barely conscious.

"Jake, can you hear me?" I whisper in his ear.

He lets out a slight moan.

"Jake," I try again. "It's me, Katherine. Jake?"

He turns his head now and sees me. The words form slowly. "What happened?" he finally asks.

"There was an explosion on the boat, a big one. Do you remember anything?"

He doesn't. I can tell by the look on his face, the confusion in his eyes—and the fear.

"You were chasing us around the deck, throwing us in the water," I continue. As I say the words, it dawns on me. "That's why we're still alive . . . *because of you.*"

"I was—"

Jake stops, wincing in pain. It hurts for him to talk, so I tell him not to. But he keeps talking anyway. Jake is always Jake, no matter what's going on around him. Even this.

"I was . . . at . . . the bow . . . with you," he manages. "Now I remember."

"That's right, that's when the explosion happened. You were the only one still on the boat. That's why you were burned."

Damn. Where's my bedside manner? He didn't need to know that, not now.

Jake struggles to look down at himself. That hurts him even more than trying to talk, and his face contorts in agony. "How bad?"

I take his hand in mine. "It's going to be okay. *You're* going to be okay. The EPIRB—you set it off, remember? They're going to come and rescue us."

I watch him trying to remember. He's breathing harder. I tell him he needs to rest.

"I can . . . still hear him," he says.

"Who?"

"My . . . brother."

It takes me a second before it clicks. He'd told me about hearing Stuart on the boat—seeing him, even—although he said he knew it hadn't really happened.

I squeeze Jake's hand. "I'm sure he's not laughing anymore," I say.

Jake's tan face is now white as a ghost's. His breathing grows more labored, and it scares me.

"You've got to conserve your strength," I tell him. *"Please."*

There's something else he wants to say. Despite the pain, he needs to tell me something. "I was never sorry," he says, his voice faint.

I don't want him to talk anymore, but I also don't know what he means. Maybe he sees it in my eyes, because of all things, he smiles. He pulls me inches closer and whispers in my ear.

"I was never sorry I loved you," Jake says.

I turn away as my tears begin to fall. They spill from my eyes, streaking down my face. It was complicated back then, when Jake and I had our forbidden summer. Stuart was away all the time, constantly, and I almost felt that he knew and didn't care about Jake and me. Maybe Stuart was moving on and wanted me to do the same.

I look out at the ocean, the lovely reflection of the moon. I look back up at the sky and all its teeming stars.

And I look at my kids, who are all still asleep. It's strange, but I don't think I've ever loved them any more than I do right now.

I squeeze Jake's hand again because there's something *I* need to tell *him.*

"Jake," I say, finally turning back to him. "Jake?"

My mouth stops.

Everything stops in my universe.

Jake's no longer breathing.

He's gone.

Part Four

ALL TOGETHER NOW

Chapter 60

"MOM, are we going to die too?"

Ernie's question shoots me in the heart, and for a few moments I'm speechless. I thought the hardest thing I'd ever have to do in my life was telling my children that their father had died. Turns out I was wrong. Breaking the news about Jake, that he didn't make it through that first night, was even harder.

When Stuart died, we all *felt* alone.

With Jake gone, we truly are.

For two days now, no less.

We've been burned beet red by the sun, and our food and water are beginning to run low, almost as low as our spirits. The sadness of losing Jake has taken the kids from overwhelming despair to something even worse. Fear.

That we all might be next.

We've been staying as close as possible to where *The Family Dunne* went down, but there's been no rescue boat, no helicopter. The only planes overhead are like ants in the sky, mere specks that we probably wouldn't see at all if not for their vapor trails. For sure they can't see us.

In short, we're lost somewhere in tropical waters, but we don't know exactly where. Apparently neither does anyone else.

So why do I keep telling the kids that we need to stay put? Why do we keep fighting the current?

For two days I've been a stubborn mule, saying that we need to give the Coast Guard more time. By now I know the kids suspect the real reason.

I'm the one who needs more time. Jake's at rest at the bottom of the ocean and I still can't let go. I can't move on. Physically. Truth is, if I were the only person on this lousy raft, I wouldn't leave. I'd stay here near Jake until I was either rescued or not.

But that's not the way it is. I now realize that. My children are on this raft with me, and I'm their mother. We may be alone out here on the ocean, but we're alone together.

And we need to be saved.

I stare through narrowed eyes at their sunburned bodies, their cuts and bruises, the sea salt clinging to their scabs. Looking between their chapped white lips and disheveled heads of hair, I stare deep into their eyes.

"No, Ernie," I answer. "We're not going to die too."

It's time to let go, to stop fighting the current.

And see where it takes us.

Chapter 61

OPERATION CHANCE ENCOUNTER has begun. That's what Ellen Pierce called it as she walked into the small, albeit well-equipped gym that the DEA offered its agents in the basement of the New York Division building.

The time was 5:20 A.M. Early with a capital *E!*

Not surprisingly, Ellen had the gym to herself. Good thing, too. This way she could pour some Poland Spring water into a towel and strategically dab her face and wet down her T-shirt without having to explain herself to anyone. Including the man she was waiting for: her boss.

She knew that Ian McIntyre worked out every weekday morning, starting at five-thirty. He was a fitness freak, having competed in iron-man triathlons up until his late forties. Now that he was a card-carrying member of the AARP, he had scaled back a little. He only did marathons. Three a year, to be exact. Boston, New York, and Philly, his old hometown.

Needless to say, the man was hard-core—all the more reason why Ellen had to go through this little charade just to have a private chat with him.

During the day, on Uncle Sam's time and dime, Ian McIntyre did everything pretty much by the book. The subject matter of work conversations he had with agents was logged in what was famously known as "the Tomb." In the era of knee-jerk congressional hearings, it was a pretty smart thing to do, actually.

There was also another benefit. The Tomb kept agents from wasting McIntyre's time. Because when it came to far-flung hunches, no one liked to go on record. It certainly didn't bode well for your annual performance review.

Sure enough, at five-thirty sharp, Ian McIntyre came bouncing into the gym via the men's locker room. Immediately he did a double take as he spotted Ellen Pierce stepping off a treadmill. He wasn't used to having company at this early hour.

"Good morning, Ian," said Ellen, wiping the Poland Spring "sweat" from her brow.

"Morning, Ellen. What a surprise. I didn't know you even worked out here."

"I don't. A pipe burst last night at the gym in my apartment building. So here I am, bright and early."

McIntyre nodded as he dropped down to the floor mat to stretch. Ellen wanted the segue to seem natural, so she waited a few moments, toweling off the handrails on her treadmill.

Then, as nonchalantly as possible, she asked, "Hey, have you been following that whole thing with Peter Carlyle's family?"

"You mean their sailboat disappearing? Yeah, a little bit. Horrible, huh?"

"Really horrible. Those kids, his wife. I never thought I'd feel sorry for the guy."

McIntyre gave her a quick, knowing

smile. "You and me both. At least for his family."

She opened her mouth as if to speak but stopped. This was the moment of truth.

"What were you about to say?" asked McIntyre.

"Oh, it's nothing," said Ellen with a shrug. "It's just that I got this feeling when I was watching Carlyle on *The Judith Fox Show.*"

"What kind of feeling?" he asked.

"Something kind of strange. It was as if he—"

McIntyre cut her off like an ax. "Stop right there," he said. "I don't want to hear it."

"Hear what?"

"Whatever you're about to tell me."

"You don't even know what it is, Ian."

"I don't have to, Ellen. This isn't the time or the place."

"Just hear me out, will you?" she asked. "It's the way Carlyle was acting. Something's not right. I'm a hundred percent on this. Carlyle *knows* something."

McIntyre stood up from the mat. In less than two seconds he was directly in Ellen's face. "Listen to me," he began. "The guy's a first-class A-hole and he made us look bad in court and blew up your case. I know you're still mad, and I can understand that. But what I won't understand—what I won't *tolerate*—is one of my agents letting her anger affect her better judgment. You keep that imagination of yours in check, you got that? That goes for your female intuition, too."

Ellen stared blankly at him. *Imagination? Female intuition? How about street smarts and common sense?*

"I said, have . . . you . . . got . . . that?"

She finally nodded.

McIntyre turned and walked over to the nearest treadmill. Before stepping on, he turned back. "Oh, and the next time you want to fake a workout so you can have my ear, try not to make the sweatstain so perfect on your little T-shirt, okay?"

Ellen grimaced. *Ouch. Busted.*

So much for Operation Chance Encounter.

It was time for Plan B.

Chapter 62

IT WAS BARELY 9 A.M. in Miami and the temperature outside the Coast Guard base was already pushing up into the high eighties, and it was humid.

As for the temperature inside, it wasn't much lower. The central AC was seemingly waving the white flag again, and the vents in Andrew Tatem's office were trickling the lukewarmest of lukewarm air.

Great, just great. Splendid . . . and now things get really hot, right?

Tatem picked up the phone and dialed. As much as he hated to take shit from anyone, that's exactly what he was about to do in a big, unpleasant way.

"May I speak with Peter Carlyle, please? This is Lieutenant Tatem of the Coast Guard."

Another night had come and gone without finding *The Family Dunne* and its crew. After ordering the search effort to continue around the clock and adding a slew of helicopters and man-hours, Tatem and his Coast Guard unit had turned up absolutely nothing.

Now, in what had become a twice-daily routine, Tatem had to call New York and share the news. Or rather, his no-news.

"I don't get it!" barked Carlyle over the phone, his patience clearly waning, if he ever had any. "You said you had their coordinates, am I right? Didn't you tell me that, Lieutenant Tatem? I made a note of it."

"We thought we did." *The bastard is making notes. For the lawsuit, right?*

"What about your maps? Are you sure you're reading them right?"

Tatem closed his eyes, blinking long and hard in an effort to maintain his usual even keel. *Reading our maps right? What does he think we're using, an old foldout*

Rand McNally from the glove compartment?

"Mr. Carlyle, this is one of the largest search efforts we've ever made. I assure you that we're doing our very best," said Tatem.

"Then your best needs to get a whole lot better," he heard back. That was followed by a loud *click!*

Carlyle had hung up on him, and he wanted Tatem to know he'd been cut off.

Oh, well.

Such abuse was nothing new to Tatem. He was used to family members expressing their frustrations. More important, he understood it. It was only natural. Very human. And thus forgivable.

What struck Tatem as being a little odd, though—or at least different—was that he wasn't getting the abuse face-to-face.

He'd been involved in over a hundred search-and-rescue efforts for people missing at sea. Most of the time, "loved ones" felt compelled to travel to the base, especially if they could afford it. They wanted to be closer to the action, feel more part of the effort. "It's the least we can do," he often heard.

Not Carlyle, though. He wanted to know everything that was happening, only he wanted to know it while he was back home in Manhattan.

Granted, his rushing down to Miami wouldn't make any difference in the search effort itself. In fact, as the search dragged on, it could only complicate things, especially since the media had really latched on to the story.

Carlyle's appearance on *The Judith Fox Show* had all but set the table.

Now, nearly three days later, with the Dunne family still missing, the feeding frenzy would only get worse.

So why was Carlyle still up in New York?

Chapter 63

I WANT TO SCREAM! I want to let go with a Grand Canyon–deep, ear-piercing primal scream that rattles the heavens and whoever may or may not be up there holding on to the deed for this planet.

We're all part of something much bigger than ourselves?

I'm losing faith, Dad. I'm feeling so small and insignificant you wouldn't believe it.

We've been drifting for two days, and the view hasn't changed. Everywhere we look it's just ocean and more ocean. Nothing else exists in our universe.

This raft may still be inflated, but the blistering sun combined with our dwindling food and water has let the air out of all of us. We're exhausted, zapped. Numb.

The kids at least have been able to sleep. Not me. Here it is, the sun about to rise on another day, and I feel like I'm back pulling thirty-six-hour shifts as an intern. Only this is so much worse. Back then I always knew that things would get better, that the shift would end.

Which brings me to my leg.

The bone may be mending, but the skin around the wound has turned a very unfortunate shade of green. Even if my medical background consisted merely of watching *Grey's Anatomy* or *House,* I'd know that the one thing I feared has happened. It's infected. I'm infected. A raging fever can't be too far behind.

I haven't said boo to the kids about any of this, nor do I plan to. At least not yet. They've got enough on their minds. So I'm keeping my leg covered and hoping against hope that the scenery changes for us soon. Really soon!

Actually, I'd laugh out loud if I had the strength.

For the longest time, years and years, I've wanted to buy a great beach house on Martha's Vineyard, or maybe Nantucket. It would be my escape from Manhattan—something with a private deck, a couple of chaise longues, and, most important, an amazing ocean view.

Ha!

To hell with wishing for that anymore. All I want to see now, and forever, is land.

I want to be rescued! I want my kids to be safe!

Then maybe I'll finally be able to sleep.

I'm about to close my eyes and try yet again to sleep when both my lids suddenly pop open like jack-in-the-boxes.

Oh!

My!

God!

Is that a mirage? Am I so ridiculously sleep-deprived that I'm seeing things?

No! It's for real, all right. I think it's real, anyway.

Way off in the distance, amid the first hint of sunrise, is the most beautiful sight in the world.

"Kids!" I yell. "Wake up! Wake up!"

They slowly begin to stir—*too* slowly, I

decide—so I supply them with a little added incentive at the top of my lungs. It's a Grand Canyon–deep, ear-piercing primal scream that rattles the heavens and whoever may or may not be up there holding the deed to this planet.

"LAND HO!" I announce.

Chapter 64

AS FAST AS YOU CAN SAY . . . well, "Land ho!" we turn into the Dunne family Olympic paddling team.

This is incredible. It's so fantastic. Unbelievable.

As we scoop frantically with paddles and hands, our pain and exhaustion take a distant backseat in the raft. I even forget about my leg.

We're gunning for a mere speck of green on a blue horizon, but the kids are just as sure as I am. It's an island. And we can't wait to get there!

Especially our empty stomachs.

"I hope they have a McDonald's!" chirps Ernie. "You think?"

We all burst into laughter, and it feels great. Humor, much like our rations, has been in very short supply the past couple of days.

"Screw that burger nonsense," says Mark, showing no letup on his paddling. "I want the whole cow, a big-ass porterhouse steak! Maybe there'll be a Morton's on the island! Ruth Chris. Flames!"

"Or maybe a really great pizza place," says Carrie, getting in on the act. "I could eat an entire large pepperoni pie all by myself! I'd do it, too!"

Talk about a couple of sentences I never thought I'd hear from her...

"What about you, Mom?" asks Ernie. "What kind of restaurant do you want?"

I need to think about it for only a split second. "Room service!" I belt out. "I want the entire menu delivered to me as I lounge on my comfy pillow-top bed at the St. Regis."

"Works for me!" says Carrie. "Order up!"

"That would be so cool, if there's a hotel," adds Ernie.

"Hey, I don't care if all this island has is a Motel 6," says Mark. "Just as long as it's a bed and not this lousy raft with its Hail Mary box buffet."

Our shoulders and arms ache as we continue paddling, but it's the best pain in the world. In the back of my mind, I can't help thinking about Jake and wishing he were here to see this.

I feel tears welling up in my eyes. I can't hold them back; I don't even try. Sadness? Joy? Both, I realize.

I also realize how proud Jake would've been of all of us. We've hung in there, toughed this out together.

Like a real family, *the* family Dunne, the one that really matters.

Chapter 65

WE'RE ABOUT four hundred yards from the island. Then three hundred. And suddenly Ernie stops paddling.

"Hey," he says, raising a hand to shield his eyes from the sun. "Where is everybody?"

We all stop and squint. We're finally close enough to shore for a good look-see at the beach dead ahead. But no matter where we look, we don't see a single person.

We don't see much of anything, actually. No houses, no huts, no construction of any kind.

No sign of life.

"Big deal. So it's a secluded beach," says Carrie with a shrug. "Keep paddling, my hearties. Look how beautiful it is!"

She's certainly right about that. The sand, a gorgeous pastel pink, is practically sparkling under the morning sun, while in the background huge sweeping palms gently lean forward as if each tree is listening to the surf. It's the very definition of unspoiled.

"I bet you ten bucks only the locals know about this beach," says Mark. "They probably keep it a secret from the tourists."

"Yeah, it would get way too crowded," adds Carrie warily. "It's not very big."

No, actually it's very small. In fact, the whole island looks small, at least from this angle. For all I know—and hope—my pillow-top bed at the St. Regis is waiting for me on the other side.

"Let's keep paddling," I say.

We're churning on nothing but a mix of adrenaline and curiosity now, our mild joking giving way to a hushed silence. We're staring straight ahead at the best news we've had in four days, if not our entire lives—land!—and yet there's no escaping this weird feeling among us. It's as if Ernie's question is echoing in all our heads. *Where is everybody? Or anybody, for that matter?*

We keep paddling, we keep looking at the perfect beach.

With nobody on it.

Chapter 66

FROM LAND HO to land here.

The kids hop out into waist-high water and pull the raft up onto shore with me still in it. I'm nowhere near able to put any pressure on my broken leg, so Mark carries me over to a spot on the sand and sets me down with great care. I have never seen him acting like this, and it's impressive. *Mark* is impressive.

No one says anything as we all look around, our necks craning left and right.

Finally Ernie sums it all up. "I get the feeling we're a long, long way from any McDonald's, or even a Taco Bell."

I'm afraid that's right. If first impressions count for anything, it's hard to imagine there being Happy Meals, or for that matter a steakhouse, on this island. As for a five-star hotel, that's not looking too promising either. Or a telephone.

Especially when the only footprints on this beach are ours.

"There's no way this is a deserted island," says Carrie, as if trying to convince herself. "I mean, there's no way . . . Right?"

"It's highly unlikely," I assure her while trying to convince myself.

"Yes, but it is definitely possible," says Ernie matter-of-factly. "I saw this movie in my science class that said there are a lot more deserted islands than people think."

Mark rolls his eyes. "That movie was probably made fifty years ago. At worst, this place might be uninhabited at the moment, but it's not *deserted.*"

"What's the difference if there's no one here to help us?" asks Carrie.

"A big difference," says Mark. "It means that somewhere on this island there's probably a house, or a couple of houses, with a satellite link. *E.T., phone home*—you follow?"

Carrie nods, cowering slightly at the thought that her younger, pot-smoking Deerfield brother has shown up his older, wiser, better-SAT-scoring Yalie sister. Sibling rivalry knows no bounds, even on an island.

"So what are we waiting for?" asks Ernie. "Let's go find a phone."

Of course, I'm not about to go anywhere. Not unless a pair of crutches were suddenly to fall from the sky. Even if they did, I'd be having second thoughts about this proposed trek. Something doesn't feel right to me.

"Whoa," I say, raising my palm like a traffic cop. "Maybe that's not such a good idea right now."

"Maybe what's not such a good idea right now?" asks Mark. "Calling the Coast Guard?"

"Going off exploring the island right away. The sun's not even all the way up yet."

"It doesn't matter. All we've done so far is trade in a raft for a beach. We still need to find help. And help's *that* way."

He points beyond the beach as Carrie and Ernie nod in agreement.

"He's right, Mom," says Carrie. "We have to find out what's here."

I know they're both right. That's the problem.

"Okay, here's the deal," I say, sounding exactly the way I feel—like a nervous mother. "The three of you absolutely have to stay together and look out for one another. Whatever you do, *don't get separated.* And there can be no fights."

Mark salutes. "Gotcha, Doc."

"I'm serious, you guys. Don't take too long, either."

"Don't worry, we'll be quick," says Carrie. "We won't leave you here long. And we'll be on our best behavior."

As the three of them walk off, Mark shouts over his shoulder, "If we're not back in a couple of hours, call the Coast Guard!"

Chapter 67

I KNOW I TOLD THEM to be quick. But I didn't mean *this* quick. This is either very good or very bad.

In less than twenty minutes the kids are back. As they emerge from the palm trees and trudge across the beach, I notice something dangling from Mark's fingertips.

"What is that?" I call out. "What did you find?"

"The only sign of civilization here," he answers.

He holds it up for me to see. It's caked with sand, and the label has completely worn off. But the shape is unmistakable. Classic.

It's a Coke bottle.

"Yeah, we found it right beyond the beach," says Ernie.

"That's it? No house with a satellite link?" I ask.

"No *anything*," says Mark. "No roads, no signs, and definitely no people." He glances at the old Coke bottle. "At least, not recently."

"Are you sure? You guys weren't gone for too long."

"We didn't need to be," he says. "It's literally a jungle out there, *thick,* and nothing more. This island is deserted with a capital *D.*"

"So now what do we do?" asks Carrie.

It's a good question, and one I don't immediately have an answer for. I'm too busy thinking about all the awful signals I'm beginning to get from my body.

What began as a low-grade fever is starting to climb. I don't need a thermometer, I can feel it—much like the chills I'm also having. The result is a cold sweat from head to toe. The only reason the kids don't notice is that we're all sweating in this heat, too.

Meanwhile, Mark seems to have more energy and ideas than I've seen from him in a year. "I think we need to do a few things," he says. "First we have to be able to signal boats and planes, right? We should spell out *SOS* with rocks and prepare a big fire we can light. We also should figure out where we'll sleep tonight."

"I vote for somewhere with a roof," says Ernie, pointing out over the water.

We all turn to look at some very ominously dark clouds on the horizon.

"Shit, I thought we were done with storms for a while," says Carrie with a groan.

"Yeah, just like we all thought we were saved," says Mark, kicking at nothing in the sand. He's pissed. Suddenly he rears back and heaves the Coke bottle into the surf.

"Hey, don't!" objects Ernie.

Mark bristles. "Why not? What, do you want to keep it for the deposit?"

Ernie ignores his big brother and wades into the water. He snatches up the Coke bottle floating amid the waves. "Don't you get it, Mark? This could save us!"

"Oh, yeah?" says Mark incredulously. "How would it do that?"

"It's simple, you dope. We put a message in it."

We all laugh, and I immediately feel awful. Perhaps Mark and Carrie ought to know better, but I definitely should. This is no time to be teasing poor Ernie.

"I'm sorry, honey, I know you're only trying to help," I say. "We shouldn't be laughing. We're all dopes."

"Go ahead and laugh. You'll be thanking me later."

"Oh, I'm sure," says Mark. "Tell me, Baby Einstein, what are you going to write your message on?"

Ernie appears momentarily stumped by that one. So am I, actually. Then his face lights up with an idea. "I'll write it on a piece of my T-shirt," he says. He grabs his T-shirt from the bottom, pulling it tight. "I'll tear off a section and write on that."

Mark nods, if only to play along. "Okay, and what are you going to write with? I mean, I'd love to help you out, but I'm fresh out of pens."

But Ernie's ahead of the curve now.

"I saw some red berries on a bush when we were walking before. I'll crush them and make ink." He mugs at his brother, and it's kind of cute.

"Let me guess—you saw that in another movie from science class."

"Go ahead, keep laughing. I'll have the last one, guys."

Mark walks over to Ernie and throws an arm around his shoulder. "Dude, in case you've forgotten, we've been drifting for days without coming anywhere near a boat. It would take months, if not years, before that Coke bottle could wash ashore somewhere else, so who do you think is going to find it in the meantime, Aquaman?"

Carrie laughs again, but I don't.

"Okay, that's enough," I say. "If Ernie wants to do it, let him. In the meantime, we need to get busy making some kind of camp."

"Yeah," says Carrie. "Camp Shipwreck!"

Chapter 68

LOOKING CRISP AND CLEAN in his neatly pressed white Coast Guard uniform, Andrew Tatem stepped up to the depressing bouquet of microphones in the parking lot outside his base. Beyond the mikes was the press. Their cameras liked him already. He was thirty-eight years old, just over six-one, with a Florida tan and shiny white teeth, which he was planning to keep all to himself today.

The media frenzy that he knew was coming had come all right, and the street directly outside the front gates to the base looked like an overbooked satellite-dish convention. One after another, reporters lined up before the cameras, their caked-on makeup barely withstanding the sweltering summer heat of Miami as they doled out the latest on the mysterious case of the missing *Family Dunne.*

But the pack was growing restless.

For an entire news cycle, a veritable lifetime for these media types, they hadn't been fed any new information. Tatem knew why, of course. *Because there wasn't any.*

Nonetheless, Tatem also knew he had to let them do their jobs. Reporters were a fickle bunch, and the last thing he needed right now was to have them turn on him.

Hence the press conference.

Slowly, calmly, methodically, Tatem delivered his prepared statement. *The search continues . . . no effort being spared . . . It's a big ocean out there . . . The Coast Guard remains extremely hopeful . . . I remain extremely hopeful.*

It was all true. It just wasn't new.

Which was why Tatem braced himself as he stopped, drew a deep breath, and made a simple offer.

"I'll answer your questions now."

All at once the air exploded with shouting as the reporters verbally elbowed one another in order to be heard.

"At what point will you call off the search effort?"

"Can you confirm that *The Family Dunne* issued a Mayday call before it disappeared?"

"Why hasn't the Navy been brought in?"

Tatem had given his fair share of press conferences, but they had never been like this. Not even close to this magnitude and intensity.

One man off to the side, a scraggly-haired beat reporter from the *Daily Miami,* was particularly relentless. Florida was this guy's turf, and he clearly didn't want anybody to forget it.

"What's your reaction to the rumor that you're about to be replaced as the officer in charge of this search effort?" he asked.

Tatem blinked. *Replaced*?

"I'm certainly not aware of any such rumor," he answered.

The reporter turned to the brunette next to him, muttering loudly enough to be heard.

"They never are."

Tatem ignored the unpleasant remark, not to mention the overwhelming urge to leap from behind the microphones and lock this asshole in a half nelson before dropping him down to the pavement. *What's your reaction to that, punk?*

It was time to wrap things up.

"I'll answer one more question," he announced.

Immediately the shouting escalated, the gaggle of reporters pushing up closer to the microphones. As nonchalantly as he could, Tatem raised his hand to wipe away a bead of sweat from his forehead, only to hear the air explode again with the sound of clicking cameras. *Damn.* They didn't miss a gnat fart, did they?

He could see it now, his photo splashed across every major newspaper in the country. *Coast Guard Lieutenant Andrew Tatem on the hot seat,* the caption would read.

Or, worse, *Andrew Tatem only hours before being replaced in Miami.*

He suddenly wished he'd never heard of the Dunne family and their damn sailboat. He had felt sorry for them, but in the media's intense glare—this ridiculous 24/7 circus—the feeling had shifted to intense frustration. Even some anger.

What the hell happened to that family? It didn't make any sense so far.

Tatem suddenly saw something out of the corner of his eye. It was Millcrest. His lieutenant was walking straight toward him with that familiar look on his face.

There was something Tatem needed to know.

And it couldn't wait.

Chapter 69

TATEM STEPPED BACK from the microphones as Millcrest whispered up against his ear.

"We found something, sir."

That was it. Four words he'd been waiting to hear. That's all it took.

Quickly copping his best poker face, Tatem turned to the crowd of reporters and announced that there was another matter he had to attend to. No one bought it, but he didn't care. As they all began shouting "What other matter?" he was hightailing it back inside the base.

Directly to the Sit Room.

"It's a life jacket from the boat," Millcrest told him along the way. "There must have been a fire onboard, because part of it was badly burned."

"You said it was from the boat. How do you know?" asked Tatem.

"Because it said so," answered Millcrest with a slight smirk. "They actually had monogrammed life jackets, if you can believe that. 'The Family Dunne' was sewn along the back of the collar."

"Only one life jacket was found?"

"So far."

"Nothing else—no other debris from the boat, the fire, whatever happened?"

"Not yet. We're circling the area again, widening the perimeter. With the jacket being scorched, though—"

"I know," said Tatem. *That's probably all they'll find.*

Millcrest grabbed the door of the Sit Room and held it open for Tatem, who immediately locked eyes with the junior officer on the radio.

"Which team was it?" Tatem asked. "Powell?"

"No, it was Hawkins," answered the officer.

"They on a secure channel?"

"Yes, and waiting for you, sir."

The officer radioed the SAR team and they answered within seconds.

"Nice catch, boys," said Tatem, which he truly meant. A life jacket floating in the ocean was the proverbial needle in a haystack.

Now came the key question he had to ask them. This was the gutwhacker.

"How far from the original EPIRB coordinates are you?"

"That's the thing," answered Hawkins, the SAR pilot, his voice echoing through the radio. "We're a whole lot farther away than any current or drift pattern could've taken them. Lieutenant, you know what that means."

Tatem fell silent. On the one hand, this explained why the search teams hadn't found anything sooner. *The Family Dunne* had never been at those original coordinates.

On the other hand, it made the situation clear to him—from a Coast Guard perspective, anyway.

It was hopeless out there.

"Sir?" asked Millcrest.

Tatem's mind returned to the room. "I'm sorry, what?"

"Would you like Hawkins to fan the area one more time?"

Tatem took a moment, squeezing his temples as if to force out the answer he didn't want to give. But had to.

"No," he finally said. "Bring 'em home . . . bring 'em *all* home. The search is over. The area's too large. *The Family Dunne* went down."

Chapter 70

PETER WAS ALONE and enjoying his morning cup of coffee in Katherine's five-bedroom, six-thousand-square-foot apartment on Park Avenue, but not for long. With the buzz of the building's intercom he was told that Mona Elien had just arrived. *Fuckin' great. Wonderful.*

Peter's first condolence call was from probably the last person he wanted to see right now. Especially one-on-one in Katherine's apartment.

Despite their socializing together on numerous occasions, Peter didn't truly know Katherine's best friend all that well, nor did he want to. It was nothing personal. Rather, it was professional.

Mona was a New York shrink. Peter *hated* shrinks, from any city. He had ever since he was a kid.

When Peter was twelve and growing up in Larchmont, his parents had caught him stealing from their wallets. His excuse was that his allowance wasn't big enough. They grounded him. At the same time they doubled his allowance, their loopy thought being that he would no longer be tempted to steal. A few months later, though, they caught Peter at their wallets again. That's when they realized it didn't matter how much money they gave him. Enough would never be enough for their troubled son.

He had to have more.

So they took Peter to see a psychiatrist. When that shrink couldn't get through to him, they dragged him to another. And another.

By then Peter loathed psychiatrists. He thought they were nothing more than smooth-talking, note-taking phonies asking bullshit questions like "How does that make you feel?"

He couldn't stand being in the same room with them anymore. There was only one way out, he decided.

Lie to them.

Peter told his next shrink exactly what he figured she wanted to hear. He said he had stolen the money to get attention from his parents, but now he was sorry he had caused them so much pain and worry.

It worked. What's more, it changed his life. Peter realized for the first time that he could lie with the best of them, and that he was born to be a lawyer.

A damn successful one, too. In fact, before meeting Katherine Dunne, he had been taking down over $2 million a year. That was enough for anyone to live on comfortably.

Unfortunately for Katherine and her kids, it wasn't enough for Peter.

He had to have more.

He was well on his way to getting it, too. All he had to do was stick to his game plan. Next up? Conning Katherine's friends and relatives as he had that psychiatrist when he was just a kid.

How fitting that Mona Elien would be first.

A shrink.

Let the session begin.

Chapter 71

THE APARTMENT'S DOORBELL sounded with an elegant chime, which he despised and would change within the week. He'd do the same to the chimes at Katherine's country house up in Chappaqua.

As Peter went to greet Mona, he stopped first in front of a gold-leaf mirror in the marble foyer. He wanted to make sure he looked sufficiently bereaved.

Not quite convinced by what he saw in the mirror, Peter furiously rubbed his eyes for a few seconds to make them good and red, as if he'd been crying half the night.

There. Much better.

"Thank you for coming, Mona," he said, opening the door.

She didn't respond. All she did was stare at him for what seemed like an eternity. There were no tears from her, no consoling hugs. Finally she spoke.

"I know what you've done," she said.

"Excuse me?" asked Peter.

It was pure reflex. He had heard her perfectly. He just couldn't believe she'd actually said it.

Relax, there's no way she could know . . . Right?

Mona held his gaze as she entered the apartment. She put her handbag down on the silk-tufted bench below the mirror in the foyer. "I can see it in your eyes," she said. "The guilt."

"Guilt?"

"Yes. You've been blaming yourself ever since Katherine and the kids disappeared. As if somehow things would've been different if you had gone with them."

"Oh," said Peter, barely able to contain his relief. *Silly rabbit. The shrink is just being a shrink.*

"It's a very common reaction, Peter," Mona continued. "But you have to know that you're not to blame for this tragedy. It's not your fault, not at all."

Peter didn't skip a beat. If he had, he might have actually laughed out loud. "I know, I know," he said with a slow, gloomy nod. "But it's been so damn hard."

With that, he shot Mona a helpless look, and she promptly responded by giving him a hug. It was like Pavlov's dog. Or was that *Peter's* dog?

For good measure, he was about to turn on the waterworks when he realized that she'd beat him to it. Her crying just happened to be genuine.

She pulled back finally. "Oh, God, look at me, I'm a sobbing mess," she said, wiping away a tear. What little mascara she was wearing had smudged beneath her eyes. She could feel it. "Let me go check on the damage."

Mona knew every room of Katherine's apartment, including the half-bath off the foyer. She closed the door behind her.

For a second Peter simply stood there, twiddling his thumbs. The next second he was eyeing her handbag on the table. Insane, but he couldn't help himself.

Quickly he approached the bag, intent

on finding her wallet. Whatever cash she had, he'd take only what she wouldn't miss.

What a rush! She could come out at any second! She could catch him in the act!

Suddenly his hand froze. He saw something next to her wallet.

It was turned on.

Chapter 72

AN HOUR LATER Peter was walking south along Park Avenue. His mind was elsewhere, though.

A tape recorder? Why would Mona Elien be taping our conversation? What is the bitch up to?

He didn't know anything beyond the obvious—that she indeed must suspect him of something. Or, at the very least, she didn't trust him.

All the more reason to be doing what he was about to do next, just to be safe.

Peter cut over to Fifth Avenue and continued south for ten blocks, until straight ahead was the fountain outside the famous Plaza Hotel. Hordes of tourists and other people on their lunch breaks were using the perimeter of the fountain as a giant circular bench. Today was no different from any other.

Good. Perfect for his purposes. Lots and lots of witnesses!

Peter was wearing a red jacket and a baseball cap featuring the near ubiquitous half Lab, half boxer logo of the Black Dog Tavern on Martha's Vineyard. He and Katherine had visited the pub—but hell, so had he and Bailey.

A mere block away from the fountain now, he gave a quick tug on the cap, pulling it down tight above his eyes—so tight, in fact, that he almost didn't see the two cops standing on the far corner chatting to a hot dog vendor.

But he was glad he did spot them. Very glad. He wrote them right into the script.

How lucky can one guy get? I guess the good Lord must be looking down fondly on me.

With a few quick glances, Peter scanned the sidewalk in front of the fountain, checking to see who was walking toward him.

His eyes breezed over the women and children, as well as anyone who looked older than him. It had to be a guy, and a younger male at that.

Bingo! There you are.

Peter spotted him about thirty yards away. Baggy jeans, T-shirt, Timberland boots, scowl.

Mr. Timberland was maybe in his late twenties—lean and fit, but definitely not a gym rat by any means. More important, he had that look on his face—the expressionless, dead stare that suggested he was a little annoyed with the world, if not outright pissed at it.

In short, Mr. Timberland wasn't about to take any shit from anybody on the street. Peter included.

Reaching into the pocket of his jacket, Peter removed a small sterling silver flask filled with Jack Daniel's. Without breaking stride, he gave the cap a twist and promptly swigged about four or five ounces of pure liquid courage.

It was showtime!

Chapter 73

PETER IMMEDIATELY CUT a hard angle across the sidewalk, lining himself up directly in Mr. Timberland's path. The distance between them quickly diminished until they were just steps apart. At the last second Peter steeled himself, and then he walked right into the guy.

Smack!

The two men collided hard, shoulder to shoulder. Before the guy even knew what—or who—hit him, Peter added insult to injury.

"Watch where you're going, asshole!" he barked.

"Excuse me?" the guy called out. The words were polite, but not the tone. Far from it. Mr. Timberland was ticked off good already.

Peter stopped and turned around to face him. "You heard me!" he shot back.

"That's right, I did. What the hell's your problem?"

Peter jabbed his finger close to the man's face. "Right now it's *you!*"

Peter could feel the eyes of several people around the fountain staring out over their stale tuna-fish sandwiches. They were beginning to take notice of this little altercation.

Peter didn't look at any of them. He kept his eyes squarely on Timberland, who was beginning to edge toward him. Within seconds they were toe to toe.

"Why don't you chill out, man?" said the guy.

Fat chance.

The only thing Peter had to make sure of now was whether he'd truly picked the right mark. It wasn't just whether the guy could take a punch, but whether he could throw one in return. Hopefully, a lot more than one.

It was time to press some buttons with this guy.

More important, it was time to press some buttons with the press.

"What are you, some kind of tough guy?" said Peter. "'Cause you look more like a pussy to me."

"What the hell did you call me?"

"You deaf or something? I called you a pussy, *you pussy.*"

Peter watched as the guy's face flushed bright red. His nostrils flared; the veins in his neck were bulging against his skin.

Yeah, he'd picked the right guy, all right. Just as with jury selection, his instincts were golden.

Peter, a southpaw, reared back, his left hand balled into a tight fist. As he let it fly, he could hear the collective gasps of all the witnesses gathered around the fountain. When the cops asked who threw the first punch, there would be no doubt. A unanimous verdict for sure.

Crack!

Peter's knuckles connected with Timberland's jaw, sending him staggering back in his boots across the sidewalk. The guy was dazed and wobbly, but he didn't go down.

Not yet.

Peter lunged forward and followed up his first punch with a couple more. "Stop!" a few good citizens pleaded. "For God's sake, stop!"

Peter ignored the looky-loos. If anything, the voices just egged him on. He did love an audience.

As blood leaked from Timberland's nose, Peter kept pummeling away until finally the guy went down.

Peter yelled at him. "C'MON, YOU ASSHOLE, GET THE FUCK UP! FIGHT, YOU BASTARD!"

That's exactly what the guy did.

He pushed up and charged Peter like a bull, wrapping both arms around his red jacket and taking him down in a flash. Faster still were the guy's fists as they connected one after the other with Peter's head as he lay flat on his back.

Peter could easily have lifted his arms to cover himself, but he didn't. At least not immediately. Not until he swirled his tongue and tasted the blood oozing from the side of his mouth.

That's when he knew. *He'd gotten what he had come here for.*

The two cops by the hot dog vendor were coming over to break things up.

"Did anyone see what happened?" one of them asked the crowd. *The jury.*

Two minutes later Peter Carlyle was in handcuffs.

Chapter 74

THE REAR HOLDING CELL at the Midtown North Precinct absolutely reeked of urine and vomit, but all Peter could smell was sweet success. His head was throbbing, his vision was still blurred, and the butterfly bandages he'd been given while being booked and fingerprinted were barely holding his face together.

But it didn't matter. He knew it would all be worth it.

To the tune of over $100 million.

"Holy shit," came a voice from the other side of the bars. "You're a mess, my man."

Peter turned to see his "one phone call" staring back at him in total disbelief.

"Nice to see you, too," said Peter. "What took you so long?"

Gordon Knowles stood clutching his custom-made Louis Vuitton attaché as a cop opened the cell for him. After a brief nod of thanks, he and Peter were left alone.

"Holy shit," Gordon muttered again. "I'm impressed."

"You oughta see the other guy." Peter shrugged. "I know, bad joke."

Every lawyer, no matter how good he was, still needed his own lawyer. In Gordon Knowles, Peter had one of the best in New York. Whereas Peter always excelled inside the courtroom, Gordon specialized in making sure his clients never had to set foot in one.

"I've got some good news and some bad news," he began. "The good news is the guy's not going to press charges. Once I explained who you were and that your family had just been declared dead, he backed off—provided, of course, that you pay any and all medical bills, plus maybe a little sweetener."

Peter shrugged his indifference. "So what's the bad news?"

"About a half-dozen TV camera crews are presently camped outside the precinct."

"Word travels fast, huh?"

"Pictures even faster. On the way here I heard that some tourist had a video camera at ringside. Your brawl should be up on YouTube in no time."

Peter groaned convincingly. "Oh, great."

"My sentiments exactly. All the more reason why I've arranged to sneak you out of here through the garage exit."

"No, I don't want to sneak anywhere," said Peter.

Gordon raised one of his bushy salt-and-pepper eyebrows. He had been expecting a thank-you. "But—"

Peter cut him off. "My public image isn't exactly of high concern to me right now," he said before dropping his head into his hands. But between his fingers, Peter was keeping a watchful eye on his attorney.

Gordon represented the first, and perhaps hardest, test of Peter's added insurance plan. Gordon was a right smart fellow; Harvard Law grads usually were. He was also one hell of a poker player, and that meant he was awfully good at reading bluffs.

Could he read this one?

If Peter was anything, he was thorough, and he wasn't about to take any chances with inheriting all of Katherine's money. Getting away with murder meant getting everyone feeling as sorry for him as possible. The sorrier they felt, the less they could ever suspect him.

So if that meant randomly picking a fight with a bruiser in the middle of Manhattan, so be it.

Because only a guy distraught over losing his family could ever do something like that.

Gordon Knowles nodded slowly. "I'm sorry," he said. "Here I am thinking like a lawyer when I should really be thinking like your friend. I'm forgetting how much you've been suffering. Katherine, the kids."

Indeed. Peter's pain was now literally etched on his face. The blood and bruises were a very public reminder of his sorrow and his loss.

"You shouldn't have to sneak anywhere,"

said Gordon. "We'll walk right out that front door together. I'm with you, kiddo."

"Thank you," said Peter. "Thank you for everything. I couldn't do this without you."

Kiddo.

Gordon called over his shoulder for an officer to open the cell.

"Oh, there's one more thing," he said, turning back to Peter. "While I know this is the furthest thing from your mind right now, I received a call from Katherine's attorney. Did you know that your three stepchildren were the only beneficiaries named in her will?"

"No, I didn't," lied Peter, who then shut his eyes briefly and shook his head.

"Well, that means—"

"I don't want the money," said Peter softly. "I just want them all back."

"I know you do. In this case, though, I have to be your lawyer and look out for you." Gordon folded his arms. "What you do with that money is your business. Give it to charity. What's my business is making sure that it's you who gets to make that decision, not someone else. Okay?"

Peter nodded slowly.

If you insist, Gordon.

Chapter 75

THE KIDS DON'T HAVE TO SAY anything to me, I can see it in their eyes. *I look as horrible as I feel.*

And I'm getting worse.

The aspirin in the first-aid kit is long gone. The infection has definitely spread, and my body's literally burning up trying to fight the poison on its own.

With the raft propped under some branches, at least I've been able to stay in the shade. Mark, Carrie, and Ernie each take turns wetting leaves every ten minutes or so, layering them on my forehead to try to cool me down. Beyond that, there's not much they can do. The fever needs to run its course.

I just don't know how much longer I can keep up with it, and how much I can stand. I've never been this sick in my entire life.

Twice already I've blacked out—the first time for a few minutes, the second for over an hour. What's going to happen the third time? *What if I don't wake up?*

It's that thought that tells me I need to talk to the kids. I need to tell them how much I love them, and also how sorry I am for the times I may have let them down. Most of all, I need to prepare them for the worst-case scenario. I know it's crossed their minds. How could it not?

It's the way they're staring at me. The fear and sadness in their eyes. They already know I might not survive. Even little Ernie knows the sad truth now.

My first instinct is to talk to them as a family. That's what this trip was all about, after all.

But I'm quick to realize that looking at the three of them together will result in a tear fest, like that hospital scene with Debra

Winger and her kids in *Terms of Endearment.* I won't be able to get through something like that.

So I decide to speak to them individually. Carrie first.

Only she doesn't want me to do it.

"I can't do this with you," she says, turning away. "You're not going to die, you're going to be fine. You're the toughest person I know."

"Sweetheart, please look at me," I beg. "Please, Carrie."

She finally does. "I'm so sorry," she says, her eyes welling up.

I wasn't expecting that. "*You're* sorry? What for? I'm the one who should be apologizing."

"No, it wasn't fair. I wasn't fair. I didn't take responsibility for myself. I blamed you for things in my life that weren't your fault."

"Some of them were. I should've been there for you more. Carrie, I should've been there."

"It's okay. *I'm* okay," she says. "I only wish it hadn't taken this trip for me to realize that."

"You and me both."

"I love you, Mom," Carrie says, and then we both cry.

Mark's next. He's not ready for this conversation either. He cracks a joke about buying a Maserati with his inheritance to avoid dealing with his emotions. Who could blame him? Certainly not me.

"You know what I'm going to say, don't you?" I ask him.

He nods. "I have to be the man of the house. Or the island, in this case. Something like that? You don't have to say it, Mom."

He's right. There's more, though. "You have to promise me something."

"What?"

"First tell me that you promise."

"That's not exactly fair. But okay—I promise. Now what is it?"

"That no matter what happens when you get off this island, you never, *ever* sell yourself short again."

He looks at me, confused. "I don't . . . understand what you're saying. Not exactly."

"I thought I was being a good mother by giving you every advantage a kid could have. I was wrong. *Really* wrong. I should've been making you hungry. Instead I made you numb."

"Is that your kind of oblique way of saying I should stop smoking pot?"

"For starters, yeah. What I'm really trying to say is that your father and I have inadvertently taught you a very harsh lesson—life is too short and too precious to waste."

He nods, a half-smile lifting the corners of his mouth. "So I shouldn't waste mine, right?"

I hold out my arms and hug him to me. "Make me proud. I know you will, Mark. You're great."

"So are you, Mom."

Finally I'm face-to-face with Ernie.

"My little man, you grew up so fast," I say. "*Too* fast."

"Not really. I'm scared, Mom. I feel like I'm *ten* for the first time ever. Or at least since I was three."

"It's okay, honey. I'm scared, too. No matter what happens, though, I'll always be with you *right here*," I say, pointing at his heart.

"What about this, though?" he says, pointing to his head.

"What do you mean?"

He takes a deep breath. He almost seems—what's the word?—*embarrassed.* "Right after Dad died, I could picture him with no problem. Now I barely can. Why is that? I'm afraid I won't be able to remember you either."

I pull him close and rock him gently. "It's different now, honey. You're a lot older. You'll remember, trust me. As for your father—"

I stop cold—my words, the rocking.

Ernie pulls back, wiping a tear from his eye. "What is it, Mom?" he asks. "What were you about to say?"

No, not like this.

"It's nothing, honey. The only thing you need to remember is that your dad loved you very, very much. And so do I. I adore you, buddy."

I just should have told you that more.

I should have told you every single day.

Chapter 76

THE DOUBLE CHAISE LONGUE sat angled perfectly toward the night sky, past a convoy of thick evergreen branches. Lying in each other's arms, Peter and Bailey stared up at a sea of stars that almost made you believe in God.

"Look, there's the Big Dipper, Daddy," said Bailey.

Peter followed the line of her slender finger, nodding when he spotted the familiar constellation glowing brightly. She was pretending she was his little girl. Cute. He kissed her forehead, pulling her tighter toward him, catching a feel while he was at it.

"Thank you for being here with me," he said.

"Of course," she replied softly.

Peter had gone to great lengths to find a place where he could be alone with Bailey—about 250 miles, give or take, from New York, deep in the woods above Dorset, Vermont.

Here, on the stone patio of a well-appointed log cabin that looked as if it could be the backdrop for a Ralph Lauren ad, Peter was sure he could escape the prying eyes and camera lenses of the paparazzi. They had already served their purpose, cultivating oodles of sympathy for him. Now they were just annoying as hell, refusing to leave him alone.

Misery truly does love company, doesn't it?

The cabin was on loan from one of Peter's attorney friends, who gladly offered it up when Peter "let slip" that he needed some time alone before the funeral for Katherine and the kids. Of course, the friend didn't need to know that *alone* meant alone with another woman. As for the funeral, Peter was well aware that a lot of people thought he was rushing things, but fuck all of them. The media glare would disappear after the funeral—he was sure of it. Once the press had closure, he was home free.

"How's your face?" asked Bailey.

"Healing," answered Peter.

She ran her hand gently over his cuts and bruises, which were still swollen around his mouth and eyes.

"I think scars are kind of sexy," she whispered. "Bruises, too."

"Then that makes me one *very* sexy guy. He beat the hell out of me, didn't he?"

The two laughed freely until Bailey suddenly stopped.

"What's wrong?" asked Peter.

"It doesn't feel right to be laughing, not with what's happened to your family. God, Peter."

"It's okay. This night is good for me, Bailey. *You're* good for me. This past week has been so hard—I don't know what I'd do without you."

About his feelings for Bailey, Peter wasn't play-acting. He really did feel better when he was around her.

"Will you make love to me?" she asked.

That might have had something to do with it.

Peter slowly undressed his beautiful young law student, who didn't have much on to begin with. A pair of shorts, panties, and T-shirt. No bra.

Completely naked and incredibly luscious, she straddled Peter and unbuttoned his jeans. By the time she reached his boxer shorts he was more than ready for her.

Slowly Bailey took him inside her, deep inside. "You feel good," she said softly.

"So do you."

Peter closed his eyes as Bailey began to rock back and forth. The way she arched her back while thrusting her hips, she didn't let a single inch of him go to waste.

"Yes," she moaned. "*Yes.* Oh God, Peter, oh God."

Minutes later she came, screaming louder than she ever had with him. It was so loud that Peter almost didn't hear the other noise nearby. But he did hear something.

"Wait, what was that?" he said, halting, holding on to her waist. "That sound—did you hear it?"

"I think that was the earth moving," said Bailey, flashing him a playful smile. "Now it's your turn."

But Peter still had his ear trained on the surrounding woods. He could swear he heard something, a clicking noise—only not the kind that any animal would make.

Son of a bitch! Had they been followed? Had the paparazzi tracked him down?

Well, yes and no.

Chapter 77

ELLEN PIERCE had a saying—actually a twist on a saying— that pretty much steered her through life: *Nothing adventured, nothing gained.* In her seven years with the DEA, she had squared off against countless gangbangers, drug kingpins, and mafioso types, one more vicious and cunning than the next. But for sheer resolve, none of them held a candle to Shirley.

Shirley, a Queens native with the accent still intact, had been Ian McIntyre's personal assistant for over a decade. She didn't so much sit outside his office as lord over the space. No one, and that meant *no one,* got to see McIntyre without an appointment—something Ellen didn't have that Monday morning.

She did have something else, though. A large black coffee and a bran muffin. A bribe.

"Here," said Ellen, stopping by Shirley's desk on the way to her office. "I thought you might enjoy a little breakfast this morning."

Shirley quickly raised a tweezed eyebrow. "Okay, Ellen, what do you want, dear?" she asked suspiciously.

"Jeez, can't anyone do something nice these days without being accused of an ulterior motive?"

"Not in this building, sweetheart. If this is your way of getting in to see Ian, you can forget about it. He's preparing for a congressional hearing and doesn't want to be disturbed until lunch."

Ellen smiled sheepishly, as if to come clean. "It was worth a try, wasn't it?"

"That depends. Do I still get to keep the coffee and muffin?"

"Of course," said Ellen. "I wouldn't have it any other way."

Indeed.

Within a half hour the coffee and bran muffin had worked their caffeine and fiber magic. Shirley somewhat urgently vacated her post for a bathroom break, allowing Ellen to waltz right into Ian McIntyre's office unannounced. *That* had been her plan.

Before he could ask why the hell she was bothering him, she tossed the first glossy picture on his desk.

"I call this one the money shot," she announced.

Even for a man as disciplined as Ian McIntyre, it was impossible not to stare at a picture of a naked couple having sex on a chaise longue.

"Is that who I think it is?" he asked.

Ellen nodded with a beaming smile. She was proud of herself. She was convinced McIntyre would be proud of her, too. His telling her to "leave this one alone" would soon be a distant memory. It was all so Machiavellian, the end surely justifying the means.

"Who's he with?" he asked.

"I'm not sure yet. It's not his wife."

In quick succession she tossed more photos on the desk, as if she were dealing cards. One after the other they fell before

McIntyre, each reinforcing the same conclusion: *Peter Carlyle was hardly a man in mourning.*

"Pretty good stuff, huh?" said Ellen. She couldn't help herself. "I told you something wasn't right, Ian."

McIntyre remained quiet for ten seconds, maybe more. Finally his eyes lifted from the pictures and bored straight into Ellen's.

Uh-oh.

"What the hell were you thinking?" he shouted, jabbing his finger. "I explicitly told you to leave this alone!"

Apparently McIntyre hadn't read *The Prince.*

"But the pictures!" said Ellen. "Carlyle needs to be investigated!"

"Based on what? Extraordinarily poor judgment with his pecker? In case you've forgotten, extramarital affairs aren't illegal in this country."

"Even when his wife and family mysteriously disappear off the face of the earth?"

"Where's the mystery? Their boat got caught in a storm, there was a fire on board—it's really sad, it's a tragedy, but it's not much of a mystery."

Just then something over McIntyre's

shoulder caught Ellen's eye. It was the television behind his desk. On the screen was a male reporter standing on a dock somewhere sunny, in front of a giant fish strung up by its tail.

He was talking, but there was no volume.

"Wait!" shouted Ellen. "Turn that up!"

Ian spun around to look. He was about to ask why when he saw the caption on the screen.

Breaking news.

Dunne family alive?

Chapter 78

PETER SAT ALONE in the first pew of the Madison Avenue Presbyterian Church, his shoulders square and his joy hidden from the view of others. He could actually feel the outpouring of sympathy from the more than five hundred people seated behind him. It made the back of his head tingle.

It was a goddamn beautiful thing. And this funeral was a necessary one.

Everywhere you looked there were long-stemmed red roses. They had been Katherine's favorite flower and the one thing Peter had suggested would be a nice touch for the service honoring her and the brats.

The rest of the planning had been handled by his executive secretary, Layla, like the song. When he had explained to her that he was in no condition to be organizing the funeral, she understood. Of course, at $120,000 a year plus bonus, Layla somehow managed to understand everything he asked of her.

"Let us pray," said the minister.

After the brief invocation, Peter listened as the silver-haired Presbyterian minister sermonized about the fragility of life and the indiscriminateness of tragedy. The guy certainly had a presence about him and was a very good orator. Slick, yet earnest-sounding.

It always struck Peter as funny and ironic how many of the world's potentially best lawyers were instead men of the cloth. They were, after all, extremely talented at making people believe in things that they couldn't necessarily prove.

"Amen," said the minister. "Now a reading from..."

The service continued, but Peter tuned

it out. Instead he was thinking about the eulogy he was about to deliver.

Talk about the ultimate closing argument.

Standing before Katherine's friends and fellow doctors, her cousins—the few that she had—along with all the brats' private school chums and chummettes, he knew this would be his moment to rise and shine. He would start strong and stoic, of course. Then he would begin to take long pauses as he fought back the tears and shared a few family stories he'd made up.

Finally he would break down, a weeping mess. This was when the cuts and bruises on his face would really pay dividends. It would be a pity-palooza. In fact, as Peter closed his eyes he could already feel the minister's embrace in an effort to console him at the pulpit. After that he was home free. And why not?

Of course, he had no idea what was happening outside the walls of the church. The breaking news had yet to break through to the congregation. All cell phones had been turned off. It was a funeral, for God's sake!

Later, when Peter turned his Motorola

1000 back on, there would be three urgent messages from Lieutenant Andrew Tatem of the Coast Guard, not to mention two from Judith Fox trying to get him back on her show.

But that was later.

It was now time for Peter's eulogy. He couldn't wait to get all of this behind him. The funeral, and especially his family.

Standing at the pulpit before the packed church, he took a moment before speaking. He couldn't help himself. He had to stop and smell the roses, didn't he? Interestingly to him, he didn't feel any regret—not for Katherine, nor for Mark, Carrie, or Ernie, who wasn't such a bad kid, actually.

Suddenly he heard whispering behind him. Peter turned to look, slightly vexed. A man, maybe in his midthirties and dressed in khakis and a polo shirt, had his hand cupped over his mouth no more than an inch or so from the minister's ear.

What the hell's going on?

The young man was the organist. He wasn't supposed to be reading e-mail on his BlackBerry during a service, but he'd been doing it anyway. It wasn't as if anyone could see him. His perch was high up in the rafters, out of sight from the pews.

Now here he was in front of everyone—and for good reason. He'd just checked the Yahoo news page while searching for a Yankees score. They were playing a day game against the Red Sox up at Fenway. How could he resist a quick peek?

That's when another headline caught his eye—a story of a giant bluefin tuna and its Coke-bottle cargo.

The minister quickly joined Peter at the podium and joyously leaned toward the microphone.

"It's a miracle!" he declared.

Chapter 79

THE WORDS ECHOED in Peter's head all the way home. *Somehow your family traveled much farther south than their EPIRB indicated. We're beginning a new search immediately. There's hope, Mr. Carlyle.*

Andrew Tatem didn't give any further details, nor did Peter ask for them when he called the Coast Guard officer back. He was still pretty much in shock.

Only minutes before, the funeral had become a non-funeral. What a scene! Five hundred people all dressed up with suddenly no one to mourn.

At least, not yet, and maybe never. No one could know for sure. Katherine and the kids still had to be found, after all.

"But they will be," the crowd kept saying as they spilled out of the church. *"They will be."*

For Peter, it was like a symphony of nails scraping against a blackboard. No wonder he couldn't wait to get home . . . to Katherine's apartment.

The second he did, he made a beeline for the well-stocked liquor cabinet in the den. Bourbon, straight up. *Very* up.

Staring at the bottle of Evan Williams as he poured, Peter couldn't help thinking about the other bottle, the one that had just ruined a perfectly good day. *A message in a Coke bottle found in a tuna?*

It didn't get crazier and more random than that. The coup de grâce? The promise of a million-dollar reward. That was $1 million of what had been *this* close to being his money!

Peter downed the bourbon and poured himself another. As he lifted the glass, his hand stopped cold. He heard a noise, something in the apartment.

Or *someone.*

He thought back to the cabin in Vermont. This was a different noise from what he had heard in the woods, or at least what he thought he had heard. He wasn't sure anymore.

But of this he was positive: someone else was in the apartment.

Slowly Peter edged his way to the entrance to the den, listening for the sound again. There it was! It was like a hissing. Or was that whistling?

Whatever it was, it was coming from his study, off the living room. Of all places for there to be an intruder. *That's where he kept his gun.*

Peter slipped off his wingtips and tiptoed out to the hallway. In the closet off the foyer was the next best weapon available, his golf bag with the Winged Foot logo. Specifically, his five-iron with the titanium shaft. His lucky club. Or would the Odyssey putter be a better choice? Shorter club, heavier head.

Before grabbing the deadeye putter, he checked the front door. Had he forgotten to lock it behind him when he came in?

No way.

The thoughts were coming fast and furious now, like the beating of his heart. The building on Park Avenue was relatively secure, although there had been a burglary two floors down the year before. Was this another one? Maybe.

But, wait—the front door had been locked. *What burglar locks himself in?*

Another thought, and this was plausible. *The television.* He'd been watching it before leaving for the funeral. Perhaps he had left it on.

All the same, Peter gripped his club, ready to swing from the heels as he slowly made his way toward the study. A few steps before the entrance, however, he breathed a sigh of relief. *Phew!*

It was the television, all right.

Peter turned the corner into the study to see a rerun of *Seinfeld* on the wide screen.

Walking over to his huge mahogany desk by the window, he put aside the golf club. He watched as the color rushed back to his white knuckles. For peace of mind, if anything, Peter removed a key that was taped beneath the desk and unlocked the bottom drawer, where he kept his gun.

The gun was gone.

"Looking for this?" came a voice.

Chapter 80

DEVOUX SMILED, A Smith & Wesson .44 Magnum dangling from his outstretched hand as he stood, calm as could be, in the far corner of the study. "What is it with you urban cowboys, always keeping a big gun locked in the fancy desk? Somebody could get hurt."

Peter was miles and miles away from being amused. His eyes burned, staring down Devoux as the word *locked* seemed to linger between them in the room. The desk, the apartment itself—everything had been locked.

"How did you get in here?" Peter demanded, turning off the television on the cutesy musical signature that signaled scene changes on *Seinfeld.*

Devoux wasn't about to explain. Instead, "We have business to discuss," he announced.

"No shit," came back Peter.

Devoux took a seat in the leather club chair nestled near the oversize fireplace. Putting his feet up on the ottoman, he balanced the gun on the armrest and folded his arms lazily across his chest.

"Make yourself at home," snapped Peter.

"What a nice home it is," replied Devoux. He glanced around, his head bobbing with approval. "I assume it becomes all yours?"

"I certainly thought so when I woke up this morning."

"Yes, it seems you have quite the resilient family."

"Would you mind explaining how they're still alive? You said no one on the boat would survive the blast. You were wrong, weren't you?"

"Maybe. Then again, maybe not," said Devoux.

"What's that supposed to mean?"

"Perhaps they weren't on the boat when it exploded. That's my best guess."

Peter rolled his eyes. "You expect me to believe that crap?"

"Actually, I don't care what you believe. You don't get it, do you? The point is not what happened. *It's what happens next.*"

"All I know is that there's an entire Coast Guard fleet gearing up for a new search," said Peter. "Call me crazy, but I think they might have a little better luck this time around. What do *you* think?"

"It would look that way, wouldn't it?" said Devoux. He reached for Peter's .44 Magnum. "Of course, looks are often deceiving."

With a flick of his wrist Devoux opened the cylinder, removing all six bullets with a quick shake into his palm. Showing them to Peter, he then returned a lone bullet to a chamber and gave the cylinder a spin. With another practiced flick of his wrist, he snapped the cylinder shut.

The next thing Peter knew, Devoux was aiming the gun directly at his chest.

"What's this look like to you?" Devoux asked.

Peter's heart skipped a half-dozen beats as he watched Devoux unveil a particularly deranged grin. This couldn't be happening, could it?

But it was.

Devoux pulled back the hammer with his thumb, his index finger holding steady against the trigger. That's when the deranged smile completely disappeared.

It was replaced by a cold, lifeless stare boring straight into Peter's soul.

Click!

The hollow sound of an empty chamber filled the study as Peter stood stunned, horrified, relieved.

"Son of a bitch, you could've killed me!"

Devoux chuckled. Then he pressed the barrel of the gun to his own head and pulled the trigger five times fast.

What the—?

Sure enough, when Devoux opened the cylinder again, there was no bullet in any chamber. It only *looked* as if he had loaded the gun. As he coolly showed Peter, all six bullets were still in his hand.

"Here's the deal," said Devoux. "Based on the EPIRB and where that tuna was caught, the Coast Guard will start searching islands in the Bahamas that are still too far north of where your family could be. Of course, the farther south you go in that area, the more uninhabited islands you find, so you're only going to have a day, two tops."

"For what?"

"To find your family first. *If* they're alive, of course," answered Devoux. "You are a pilot, right?"

Peter nodded, Devoux's plan beginning to play out in his head. Great minds think alike. So do sick ones.

To the press and the public, it would look as if the loving husband and father was desperately taking matters into his own hands. Time was everything now. No longer would he rely on the Coast Guard alone. He would become a one-man search party.

"There's only one more thing I need to know," said Devoux, holding up Peter's gun again.

"What's that?"

"Are you ready to use this thing for real?"

Part Five

FINDERS KEEPERS

Chapter 81

THE DAY'S FIRST RAY OF SUN hits my face, waking me up as it has every morning since we landed on this godforsaken island in the middle of who knows where. Only this time the feeling is different, and I can sum it up in one word.

Hallelujah!

I'm not dizzy, and I'm not dry-heaving. I'm not even sweating like a pig in a sauna.

The fever's broken. The infection, *gone.* Or at least on its way out.

I'll say it again. *Hallelujah!*

I sit up, taking a deep breath. I'm far

from a hundred percent—barely even fifty. Still, that's enough to know that I'm on the mend instead of knocking on death's door.

Hell, if my leg weren't still broken, I'd get up and dance a little jig.

Instead I settle for a good cry. I can't help it, I'm so relieved. The three biggest reasons why are lying right next to me.

They're still fast asleep, but I don't care. "Wake up, Dunnes!" I call out. "Wake up! Hey, you lazybones!"

They all stir, slowly lifting their heads to look around and see what's going on. When they see me smiling, they jolt up. They're speechless.

I'm not.

"Mark, it looks like you'll be waiting a little longer on that Maserati," I joke. "My fever broke."

He has no quick comeback, no smart-alecky reply. Instead he does something I haven't seen him do since his father died. He starts to cry.

The tears are contagious, and Carrie and Ernie join in. It's officially a Dunne family meltdown, and we couldn't be happier about it.

Only a loud, low-pitched rumble brings us back to reality. Thunder? No.

"Was that your stomach, Mom?" asks Ernie.

Any other place or time and we all would've been laughing. Not here and not now. My growling stomach is a stark reminder that we're all still stuck on this island and our rations are running dangerously low. Thanks to a few rain showers we've been able to collect some drinking water, but foodwise we're down to a handful of nuts.

"Wait," Mark whispers. "Nobody move."

I fix on his eyes staring somewhere over my shoulder. "What is it?" I whisper back.

"Something a lot better than nuts."

We all turn slowly to look. There on the sand, nibbling at a palm leaf, is a brown-and-white rabbit. It's cute. It's cuddly.

It's dinner!

Not that we'd wait that long. It would surely be breakfast if we could only figure out how in the world to catch it. I whisper again, "How should we—"

I don't even finish the sentence. Like a rocket, Mark jumps up, sprints across the sand, and hurls himself at the rabbit. I've never seen him move that fast—he's a blur.

Unfortunately, so is the rabbit. An even faster blur. It darts back into the brush, leaving Mark with nothing but a faceful of sand.

"Shit!" he yells. "We'll never catch it now."

"We don't have to," I quickly point out. "At least not that one."

"Mom's right. It's a *rabbit,*" says Carrie.

For once Ernie's too young to understand. "What's that supposed to mean?"

I reach over and give him a gentle pat on the head. "It means there's plenty more where that one came from. Rabbits like big families, Ernie. Just like us."

Chapter 82

TALK ABOUT A STRANGE NEW FEELING. Back home in New York, practically every minute of every hour of my day was accounted for. Each surgery, all my meetings and rounds, everything I did had a start and finish time. If I fell behind, I simply worked faster. And if I got ahead of schedule and had time on my hands—

Wait, who am I kidding? I never got ahead of schedule.

The point being, it's so strange having nothing *but* time on my hands. Of course, the only reason that I'm even thinking this is because I'm bored out of my skull. As I sit here with my bum leg, waiting for the kids to return from their rabbit hunt, I literally don't know what to do with myself.

Except think, which maybe isn't such a bad thing.

Mostly I'm wondering what Peter's doing, how the poor man is handling our disappearance. Not well, I can only imagine. He must be a wreck. I felt so guilty about leaving him for this trip; we were just beginning our life together. Will we still have the chance?

Yes.

We will be found.

I'll be with Peter again. I just know it will happen.

After all, we're not halfway around the planet in the middle of nowhere. We can be only so far from civilization. Off the beaten track, maybe, but it's still a track. Eventually a boat, an airplane, someone has to come our way.

I'm right, right?

God, I hope so.

Fittingly, I hear a grumble from my gut again, the sound echoing through the empty, hollowed-out cavern otherwise known as my stomach. *C'mon, kids!* I've got every finger and toe crossed that they're having luck with that rabbit—any rabbit!

Finally, after more than an hour, I think I hear them coming. I'm pretty sure...

"Mark?" I call out. "Carrie? Ernie?"

They don't answer.

I call out again. All I hear back is the sound of a slight breeze blowing through the palms. Maybe that's all it was. Or maybe I'm getting a little delirious from not eating!

I keep staring at the brush on the edge of the beach, hoping to see the kids at any moment. Instead it's something else that I see.

"Oh my God," I whisper. *"Oh my God."*

Chapter 83

IT'S A SNAKE!

It's a snake like the Great Wall of China is a fence.

It's lava green and black and slithering through the sea grass onto the beach, and there's no end to it. This snake is huge.

And it's heading right for me. I want to run. Everything inside me is saying "Run!"

If only I could. I can't even walk.

I push off the sand, struggling up to my feet. Maybe the snake hasn't seen me yet. How good is a snake's vision? Where is Ernie and his science-class info when I need him?

I'm about to scream for the kids when I stop short. I don't want to call any more attention to myself, do I? Should I back away slowly? Should I stand perfectly still?

No, that's what you do with bears! At least I think so. I don't know. I can barely think right now. I've never seen a snake this large, not even on *National Geographic.*

I try putting a little pressure on my right leg, enough so I can limp away. Damn! It hurts like hell, the pain shooting up my thigh and hip like a fireball with spikes.

Suddenly the snake stops. For a few seconds it holds itself perfectly still.

C'mon, go back to the grass where you belong, pal. There's no food here on the beach!

Except for me, of course.

And I'm afraid that's the idea. Sure enough, the mammoth snake lurches forward, its bowed head rising as if it's homing in on me. So much for not being seen.

I don't have any choice now. I scream for the kids, so loudly that my throat burns. I scream again and again.

It's no use. I hear nothing back from them. They must be too far away.

Pain or no pain, I start limping away from the snake. But the snake is faster.

Maybe if I could get to the water. Would it still come after me? Would I drown?

I turn my head, peeking over my shoulder to see how much more sand I need to cover. Thirty feet or so. Maybe I can make it! All I have to do is pick up the pace.

Frantically I begin to hop. I've got one eye watching the snake, the other watching the water.

I should've been watching the sand.

Before I know it, I'm falling backward, my heel tripped up on a piece of driftwood.

And slithering right over the wood, the snake's hideous head.

Chapter 84

IT'S GOING TO BITE ME. I know it's going to strike any second. I feel the panic surge through my bloodstream as I try to stand again. I can't get up. It's as if my body and brain aren't connected anymore.

The only thing I can manage is thrusting my palms against the sand and pushing away. I'm scooting backward as fast as I can.

It's not fast enough.

The snake is inches from my foot, its head suddenly rising. I'm thinking that any moment I'll see its fangs, then *feel* its fangs.

But I don't. The huge snake doesn't lunge or strike. Instead it crawls slowly, powerfully—*oh my God, no!*—over my legs.

That's when I realize what's actually happening.

This diabolical snake wants to do more than just take a bite out of me. It wants *all* of me.

I scream again for the kids as the reptile travels past my thighs and coils around my waist. Even before it completes the loop I can feel the immense pressure, like a fleshy vise slowly closing. The snake wraps itself around my chest as I empty my suffocating lungs for one last scream, which finally comes out as a gasp.

I thrash, trying to get loose. It's too powerful. The more I push, the tighter it squeezes. I can't breathe!

It's up to my shoulders, the scales cool and dry against my skin. I catch a glimpse of the snake's eyes as the head passes in front of me again. The eyes are jet black. They're lifeless and seem not to see me at all. Oh God, it's ugly!

The thought of dying takes over, shooting another wave of panic through my body. This one is off the charts; I'm whipping and writhing what few parts of me can still move. This is not the way to die.

Chapter 85

"HOLD ON!" I hear.

Mark runs out of the brush and scoops up the four-foot hunk of driftwood in front of me.

"Stay still!" he yells.

Gripping the driftwood like a sledgehammer, he raises it above his head. *Whack!* Again he swings, even harder. *WHACK!*

He's aiming for a narrow stretch of the snake above my left kneecap. If he misses I've got another broken leg, but I don't care so much about that. Not right now, anyway.

Mark doesn't miss. One brutal swing after another.

In the corner of my eye I can see Carrie and Ernie, too stunned to do anything except stare. Their brother keeps swinging away, not letting up.

Neither is the snake, though. The pain it's causing is excruciating. I feel like I'm about to burst wide open.

"Hurry, Mark!" I plead.

Finally the moment he's waiting for comes. The snake fights back, its head darting toward Mark with a piercing hiss. The beast's jaws are open, the fangs on full display.

"*Thatta boy!*" Mark beams. *"You dumb shit!"*

In a flash the driftwood sledgehammer turns into a baseball bat. The snake's head is away from my body, giving him a decently clear shot.

Mark unloads on the snake's head as if it's a hanging curveball. Once, twice, three times he swings, each blow more vicious than the last.

The viselike grip around me starts to loosen. The snake no longer fights back, and its head is falling toward the sand.

Going.

Going.

Gone.

Chapter 86

"TASTES JUST LIKE CHICKEN," says Ernie, grinning as he chews. *"Not."*

That gets a good laugh from the rest of us as we sit around the fire at dusk, dining on the last thing any of us thought would be our next meal: grilled snake on a stick.

"I can't believe I'm eating this thing," says Carrie.

But she is. We all are. A lot of it, too. Of course, with the size of that snake there's a lot to go around.

"Hey, it was either this or nothing," says Mark. "Guess we're snaking out."

Their rabbit hunt was an exercise in

futility. Or should I say, the three of them got a lot of exercise while chasing but never catching the few rabbits they saw.

"You know, there are some cultures that think of snake as a delicacy," says Ernie. "It's true."

"Yes," says Carrie right back, "and those people usually have bones through their noses."

"Actually, I remember reading that a couple of restaurants in Manhattan serve rattlesnake," I say. I can't believe I felt the need to contribute that grotesquerie.

Carrie shakes her head. "Not any restaurants I've been to. Now that you mention it, though, what I wouldn't give to be eating at Gramercy Tavern right now."

I can't say I blame her—I feel the same way. Only what I'd really kill for would be a big, thick New York strip.

"What about Flames, up by the country house?" I say. "In fact, when this whole ordeal is over, I'm taking you all out to dinner, soup to nuts."

"Soufflés too?" asks Carrie.

"You bet! Soup to soufflés."

I look at Mark and Ernie. I'm not expecting cartwheels, but I hardly expect their sullen stares back at me. Especially Ernie's.

"What is it?" I ask him.

"You said *when* this whole ordeal is over. What if it never is?"

"It will be, honey, trust me."

He can't. Instead he turns to Mark. "You were right—that message-in-a-bottle thing was stupid. Dumb. No one's going to find it, or us."

I'm about to chime in again and assume my reassuring-mother role when Mark gives me a subtle wave of his hand. He wants to take care of this himself.

"No, it wasn't stupid, bro. No way. You were just trying to help us," he says. "I was the one being stupid, making fun of you."

Ernie smiles as if it's Christmas morning and he's gotten everything he wanted. Meanwhile, I'm about to melt as I gaze at Mark. What happened to the spoiled prep-school stoner? He even *looks* different after battling that snake. A little taller, squarer in the jaw.

Mark turns and catches me staring at him. "And as for Mom treating us to dinner . . . I'm ordering the porterhouse, double-thick!"

he says. "What about you, little man, you want one too?"

"Absolutely!" says Ernie.

"Good. Because Mom's right, I can feel it. *We're getting off this island – soon!*"

Chapter 87

"DON'T WORRY," said Peter, caressing Bailey's smooth, soft cheek. "I'll be back before you know it."

"That's what I'm afraid of," she said. "You'll find your family, be reunited with Doctor Katherine, and before I know it I'm yesterday's news."

Peter had yet to see this hidden side of the usually tough-minded, confident Bailey. *Vulnerability.* He had to admit, it was kind of sexy, and even sweet.

"Trust me, no matter what happens during this trip, I won't be able to get you out of my mind," he said.

Bailey liked the sound of that. She picked a plump strawberry off the room-service breakfast tray and gently wrapped her lips around it. Biting down, she winked at Peter. "I trust you, Peter. But is that wise of me?"

Their night of sex and champagne had been his idea, a proper goodbye before he left Bailey and headed for the Bahamas. He had chosen the swank Alex Hotel in Midtown for a couple of reasons, both geographic. First, it was close to Grand Central Station, where he could easily lose any paparazzi who might be following him on foot. Second, the hotel was close to the Midtown Tunnel, which would be his quickest route to Kennedy Airport. His flight out was in less than two hours.

"Oh, that reminds me," he said. "I need you to do me a small favor if you can."

Peter leaned over the side of the king-size bed and fetched something from his duffel on the floor. It was a FedEx box.

"I didn't have a chance to drop this off last night before coming here. Would you mind doing that after I leave for the airport?"

Bailey eyed the shipping label. The box was addressed to Peter's hotel in the Bahamas. "Sure," she said, nodding, albeit with a slight hesitation.

Peter expected as much.

"Go ahead, you can ask me what's inside," he said.

"No, it's none of my business."

Peter feigned disappointment. "You call yourself an aspiring lawyer? What if what's inside that box is something illegal? They rarely, if ever, x-ray them. You could unwittingly be an accomplice to a crime, lose your chance ever to practice law."

Bailey reached for another strawberry and this time fed it to Peter. "I guess I'll have to take my chances," she said.

Again, Peter had expected as much. *She trusted him.*

He bit down on the strawberry, returning Bailey's wink. Then he eyed his platinum Rolex.

It was time to catch a plane and take care of some family business.

Chapter 88

IT WASN'T QUITE the Beatles landing in the sixties at JFK, but for sheer media turnout it was close enough. Early in the afternoon, the plane touched down at Lynden Pindling International Airport on New Providence Island in the Bahamas. For the "benefit" of the other passengers—but really just to heighten the drama—Peter made sure he was the very last to disembark.

A black Tumi duffel slung over his shoulder, he approached the herd of reporters assembled behind a rope curtain on the tarmac.

Gee, all this for little ol' me?

This was why Peter flew commercial. He wanted the publicity. He wanted the transparency. The press could and would question his bucking the Coast Guard and conducting his own search. He just needed to make sure they didn't question his motive.

So with his courtroom-perfected poise, Peter made it clear. "I couldn't live with myself if I thought for one second I didn't do everything I could to help find my family. Especially since I'm a licensed pilot."

The press ate it up. They always did when it was spoon-fed to them like this. Besides, it was too damn hot. Blistering, really. The sooner they could file their reports and get out of the sun, the better.

Peter thanked the reporters and promptly left them in the dust—literally. After cruising through customs and immigration, he exited through the front entrance of the airport in search of a taxi.

An LCD display out by the curb put a number on the sweltering heat: 101°, the sign flashed. Next to it a Coppertone ad warned "Don't Get Burned!" above a picture of a hapless, chubby man in a bathing suit. His skin was a decidedly nasty shade of lobster pink.

"Hot enough for you?" came a man's voice just over Peter's left shoulder.

A local? Another reporter?

Neither.

Turning around, Peter stared Andrew Tatem straight in the eyes. He recognized the Coast Guard officer from his televised press conference in Miami. Now here he was in the Bahamas, getting up close and personal with Peter. Why would that be?

"Mr. Carlyle, I'm—"

"Lieutenant Andrew Tatem—yes, of course," said Peter. "Nice to see you. How are you?"

"Good, good. You look surprised to see me."

Peter shrugged. No need to hide it. "I am. Didn't you tell me you were staying in Miami despite the search effort's moving down here?"

"Yes, that was my original plan."

"What changed?"

"That's easy, Mr. Carlyle. *You did.*"

Chapter 89

"CAN I GIVE YOU a ride to your hotel?" asked Tatem. "It would be my pleasure."

"Thanks, but I'm fine with a taxi," Peter answered quickly. "It'll get me there."

"Really, it's no trouble. In fact, it will give us a chance to talk. Come with me."

Peter eyed Tatem. Clearly the guy had an agenda and wasn't about to take no for an answer.

"Sure," said Peter, relenting. "Thank you. It's very kind. I'm at the Sheraton Cable Beach Resort."

Before he knew it he was sitting shotgun

in a black sedan that screamed government-issued.

"Mr. Carlyle, you really shouldn't be down here," said Tatem a few seconds after pulling out of the airport. He was hardly slow to make his point.

Ditto for his driving. For someone who spoke in such a measured tone, the guy sure knew how to let fly behind the wheel.

Peter watched the lineup of palm trees whizzing by his window. *Is there a speed limit in the Bahamas? Is this asswipe just trying to scare me?*

Tatem continued, his gaze pinballing back and forth between Peter and the road. "I mean, I don't care that you're in the Bahamas, Mr. Carlyle. What I'm saying is that you shouldn't be trying to conduct your own personal search effort."

Peter rubbed his chin as if he were actually considering Tatem's point of view. He wasn't. Having the guy greet him at the airport might have been a surprise, but his "advice" wasn't. Of course he didn't want Peter doing *his* job. What good could come of that?

"Are you afraid that I might get in the way?" asked Peter.

"To be honest, yes."

"It's a big ocean out there."

"I think you know that's not what I mean."

"Yes, you're afraid that I'll just fuel the media frenzy. Point taken."

Tatem nodded. "It's hard enough to oversee a search effort, let alone having to manage the press."

"So don't manage them," said Peter.

"With all due respect, you of all people should know that's not realistic."

"*With all due respect,* I think what you're really afraid of is that I'll find my family first."

Tatem shot him a steely look. "I promise you, that's not the case. I'm not built that way."

"Good. Then I don't see what the problem is. I just want them found, Lieutenant, that's all."

"So do I. That's what we're trained to do."

"Oh, I see," said Peter. "You want me to leave it to the professionals?"

"For lack of a better phrase, yes."

"You mean the same professionals who had already called off the search?"

That got Tatem's goat. He bristled. "You know as well as I do that the boat's coordinates—"

Peter cut him off. Enough was enough. "Listen, I'm doing what I came down here to do," he said sternly. "If you don't understand it, or don't like it, tough shit."

A silence fell over the sedan, and Peter loved every second of it. He figured that was the end of the discussion. What else could Tatem say or do, except drop him off at his hotel?

"As I said, I'm at the Sheraton Cable Beach," said Peter. "Do you know where that is?"

Tatem answered with a clipped "Yes."

They were five or six miles out from the airport now, speeding along a curvy stretch of road that hugged the coastline.

"Are we close?" asked Peter.

"It's about a mile or so," Tatem answered.

The car went silent again. A beige-and-tan sign for the Sheraton soon appeared, and Peter heaved a sigh of relief. The entrance was directly behind it. Lush tropical gardens, a spectacular white-sand beach, casuarina trees blowing in the wind.

But Tatem didn't slow down.

Instead he sped up. Gunned it, actually.

Blowing right by Peter's hotel.

Chapter 90

FOR THE FIFTH TIME Peter asked—no, *demanded*—to know where Tatem was taking him.

For the fifth time Tatem ignored him, acting as if Carlyle weren't even there in the car.

Right up until they drove through the towering wrought-iron gates of the U.S. embassy in the heart of downtown Nassau.

"Follow me," said Tatem after parking the car in front. Not a request—an order.

So Peter followed Tatem into the embassy and down a long, narrow corridor. If the building had air conditioning, it was broken. The place was hot, a few rocks and a ladle short of a sauna. There were ceiling fans overhead, yet all they did was make sure the stifling air was evenly distributed.

At the last door at the end of the corridor, Tatem stopped. "Go on in," he said, stepping aside.

Peter stared at the closed door, beads of sweat trickling past his sideburns. This Tatem was tougher than he had sounded over the phone. "You're not coming with me?" Peter asked.

"No. Out of my jurisdiction, as they say. I'll wait for you out here."

Tatem turned and walked off, leaving Peter alone. And wondering, *What the hell's going on?*

Through another door down the hall Peter could hear a radio, the muted sound of Bob Marley's "Could You Be Loved." The song that really would've nailed the moment was by the Animals: "We've Got to Get Out of This Place."

The exit sign hanging over a nearby stairwell was practically calling out Peter's name. That's when the door suddenly opened before him.

"Hello, Peter," she said.

They were standing face-to-face, yet another surprise for the day. This one was a doozy, and couldn't have been more unpleasant or threatening.

The last time Peter had seen Agent Ellen Pierce, she had been sitting in a Manhattan courtroom shooting daggers at him with her intense yet unquestionably beautiful brown eyes. She had dedicated two years of her life to investigating and finally nabbing a Brooklyn crime boss who was running a hundred-million-dollar drug ring.

All it took was two weeks for Carlyle to set the bad guy free.

When the jury came back with their not-guilty verdict, she actually yelled "Fuck!" in the courtroom. It even brought a smile to his face.

So what was Ms. Pierce doing here? Why would she possibly need to speak to him now? About what?

He had a pretty good hunch.

"Don't tell me," began Peter, raising both his palms. "You want to talk me out of searching for my family, too."

Pierce smiled. She was wearing a white

polo neatly tucked into a pair of tan linen slacks. DEA island wear, perhaps?

"Oh, no," she said. "I think it's great that you want to search for them." She motioned for Peter to have a seat at the small conference-room table behind her. "But before you do, I think there's something you need to know. I'm here to *help* you, Peter."

Chapter 91

JAKE DUNNE, A drug runner? Uncle Jake a bad guy? Was it possible?

It sounded crazy coming out of Ellen Pierce's mouth and even more so when he repeated it in his head. He couldn't picture it, not for a minute. It was obviously no joke, though. The DEA was known for a lot of things, but comedy wasn't high on the list. In fact, it wasn't on the list at all.

"Jake Dunne's been on our radar for well over a year now," said Agent Pierce, folding her lean arms on the table. "He's been spotted repeatedly with a known smuggler, and his travel patterns have been suspicious, to say the least. Unfortunately, beyond that, we've not been able to prove anything. Close, but not quite. Nothing that would hold up in court."

"Even if your suspicions about Jake are true, what does that have to do with my family's disappearance?" asked Peter. "They were hit by a storm."

"Yes, they were," said Pierce. "What we don't know for sure is whether that storm is the real reason the boat went down. There remains another possibility—that Jake was pulling double duty on this trip, captaining the boat while also making a dropoff."

"A dropoff *where?*" asked Peter. Agent Pierce definitely had his interest now. This was sounding better and better.

"That's the thing. They're mostly done on open water. You've got two boats and no one else around for miles. If that's what Jake Dunne had planned and there was an altercation of some kind—a disagreement about money, perhaps—I'm afraid your wife and stepchildren may have paid the price. It's a working theory, anyway."

"But the note in the bottle—they're alive," said Peter. "At least, I'm praying they still are."

"I'm praying for the same thing, Mr. Carlyle. In fact, I'm banking on it," she said. "And having seen firsthand in a courtroom how determined you can be, I'd say the smart money's on your finding them first." She reached into her pocket. "That's why I want you to have this."

Pierce placed a sleek black cell phone on the table. It wasn't any kind of phone Peter had seen before, and he thought he'd seen them all. He picked it up, staring at it as if it had just fallen from the sky.

"Yeah, I had the same reaction when I first saw it," said Pierce. "Here, let me show you how it works. Piece of cake, really. You don't have to be a techie."

She took it from Peter's hands and opened it like a compact for makeup. On one side was a keyboard, on the other what looked like a solar panel.

"It's a satellite phone, isn't it?" asked Peter.

Ellen nodded. "The best Uncle Sam's money can buy. Waterproof, shatterproof, with a carbon nanotube battery that lasts over a hundred hours a charge. You can call from anywhere on the planet at any time. Perfect signal, completely encrypted. No one can listen in."

"Very cool," said Peter. "Why do I need it?"

"Because no matter where you are, you need to contact me the second you find Jake and your family. I have to know before the media does—even before the Coast Guard, if possible."

"I got that part, Agent. But *why?*"

"If there were people who wanted Jake Dunne dead, it's safe to assume they still do. That's why we have to get to him first—for his protection and, more important, for your family's. At the very least, they're out there with a drug runner."

Peter blinked long and hard. "This is weird," he said. "I mean, the fact that you're helping me. You don't even like me."

"You're right, I don't. That said, you have your job to do and I have mine." Pierce smiled. "Now do me a favor, will you? Go find your family."

Chapter 92

THERE WAS THIS ONE NIGHT BACK when I was a resident at the Cleveland Clinic, and I was supposed to be catching an hour nap in the middle of a twenty-four-hour shift. It was my only chance to get some much-needed rest, and I was exhausted.

But I couldn't sleep. I was too tired. So I turned on an old Sony Trinitron in the doctors' lounge and started watching this documentary on Ansel Adams. Or was it Franklin B. Way? I can't remember. Anyway, what I do remember is the phrase they used to describe this time of day, when supposedly the light from the sun is perfect for photography. "Magic hour," it's called.

Magic hour.

As I sit here on the beach, staring out over the ocean as the sun kisses the horizon, I'm pretty sure this is what they were talking about on the TV show.

It's beautiful.

It's also ironic. Back home I almost never saw sunsets. Hell, I barely saw the outdoors. Most of my days were spent standing in a sterile, windowless room, my view alternating between heart monitors and the real thing pulsing on a table in front of me.

No regrets, though. I never lost sight of the good I was doing. But like I said, it's ironic. It took all of this to happen before I could really appreciate something as simple as a sunset.

"Hey, Mom," says Ernie, running over to me. He stands sideways, displaying his profile. It's obvious, in a very cute way, that he's sucking in his stomach a little. "How much weight do you think I've lost?" he asks.

Indeed, my pudgy little man is a lot less

pudgy than at the start of the trip. He's probably lost seven or eight pounds, and it shows. Better yet, it's seven or eight pounds more than he was ever able to shed back home.

I look at his face, the pride written all over it. Then I glance down at his stomach. I'm ready to *gush* about how thin he now looks.

And that's when my eyes nearly pop out of my head.

There's a boat sailing out of Ernie's belly button!

"What is it, Mom? What's wrong?" he asks, looking down at himself in horror.

"Nothing's wrong!" I answer with a jolt. "It's all right!"

In fact, it's better than all right.

It's magic!

Chapter 93

I CAN BARELY GET THE WORDS out of my mouth fast enough. "Ernie, where are your brother and sister?"

"They're picking berries," he says. "Why?"

"That's why!" I say, pointing out to the horizon. "Look at what's there."

Ernie turns to see what I see—a huge sailboat, close enough that we can actually make out the shape of the sails. It's not a blip like the other boats we've seen, too far away ever to notice us.

We've got a chance with this one. A real chance!

"Hurry! Go get Mark and Carrie," I say. "We need to light the fires! Ernie, run!"

Ernie races as I push myself up to stand. If I could, I'd be doing jumping jacks or cartwheels, anything to attract attention. *Please, let there be someone on that boat with binoculars!* I pray. *Look this way. I can see you, so you can see me.*

"Holy shit!" yells Mark seconds later, bursting through the brush onto the beach. Carrie's behind him. They both outran Ernie, who finally brings up the rear.

"See! See, I told you!" says Ernie.

"Yeah, now let's make sure they see us!" says Mark, heading for our campfire.

He grabs our ready-made "match," a thick stick wrapped with a swath of one of our blankets, and douses it with the rubbing alcohol from the first-aid kit. As he dips it into the fire and sprints to our three piles of leaves and branches, he looks like he's carrying the Olympic torch.

"Here goes nothing," he says, lighting the piles.

They ignite immediately, their orange glow matching the sky almost perfectly.

With the last of the sun disappearing, all

we can do is stand here on the beach, our gaze bouncing back and forth between the boat and the flames as if willing them together.

"C'mon," pleads Carrie. "They have to see us!"

This has to be our moment—has to be. We deserve it. So we wait to be spotted, the fires roaring in their perfect triangle. I'm fifty feet away and I can still feel their heat. I keep thinking that at any second we'll see a signal from the boat. A flash of light, a flare shot high into the sky. Something.

Anything.

I look at the kids and I see exactly what I feel—hope. But as five minutes turn into forty, without any signal from the boat, it fades. Slowly. Painfully. Our fires are beginning to die down. It's getting dark on the beach, in every sense of the word.

I want to cry. I don't. *I can't.* For the kids' sake. For my own sake, too. But this is so cruel.

"There'll be another boat soon, you'll see," I say instead, trying to lift everyone's spirits.

The kids know exactly what I'm trying to

do. But rather than calling me on it—something they always used to do—they go along with me.

It's as if we all suddenly realize that even though we've had our hopes dashed today, that's better than having no hope at all.

How can it be that the more life throws at us, the stronger we become?

Chapter 94

SITTING AT A SECLUDED BACK TABLE in Billy Rosa's, the diviest of dive bars on the outskirts of Nassau, Devoux glanced at his Glashütte Pano Navigator watch yet again. He'd made the trip down to the Bahamas for one reason and one reason only. *Insurance.* If Carlyle needed backup, he'd be close by to intercede. But he was hoping that it wouldn't come to that.

He knew they couldn't afford even the slightest hiccup. Everything had to go as planned, tidy and neat. Like clockwork.

But here was Carlyle, over a half hour late. They were supposed to be discussing his flight plan one last time, and exactly how he should commit the murders. *What the hell was keeping him?*

"It's not what, but *who,*" explained Peter when finally he arrived, a few minutes later.

Peter then shared his recent conversation with Agent Ellen Pierce. The upshot was surprisingly simple, not to mention being an amazing case of serendipity. Jake Dunne was taking the fall for everything.

"Talk about a lucky break, huh?" said Peter before letting go with one of his obnoxious chuckles. He leaned in, his voice cutting back to a whisper. "For a minute there, I almost believed the bitch."

Devoux rubbed his square chin, not yet sold either way. "What tipped you off?"

Peter reached into his pocket. "*This,*" he said. "She gave it to me so I can call her the minute I find Katherine and the brats."

Staring at the satellite phone, Devoux nodded knowingly, a rocket on the uptake. "There's a tracking device inside."

"Exactly."

"You sure you're not just being paranoid, Peter?"

"No, she suspects something, all right. I'm not sure how or why, but she does."

Now it was Devoux's turn to reach into his pocket. He pulled out a Swiss Army knife, classic red.

"Give me the phone," he said.

"What are you going to do?" asked Peter.

"Just give me the phone."

Peter handed it over. "Be careful with it, okay? She can't think I tampered with it."

Devoux bypassed both the foldout scissors and the Phillips-head screwdriver on his knife. He went straight for the blade, wedging it hard between the seams of the phone.

With a flick of his wrist he shucked the phone open like an oyster.

"Trust me," he said. "If you're right about your little agent friend, tampering will be the least of our problems."

Chapter 95

THE AREA SURROUNDING Billy Rosa's bar wasn't exactly conducive to a stakeout. Come to think of it, thought Ellen, it wasn't conducive to much of anything. To the left of the bar was the scorched frame of a burned-down warehouse, to the right a junkyard of rusted-out cars and trucks. Dotting the rest of the otherwise barren, sandy landscape was a smattering of withering sea-grape trees and bleached-out grass.

All in all, it was hardly a tourism brochure for the Bahamas in the making.

Still, Ellen made do.

First she parked her rental, a dark blue Honda Civic, amid the junkyard of cars, propping up the hood so it would blend in. Second, she nestled behind one of the sea-grape trees about seventy-five yards from the bar's main entrance.

Third, she waited.

Despite the obvious fact that the sun was setting, the heat remained brutal. She was sweating from every pore, and her clothes were absolutely drenched. Even the leather strap of the high-powered binoculars draped around her neck was soaking wet.

Of all the places to have a drink on this island, why here, Peter Carlyle?

Ellen continued to wait, occasionally glancing at the receiver in her hand, which was picking up a signal from the phone she had given Carlyle. The receiver's screen, about the size of a credit card, glowed bright with a 3-D topographical map of the area, a red dot indicating Carlyle's location right smack inside Billy Rosa's bar.

She smiled. She had turned the creepy lawyer into a human LoJack device. Good thing, too. Now she didn't have to follow him around the clock.

Just when it counted.

Like right now.

Staring at the entrance to the bar, Ellen scanned the dozen or so cars lined up in front. Some of them were only a notch above the clunkers in the adjacent junkyard, the rest being either modest compacts or Jeeps.

Then there was the one on the end. All she could think of was that bit from *Sesame Street: One of these things is not like the others. . .*

It was a black Mercedes 600CL coupe. Ellen was no car fanatic, but she had learned a thing or two over the years while tailing drug dealers. When it came to Ferraris, Porsches, and Mercedes-Benzes, she could moonlight as a reporter for *Car and Driver* magazine.

Boasting over 500 horsepower and a price tag hovering around a hundred and fifty grand, the 600CL stood out no matter where it was parked. But here, outside Billy Rosa's, it might as well have been painted purple with pink polka dots.

And the more Ellen stared at it, the more her gut told her the 600CL was somehow connected to Peter Carlyle.

Two minutes later her gut proved right.

Carlyle stepped out of the bar.

He wasn't alone.

Ellen quickly peered through her binoculars. With Carlyle was a man of about the same height and build, maybe a little younger. He wore white linen pants, a blue silk shirt, and dark, mirrored sunglasses. And he was easily as creepy as Carlyle.

After chatting for a moment, the two went their separate ways. There was no handshake, barely even a nod from either of them.

Carlyle walked over to a white Buick Lucerne. The Mystery Man climbed behind the wheel of the hot Mercedes.

Ellen lowered the binoculars, waiting for both cars to leave. *Whatcha up to, Peter? Who's your new friend? Anybody I should know about?*

Only one way to find out.

Chapter 96

HURRY!

Ellen sprinted to her rented Honda and slammed the hood shut. After climbing in, she snapped her wrist hard against the key and gunned it. The puny four-cylinder engine instantly squealed its disapproval.

Talk about a mismatch! Could she even catch up to the Mercedes, let alone follow it?

She sure as hell was going to try.

The Mystery Man was the break she needed, she was pretty sure of it. She knew he didn't look kosher. As for Carlyle, she'd catch up with him later—not a problem, thanks to the transmitter.

No, the problem lay straight ahead, speeding down the dirt road. That Mercedes was already a blip on the horizon. Soon she wouldn't be able to see it at all.

Or maybe not.

Ellen blinked with disbelief. *The blip was getting bigger.* No lead foot for the Mystery Man; it was more like helium. He was taking his own sweet time.

That probably had something to do with the quality of the road, she thought.

While Carlyle had left the same way Ellen had come, the Mystery Man was heading the other way, fittingly into the unknown. It was a dirt road, bumpy and winding. Not a building in sight. Not even a sign or a billboard. If Billy Rosa's bar was isolated, this direction was damn near off the map.

Suddenly Ellen had to do what she least expected: hit the brakes. She was getting too close to the coupe and had to pull back lest she arouse suspicion.

Where are we going, Mystery Man?

He wasn't telling, not yet.

One mile became another, and another

and another. Ellen's eyes stayed focused on the back of the Mercedes. Her mind, however, began to drift. Out of nowhere she heard a voice from her past. It was her grandfather, as if he were sitting right next to her, riding shotgun. In his thick, raspy staccato he was invoking one of his favorite expressions.

Take the devil you know versus the devil you don't.

Back in those days, when Ellen was a young girl, she never really understood what it meant. That's probably why she forgot about it.

Until now.

Ellen glanced down, peeking through the steering wheel at the speedometer. The Mystery Man was puttering along at no more than thirty miles an hour. Wherever they were heading, they weren't in any hurry.

Then, in a flash, all that changed. The Mercedes took off like a missile, all 500 horsepower firing at once. Before Ellen could speed up, it was gone behind a wall of dust.

Shit!

Ellen's foot found the gas, but it was

probably a lost cause. No contest, right? She couldn't see the Mystery Man now. She couldn't see *anything.*

Including the bullet heading straight for her head.

Chapter 97

AN INCH.

Maybe two inches.

That's how close she came to dying on the dirt road somewhere in the Bahamas.

The bullet ripped through the windshield, buzzing Ellen's right ear amid shards of broken glass. She had no idea what was happening. Until...

Duck!

Dead ahead, the Mystery Man was standing squarely in the middle of the road, staring down the barrel of a 9-millimeter Beretta.

As he fired again, Ellen flung herself against the seat, her foot jamming the brake pedal. *Smack!* went her forehead against the glove compartment as the car slowly skidded to a stop.

For a second she lay there, her head throbbing, the brainwaves scattered. She listened for another shot. It didn't happen right away. Instead she heard something worse. *Footsteps.*

He was coming for her.

My gun! Where is my gun?

She reached down her right leg. She could feel the shin holster, the rippling grain of the worn-out leather. But no gun.

She never kept it strapped. It must have fallen out!

The footsteps stopped. Ellen twisted in a panic, looking up at her driver's side window. There he was! He was right there!

His body blocked out the setting sun, a badass eclipse if ever there was one. He raised his arm, cocking the gun with absolutely no remorse in his eyes. This guy, this Mystery Man, had clearly killed before.

And he was about to do it again.

No!

Ellen threw the car's shift in reverse, her foot hopscotching from the brake to the gas. Suddenly a second shot shattered the driver's side window.

Am I dead? Badly wounded?

No. He missed!

Accelerating backward now, she kept her head tucked just below the dash. With one hand she gripped the steering wheel, struggling to keep the car straight if she could. With the other hand she searched frantically for her gun, feeling blindly under her seat.

There!

She wrapped her fingers around the grip and pulled it up to her side. The chill of brushed steel had never felt so good.

Then, spinning the steering wheel like a top, she threw the car into a seemingly endless three-sixty. One wall of dust deserved another.

It's my turn, you son of a bitch.

Chapter 98

THE DIRT ROAD WAS no longer a road—it was more like a Kansas-style tornado.

With the dust funneling round and round, Ellen peeled off her second three-sixty, backing up the car about a hundred yards.

She threw it into park for all of five seconds, just long enough to lift her feet and kick out what remained of the front windshield. As the glass splintered across the hood she raised the gun.

Then she hit the gas.

The little blue Honda choked and sputtered its way past thirty, forty, fifty miles an hour. When it finally emerged through the dust, it was pushing past eighty!

Are you still there, Mystery Man? Are you waiting for me? Well, here's a little surprise for you. Today you're going to get shot, not me!

The split second she saw him, Ellen started firing. He was still smack in the middle of the road, precisely where she'd left him. Only there was one big difference now. His gun wasn't visible.

The psycho was standing there, not firing back. What? Did he have a death wish?

Fine! She had no problem giving him exactly what he wanted.

Ellen was a crack shot, but shooting from a speeding vehicle over a bumpy road wasn't exactly target practice at the range. On her third pull of the trigger, though, her brain made all the necessary adjustments. *She was locked in.*

But then she watched as the Mystery Man pulled the Beretta from behind his leg.

Chapter 99

DEVOUX WHIPPED HIS ARM FORWARD, locking the elbow before firing just one shot.

Bull's-eye!

With a thunderous *pop* the right front tire exploded, shreds of rubber spinning wildly round and round as the little car weaved out of control.

The rest was pure physics. He could tell she was trying to hit the brakes. It didn't matter. *You're way too late for that, sweetheart. It's all over – you just don't realize it yet.*

The two left tires lifted off the ground.

Then it was all four. Her car launched into the air, flipped once, twice, and then landed with a crushing thud upside down, the roof buckling into a zigzag of twisted metal.

The engine hissed as flames shot out from the grille, the smoke black and thick. As the dust settled, Devoux stood and watched with his gun still drawn, waiting for any sign of life.

What he saw was her hand, streaked with blood, reaching out from the driver's side. She was clenching the dirt; she was trying to pull herself out.

Scrappy little thing, isn't she?

Though not for much longer. Devoux began to walk forward, then to jog. It was time to finish her off, DEA agent or not.

It had to be done. She was a loose end, a fly in the ointment, and a risk he could ill afford to take. As long as she was alive, she'd be looking for the goods on Peter Carlyle, and she just might find something.

That's when he stopped short.

Coming fast up the dirt road was another car. He was about to have company, an eyewitness, maybe even plural.

But there was still time. He fixed his eyes

back on Agent Ellen Pierce, about to run over and shoot her dead.

Shit.

Her other hand was reaching out of the overturned car. This one was holding her gun. Slowly, clumsily, she was taking aim at him again.

Time to go. Devoux retreated to his Mercedes and fishtailed as he sped off. Looking in the rearview mirror, he could see a shaky and bloodied Agent Ellen Pierce stumbling to her feet, staring down the road at him.

Kill ya later, sweetheart.

Chapter 100

LIEUTENANT ANDREW TATEM high-tailed it into the emergency room of Princess Margaret Hospital in Nassau and was immediately escorted to a nearby examining room. That was one of the fringe benefits of being a man in uniform and an officer. Most people dropped everything in order to help you. It was a good thing.

The message relayed to him from the headquarters of the Bahamas Air Sea Rescue Association, BASRA, was only that Ellen Pierce was at the hospital. He didn't know why. He didn't even know whether she'd been hurt or it had been someone else.

That little mystery got solved the moment he saw her lying in the bed. It was her all right, and she was clearly a patient. Cuts, bruises, lots of bandages from head to toe.

"Christ, what happened?" he asked.

"Car trouble," she said, her sense of humor still intact. "Flat tire, actually."

Ellen described her showdown with the pistol-packing Mystery Man from Billy Rosa's bar. She had no doubt that Carlyle had arranged to meet him there. As to why exactly, she wasn't sure, but she had her suspicions, none of them good.

So did Tatem.

"We can't let him fly out of here in the morning," he said. "We've got to ground him."

"Believe me, I've been lying here trying to figure out how we can. Legally, that is."

Tatem rolled his eyes. "You almost got killed today. At least to buy us some time, I think your office would understand if we concocted something to keep Carlyle on the island. Don't you agree?"

Ellen shot him a sheepish look.

"What's wrong?" asked Tatem. "What am I missing here?"

She glanced over his shoulder, making sure they were alone. The nurse in the hallway seemed safely out of earshot. Besides, her vote didn't count.

"You see, technically I'm not here," said Ellen.

"I don't follow."

"Let's just say that my boss back in New York didn't exactly share my concerns about Peter Carlyle. I'm kind of . . . on vacation down here."

Tatem rolled his eyes again, her confession sinking in. "Let me get this straight—you contacted me on your own? You're flying solo on this, with no clearance?"

"Bingo."

"I hate bingo. Christ, that's why you wanted me to play airport courier for you. You couldn't be seen with Peter Carlyle."

"I'm sorry," she said. "I'll make it up to you. I don't know how yet, but I will."

"I'll make sure you do," he said, allowing a smile. Above all else, Agent Ellen Pierce certainly showed initiative, and guts. He liked that. She was trouble, sure, but his kind of trouble. Never mind that she was also very attractive—even all banged up in a hospital bed.

"Here's the problem," she said. "If Carlyle somehow has it in for his family, the only way to ground him would be to lock him up. To do that, we need evidence."

"Which we don't have, of course. Do we?"

"Not yet." She thought for a second. "Wait, what about that life jacket your guys found, the burned one? How fast can we have it tested for explosives?"

"That depends. You plan on bringing anyone up to speed? The feds, perhaps?"

Ellen shook her head.

"I didn't think so," said Tatem. "The Coast Guard isn't exactly an investigative unit, although I do know a pretty decent lab guy in Miami. Figure eighteen hours—twenty-four."

"Good enough, I guess."

"And in the meantime?" he asked. "What are we supposed to do?"

"Simple," she said. "We pray your Coast Guard boys find the Dunne family before that bastard Carlyle does."

Chapter 101

PETER WAITED IN HIS HOTEL ROOM the next morning until he heard the five magic words. At 9:15 his phone rang. "You have a FedEx package," said the front desk. Now he had everything he needed.

Securing a private plane had been no problem. In fact, he had his pick of aircraft. Under the guise of being Good Samaritans, about a dozen aviation leasing outfits were willing to offer—for free, no less—the use of one of their planes.

Of course, their real motivation just might

be the gobs of free publicity they would attract thanks to this ultra-hyped media story.

Everyone's an opportunist, right? Nothing new about that. Greed is always at the core of human nature.

By 9:45 Peter was out on the tarmac at Pindling International, performing the requisite visual inspection of his loaner plane. It was what they called an amphibian, able to take off and land on both the ground and the water.

Slowly he circled the aircraft. The Coast Guard had probably begun its new search at the crack of dawn, but Peter didn't care about its head start. *Good luck, fellas. You'll need it.*

While its complex computer models were busy trying to reconcile a bogus EPIRB signal, a found life jacket, and the migrating habits of giant bluefin tuna, Peter's search area would be based on the one thing the Coast Guard didn't have: the actual coordinates of where *The Family Dunne* went down.

Peter climbed aboard the plane and strapped himself in. Even in the private confines of the cockpit he still felt the need to glance left and right, like a kid about to cheat on his math test, before going over his flight plan one last time, reviewing exactly how he should commit the murders. The preflight checklist followed. All instruments and gauges were operational. Everything responded. No glitches. At least, it seemed that way.

Peter wasn't a hundred percent focused on his instrument panel and he knew it. He also couldn't help it. His mind was elsewhere. It was impossible not to dwell on Katherine and the brats, namely on what he had in store for them. His *post*flight checklist.

1. Kill them all, whoever had survived the explosion.
2. Bury the bodies.
3. Pretend to search the area for a few more days.
4. Tearfully give up, undoubtedly before tons of news cameras from around the globe.

The voice of the tower crackled through Peter's headset. "Mr. Carlyle, you are cleared for takeoff on runway A-three. On a personal note, here's hoping you find your family."

Peter thanked the voice from the tower, grinning behind his sunglasses.

Be careful what you wish for, pal.

Chapter 102

THE DAY WAS A PILOT'S DREAM, all right. Nearly perfect visibility. With barely a cloud in the sky, Peter could see everything from his perch at three thousand feet.

Everything, that is, except Katherine and her obnoxious brat pack. Plus their uncle, of course.

He'd covered a half-dozen islands along the southernmost tip of the Bahamas that qualified as uninhabited. Sure enough, they were still uninhabited.

There remained two ripe prospects in his mind, and he had the coordinates for both.

A half hour later, that was down to one.

Peter wasn't given to self-doubt, and that wasn't changing as he steered the plane due east and throttled up. It was Devoux's work he was beginning to question.

With his charts and graphs, the guy had certainly made the search seem like a slam dunk. *Of course, that expression had some interesting history with the CIA, didn't it?*

Peter still had an unfair advantage over the Coast Guard. Its search wouldn't expand this far south until the following day—at the earliest. Still, what good was having the extra time if he came up empty?

Peter increased the throttle and the plane responded seamlessly. He very much liked the way it handled. Even when pushed, she still felt smooth. *Very* smooth. With the engines purring, he gave the throttle one more nudge. *Why not get there a little faster?*

Out of nowhere, the plane answered with a loud sputter. *That's why.*

Jolting up in his seat, Peter looked out his side window to see the left propeller slowing down. Then it stopped.

Immediately the wings seesawed, the plane lurching hard left. Peter threw his weight against the control stick, struggling to steer it back to the right.

Again he looked out the window—both sides now—checking the ailerons on the rear edge of the wings. They looked intact, but he was still losing roll control.

Peter's gut shot up into his throat as the small plane began to spiral downward. Once, twice, he tried to restart the engine, but with no luck. The nose of the plane plunged farther and farther south. Within seconds there would be nothing he could do.

Except crash into the sea.

Was this God intervening? Was there some kind of cosmic justice after all? Nah!

Peter shook his head, clenching his jaw. With one last heave he pulled back on the control stick, trying to bring the plane out of its spin. If he could level the plane, he'd have another shot at restarting the engine. *That's it, baby, straighten out! You can do it.*

The left engine stirred, then stammered, the propeller clicking, clicking, clicking...

Then catching.

Sweet music to his ears, the engine fired up, kicking out a burst of air and sending the plane hurling forward out of its spin. Only when it leveled out a few hundred feet over the water did Peter remember to breathe.

"Unfuckingbelievable!" he shouted.

But that was only the half of it. Peter stared out over the nose of the plane, quickly lifting his sunglasses. The island! Twelve o'clock, straight ahead! Were those animals?

No, they were people.

And not sunbathers, either—not tourists enjoying a secluded day at the beach.

Back on went the sunglasses. He throttled down, the plane swooping lower and lower. He wanted to get closer, close enough to know for sure that what he was seeing was for real.

That it was the Dunnes.

Chapter 103

I'M NOT THE FIRST TO SPOT IT, Mark is. He yells so loud that I think I'm back in the ER and there's a big problem.

But the second I turn to see him down by the water, his arm outstretched and pointing feverishly into the sky, I know he's screaming for joy.

The next second we all are.

Carrie and Ernie, sprawled in the shade by the top of the beach, jump up like two jack-in-the-boxes. They practically trip over each other as they sprint to join their brother.

No one says a word about lighting the fires. *We don't have to!*

That's how close this low-flying plane is. It's coming straight toward us, no mistake. There's no way it can't see us.

Still, just to be sure, Carrie runs over to our SOS spelled out with rocks. I actually laugh as she elaborately motions to it with her hands. She looks like one of those silly prize girls on *The Price Is Right.* Wow, this is really happening! We're about to be rescued!

Yesterday we thought our ship had come in. Today, for real, our plane has!

It's only a few hundred yards away and dipping lower, as if to say hello, signaling that it's seen us.

That's when Mark screams out again. "Look!" he says. "It's got pontoons!"

He's right. I was so happy to see the plane, it never occurred to me where it might land.

No problem at all.

It's got a runway as big as the ocean.

With a giant *whoosh!* the plane sails right overhead, its wings angling into a steep turn. I catch a glimpse of the pilot—or at least the silhouette of the pilot. It looks like a man, or maybe I'm just assuming that. I really can't tell for sure. But if it is, he's going to get the biggest hug of his life, whoever he is.

"It's coming around to land!" yells Mark. "He's coming! He's coming!"

We watch the plane circle back at the far end of the beach. The wings level out no more than a couple of hundred feet above the surface. In all my years of sailing, I've never actually seen a water landing.

Talk about a memorable first time.

The plane approaches, its twin propellers like two perfect circles against the sky. Any second now it will begin to dip toward the surf, those pontoons gently easing down.

But that expected moment never comes.

Right before our eyes—so close, so very, *very* close—the plane continues straight past us, the roar of its engines drowning out our screams.

"Noooooo!"

Stunned, we watch as it flies off into the distance. It doesn't turn around, it doesn't come back. Instead it disappears over the horizon.

Gone.

How could what just happened here possibly have happened? Who was that maniac who just buzzed us?

Chapter 104

CHRIST, IT'S DARK...

Not that Peter was complaining. This was exactly what he had been waiting for, the cover of night. The darker, the better.

Walking through the thick and tangled brush, he kept his flashlight low, shining it ahead only enough to see where each step was about to land. Anything more would've been too much. It would make him into a walking lighthouse.

He was an uninvited guest, after all—the ultimate surprise visitor—and the whole key to his plan was keeping it that way until the very last moment.

Now he just had to find his lovely family, once and for all, and finish them off.

The plane was anchored on the other side of the island. Earlier he'd cut the engines and performed a near-silent "dead drop" a few miles from shore. *Hey, kids, don't try that at home — trust me on it.*

For one thing, there are no do-overs.

It took hours for the current to drag the plane close enough to the island, but hours he had. If he'd really thought about it, he would've included a few magazines in the FedEx box.

Other than that, though, he'd packed everything he needed. One fold-up shovel. The flashlight. Some double-braided rope. Of course, the most important was his Smith & Wesson .44 Magnum. And yes, he was ready to use it. The murders wouldn't be a problem for him.

Peter pressed on. The night air was warm and still, peppered only with the high-pitched chirping of some kind of bird. Short of that, the only distinct sound was the pounding of his heart. The adrenaline was now gushing through his veins. Maybe the murders would be a small problem.

Finally, through a clearing, he saw it.

Distant but definitely there. It was a small orange glow.

Their campfire.

The edge of the beach was only a few yards away. Reaching it, he immediately kicked off his docksiders and wet his feet, made sure he was balanced in his stance.

Each step he took now was silenced by the squishy give of the sand. He was quiet as a mouse.

As he got closer, his eyes began to distinguish among the shapes near the fire. Bodies. All horizontal. Fast, fast asleep. No one seemed to be stirring. He could even hear some snoring.

One big happy family.

But who was who? Peter wondered.

Did it even matter?

For some perverse reason, it did. Yes, the first shot would be reserved for Katherine. He had nothing against her, really. There was no need for her to see the kids slaughtered.

Peter took one more step forward, his eyes squinting down to narrow slits.

Until . . .

The light from the fire shifted ever so

slightly, illuminating Katherine's face for only a split second.

There you are, sweetie pie!

With a stiff arm he swiftly raised his gun in front of him, the barrel aimed squarely at Katherine's head, right between her eyes. All he had to do was pull the trigger.

At least, that's how it might have looked.

"But trust me, ladies and gentlemen of the jury, I was there to save my family, not to kill them."

Part Six

TRUST NO ONE

Chapter 105

PETER'S ASSEMBLED DREAM TEAM of lawyers looked like an ad for Paul Stuart suits as they conversed in hushed tones around the defense table. As for Peter himself, having traded in his flashy Brioni for a Brooks Brothers gray flannel, he kept his focus squarely on the jury as they were led back into the courtroom after a one-hour recess for lunch.

That's right, people, make eye contact with me. Only an innocent man can stare a jury straight in the eyes, right? That's been my experience, anyway.

"All rise!" bellowed the court clerk.

Judge Robert Barnett, midfifties with slicked-back gray hair divided by a razor-sharp part, made his way to the bench and further cemented his reputation as a no-nonsense, no dilly-dallying man even before he sat down. He dispensed with any idle chitchat—not even a "Please be seated"—and asked the prosecution to call their first witness.

Nolan Heath, the lead prosecutor, promptly stood and straightened his rep tie before adjusting his wire-rimmed glasses. Heath was a deliberate and pensive man, his expression always like that of a chess player considering his next move.

"Your Honor, the prosecution calls Mark Dunne."

Mark, pot-free for over four months now, rose quickly from the first row behind the prosecution table. If anything, he looked a little too anxious to testify. Who could blame him? He had something to say here, something hugely important.

As he was sworn in, he stared at Peter Carlyle, his hatred of the man on full display for all to see.

Heath said, "Mark, would you please describe the events, as you recall them, of the night of June twenty-fifth earlier this year?"

Mark nodded and took a deep breath. That was something Heath had repeatedly reminded him to do on the witness stand. *Breathe. Think, then speak.*

Slowly Mark began to answer. "My sister, Carrie, and I had been taking turns watching over our campsite on the island while everyone else slept. A large snake had attacked our mother a few days earlier, so we wanted to make sure nothing snuck up on us during the night. Carrie and I were vigilant.

"Anyway, a few hours in I heard something. It was dark, but I knew it wasn't just the wind blowing. Or even an animal. They're quieter. Sure enough, I could see someone approaching. I mean, I couldn't tell who it was, but I knew it was a person."

Heath nodded. "You must have been excited, right? You thought you were about to be saved."

"Yeah, that's what I thought at first," said Mark. "Then I wondered why the person wasn't calling out to us or anything. It didn't make any sense. That's when I saw the gun in his hand."

"So what did you do?" asked Heath, as if he were hearing the story for the first time.

"I protected my family as best I could. As soon as I saw him raise that gun and point it at my mother, I hit him with a heavy branch. Thankfully, it knocked him out."

"And when you say *him,* who are you referring to, Mark?"

Mark pointed, jabbing his finger as he had done when he spotted Peter's plane flying toward the island. "*Him* right there. Peter Carlyle. My stepfather. *The son of a bitch!*"

The courtroom buzzed until Judge Barnett banged his gavel. "Young man, I won't tolerate that kind of language in my courtroom. Do you understand?"

Mark nodded dutifully before turning back to Heath. No one would ever know by the prosecutor's expression that he was extremely proud of his young witness. Mark had delivered the son-of-a-bitch line exactly as he had been told.

"No further questions, Your Honor."

Chapter 106

JUDGE BARNETT MOTIONED to the defense table. “Your witness,” he announced.

“Thank you, Your Honor,” cooed Gordon Knowles, presumptive captain of Peter’s dream team. He stood up and nodded politely at the jury.

Then, as if to please the impatient judge, he turned to Mark and got right into it.

“You just testified that you were on guard duty that night on the island. So in a way you were sort of looking for trouble, weren’t you?”

Heath bolted up from the prosecution

table. "Objection, Your Honor! He's putting words in the witness's mouth."

"Sustained," muttered Judge Barnett with a disapproving glance at Knowles. "You know better than that, Counselor."

Yes, he did.

And he would do much better, too.

"Tell me, Mark," he continued before quickly stopping himself. "You don't mind if I call you by your first name, do you?"

"Not at all, *Gordon.*"

The jury chuckled.

"Fair enough," said Knowles, pretending to laugh along. "Now, Mark, when you first saw Mr. Carlyle arrive at your campsite on the island, could you see what he was wearing?"

"No, I couldn't," answered Mark. "As I said, it was dark."

"Yes, it was, wasn't it? *As you said,* you didn't even know who the person approaching was until after you attacked him."

Heath was halfway through his objection when Knowles rephrased. "I'm sorry," he lied. "Sprang into action, I should've said."

Judge Barnett frowned. "Get to your question, Counselor."

"Gladly, Your Honor. My question is this. Mark, if you had known that it was Mr. Carlyle, would you have hit him with that heavy branch?"

Mark blinked a few times as if trying to keep his mental balance. He saw where Knowles—*Gordon*—was going with this line of questioning and didn't want to be tripped up. Not by this prick!

"He had a gun," Mark answered, slowly and distinctly.

"That's not what I asked," said Knowles. "If you had known who it was, would you have hit him with that branch?"

Mark fell silent again.

Judge Barnett leaned toward the witness stand. "Please answer the question, son," he said.

"No, I wouldn't have hit him," said Mark softly.

"Why is that?" asked Knowles.

"Because he was my stepfather."

"Someone who would have no reason to harm you or anyone else in your family, right?"

"But he had a gun!" Mark repeated, his voice cracking.

"Yes, he did," said Knowles. "For the same

reason you claim to have jumped him. *For self-defense.*" He turned to the jury, throwing up his arms in mock desperation. "After all, Mr. Carlyle had more than large snakes to worry about that night. As I mentioned in my opening statement, he had been told by none other than a federal agent that drug traffickers may have been involved in his family's disappearance. So Mr. Carlyle came prepared. He had a gun *for self-defense.* It makes all the sense in the world."

Heath stood to object again, but it was too late. A few members of the jury were shrugging in agreement. *Gun ≠ guilty.*

The damage was done.

So was Knowles.

"No further questions," he announced.

Chapter 107

PETER'S EXTRADITION from the Bahamas was one thing, but this trial is definitely another kind of circus. I don't know how much more of it I can take, and this is only the beginning! The madness has just begun.

It's not just the trial itself, though. It's what it represents—what this feels like for the kids and me.

It's as if we're taking the trip all over again.

We were finally getting on with our lives and moving forward. I had filed for divorce as soon as I got home, and it would be final in just a few weeks. The incessant media coverage had died down—no more pictures every day in the paper or boldface mentions in the gossip columns. Even my broken leg had healed nicely.

Then, *pow!* the trial throws us right back on *The Family Dunne* and we have to relive everything.

No wonder I'm back on the couch in Mona's office. Once again, I thank God for her soundproof walls.

"Damn it! Damn it! *Damn it!*" I yell, barely a minute into our session. "This is so unfair to the kids."

With the trial taking up almost the entire day, Mona agreed to see me late for what she's calling a "gripe and grub." Translation: after I vent to her for an hour, we grab dinner together at the restaurant of her choice. My treat—my very expensive treat.

I quickly apologize for the yelling, and as usual Mona tells me it's more than okay.

"In fact," she says, "I think it's good for you."

"Maybe," I reply. "What would really be good for me is seeing Peter locked up behind bars. That can't happen soon enough."

"At the same time, you need to prepare yourself if—"

I lift my hand, telling her to stop right there. I don't even want to hear those two horrible words.

Not guilty.

What Peter did—and I'm convinced way beyond a reasonable doubt that he did indeed do it—is hard enough to swallow. The idea that he might not be punished makes me want to throw up.

Others agree with me. Not the least of whom is Agent Ellen Pierce. She risked her job, if not her career, following her gut about Peter Carlyle, Esq.

"What did you think when Agent Pierce first approached you?" I ask Mona.

"I didn't know what to think. At the time I thought you were dead. That was shocking enough. The idea that Peter might have been responsible . . . Well, the least I could do was carry that tape recorder for her. I just wish it had helped."

"Isn't it ironic, though?" I say. "The person who I thought I trusted the most was trying to kill me, and the people who I thought I couldn't count on—my kids—were the ones who ended up saving my life."

"That's definitely the word for it," says Mona. "To think you were sitting right here in my office before the trip, wanting so desperately to save your family." She smiled. "It almost killed you, but mission accomplished. You all came out better for it."

We both fall silent, suddenly realizing that's not entirely true.

We didn't *all* come out better.

"I'm sorry," says Mona. "I didn't mean to forget Jake. I haven't. None of us have."

"It's okay," I say. "Sometimes I wish I could, if you know what I mean. Hardly a day goes by that I don't think about him."

"What about the kids? Have they dealt with it?"

"Mark and Carrie have. They're older. For Ernie it's taking a little longer. He really looked up to Jake."

I hear myself say that last sentence and I know exactly what Mona's thinking. Probably because I've been thinking the same thing.

"It's time, isn't it?" I ask Mona.

"Yes," she answers. "I think it is."

Chapter 108

"YOUR WITNESS, Mr. Knowles."

Gordon Knowles thanked Judge Barnett with a sharp nod as he rose from the defense table. Agent Ellen Pierce was a key witness for the prosecution, and he was champing at the bit to cross-examine her and take her testimony apart.

"Agent Pierce," he began, his tone as warm and inviting as a bed of nails, "you just testified that you followed my client to Vermont, where you trespassed on private property and secretly photographed him with a woman. Do you think that proves beyond a reasonable doubt that Mr. Carlyle was planning to kill his family?"

Ellen answered quickly and confidently. "No, I do not."

"Earlier today we heard testimony from an explosives expert who said his lab found traces of RDX, a military-grade explosive, on the life jacket salvaged from the Dunne family's boat. Do you think that proves beyond a reasonable doubt that Mr. Carlyle was planning to kill his family?"

Ellen, dressed modestly in a black pantsuit and simple white blouse, glanced over at the jury, as if to express her dissatisfaction with this line of questioning. She was being walked like a dog by Knowles and she didn't like it. Not one little bit.

It was time to bite back.

"What I *think* is that the jury might start to wonder if all these coincidences, as you'd like to call them, are something more than just a coincidence," she said.

Judge Barnett didn't wait to hear Knowles's objection to intervene. He quickly turned to the jury box. "The jury will disregard the unsolicited speculation by the witness." He then fixed his disapproving gaze on Ellen. "Ms. Pierce, please just answer the question."

"Sorry, Your Honor," she said. She wasn't sorry, of course. In fact, she felt quite content that her point had been made. Somebody needed to make it if justice was to be done here.

"To repeat the question, Agent Pierce—"

She cut him off. "No, I don't believe that the trace explosive alone proves beyond a reasonable doubt that Mr. Carlyle was trying to kill his family."

Knowles smiled with smug satisfaction. "Agent Pierce, you were suspended by the DEA for your reckless actions in pursuing my client, correct?"

Instinctively Ellen looked over at Ian McIntyre, seated behind the prosecution table. She was somewhat surprised that he had come to lend his support. It almost took the sting out of the three-month "vacation" he had given her.

"I don't think the word *reckless*—"

It was Knowles's turn to interrupt. "Were you or were you not suspended from duty?"

"Yes, I was."

"Indeed, you had been told explicitly by

the head of your division *not* to pursue Mr. Carlyle, correct?"

"Yes."

"Nonetheless you met with Mr. Carlyle under false pretenses and lied to him about Jake Dunne's being suspected of drug smuggling, didn't you? In fact, you warned Mr. Carlyle that if he found his family, they were still potentially in danger."

"What I was trying to do—"

"Yes, that is the question, isn't it? *What were you trying to do?* Was it some kind of revenge?"

Every ounce of Ellen was now telling her to keep her cool, not do this jerk-off any favors by getting emotional. Still, she had to defend herself. "That's preposterous," she said firmly. "There was no revenge. That's utterly absurd and insulting."

"Is it, though? The head of your division himself said that your judgment may have been clouded because of a trial a few months back in which Mr. Carlyle successfully defended someone you had vigorously investigated."

"Trust me, the only clouded judgment was the verdict in that case," replied Ellen. She knew she should've just answered straight, but she couldn't help herself. Not anymore. "Sometimes justice truly is blind," she added.

Knowles shook his head. *Tsk-tsk!* "It sounds to me, Agent Pierce, as if you have serious contempt for our legal system."

"No," said Ellen, looking him squarely in the eye. "Just for defense attorneys."

Chapter 109

ONLY ONE DAY of school. That's all I'm allowing the kids to miss for the trial, I tell myself.

For Carrie, that's one day too many. She wants nothing to do with Peter, even if it means seeing him locked up for the rest of his miserable life. Hopefully it will.

Anyway, that's fine with me. Carrie's exactly where she should be—enjoying her sophomore year at Yale. There's no more school nutritionist, no more school psychologist. Just school. Her body weight is back up to normal, and something tells me it's going to stay that way.

Mark, of course, had to miss a day of classes at Deerfield in order to testify. I'm so proud of him, and I think he did a fine job under the circumstances. He, on the other hand, is a little bummed about the way Peter's buddy-buddy lawyer—"the dickwad"—played hardball with him.

Speaking of bummed...

It's Ernie.

After an early dinner with Nolan Heath to discuss my testimony tomorrow, I return to the apartment and relieve Angelica for the evening. She tells me Ernie's in his room doing his homework.

In a lot of ways Ernie should be on cloud nine with the rest of us. It was his idea to put the note in the bottle. *He* saved us. And from the moment we flipped that transponder back on in Peter's plane, his was a hero's welcome. From the *Today* show to *Larry King* to *On the Record with Greta Van Susteren,* he did more than a dozen TV interviews. In every article written about our ordeal, he always got the most ink.

Except he never really enjoyed any of it, even though it was always his choice whether to make an appearance or not. He smiled for the cameras, saying and doing all the right things like the trouper he is. But I'm his mother. I could tell. And after more than four months, this funk of his hasn't gotten too much better. I blame myself, of course.

Gently I knock on his half-open door. "Mind if I come in?" I ask.

He's sitting at his desk in the far corner. "Sure," he says, his eyes fixed on the glowing rectangle of his iMac. "Hi, Mom."

"How's your essay coming?" Five hundred words on the Emancipation Proclamation. Not counting *a*'s and *the*'s. This is what I get for cutting back my hours after returning to the hospital, something I was so sorely missing: the details of my kids' lives.

"Three hundred and eighty-seven words . . . and counting," Ernie answers, his fingers tapping away on the wireless keyboard. "I'll make it."

"Absolutely."

I browse around his room for a minute, not wanting to get into it right away. I glance at a poster of Albert Einstein, the one in which he's famously sticking out his tongue.

Then I stop in front of a framed photograph of Ernie with those two fishermen, Captain

Steve and his first mate. Jason? No—it was Jeffrey, I remember. What a couple of characters those guys are. Look how they're smiling, too! Then again, that shot was snapped right after I gave them their reward. Who wouldn't be smiling?

I certainly was. Best million dollars anyone could ever spend.

"Are you scared?" asks Ernie out of nowhere, breaking the silence in the room.

"You mean about testifying tomorrow? I guess I'm a little nervous," I say. "You'll be there to support me, right?"

He nods. The one day he's chosen for attending the trial is when I'm scheduled to take the stand. I can't begin to explain how good that makes me feel.

"Ernie, there's something I want to talk to you about," I say.

Maybe it's the tone of my voice, the notion that we're not about to discuss the weather or anything else that's trivial in our lives. He turns away from his computer and stares right at me. "What is it, Mom?" he asks.

I sit down on his bed, taking a deep breath before I begin. I've been planning this conversation in my head for years, all along thinking that I could prepare myself properly, not get too emotional.

So much for that.

"Why are you crying, Mom?"

I tell him the truth. "It's Jake," I say. "I still miss him a lot."

"Me too."

"I know you do, honey. That's what I want to talk to you about."

"Did I do something wrong?" Ernie asks.

"No. Absolutely not." *I did. But it's the best mistake I ever made, something I'd never change.*

I stare at Ernie, his eyes and face, and it's as if I can see him more clearly than ever before, as if I know who he really is.

"Mom?" he asks. "Is there something you want to tell me?"

"Yes, honey, there is."

And so I do.

I tell Ernie who his father is.

Chapter 110

AFTER A NIGHT of telling the whole truth and nothing but the truth to Ernie, I promise to do the same in court the next morning.

So far, so good.

As I wrap up my testimony for Nolan Heath and his prosecution, my only complaint is the hardness of the witness chair. Would it kill them to include a cushion on this thing? Seriously, though, I think I'm doing okay. The jury seems to believe me, if not to feel downright sorry for our family. The elderly lady on the end of the first row looks as if she wants to bake us cookies.

That said, I'm not sure how much anything I have to say matters. The most I can prove is that I'm a woman who got duped by one of the best. I thought I was marrying a really great guy. How was I supposed to know that charming Peter Carlyle was a lying, cheating, murderous lout?

That was the point, I guess. I wasn't supposed to know who Peter was. Sometimes I still find it hard to believe. *My husband tried to murder my entire family.*

"Your witness," Judge Barnett announces. I immediately feel a twinge.

All it takes is Gordon Knowles rising from the defense table for me to realize that "so far, so good" only gets you so far in a murder trial. The real test is about to come.

"Dr. Dunne, this sailing trip with your children was your idea, wasn't it?" he asks.

"Yes," I answer.

"Mr. Carlyle had nothing to do with arranging it, am I correct?"

"Yes. Although he did know about it well in advance. Months in advance, actually."

Knowles grins. "Oh, I see. Because he knew about it in advance, you're suggesting he had ample time to plot your family's murder."

"I'm just saying—"

"Of course, lots of people knew in advance that you were taking this trip—for instance, the people you work with at Lexington Hospital."

"I'm pretty sure no one there wants to see me dead."

"What about you, Dr. Dunne?"

I'm taken aback. "I'm not sure I understand the question. Could you rephrase, please?"

"You've been under the care of a psychiatrist for some time, haven't you?" asks Knowles.

"Yes, I see a therapist. Lots of people do."

"Are you on antidepressants?"

In a flash I can feel my blood, comfortably on a low simmer up until this point, begin to boil. The word *incredulous* doesn't even begin to describe how I feel. "Are you suggesting I had something to do with all this?" I ask with a shaky voice.

"Your Honor, could you please instruct the witness that I'm the only one permitted to ask questions right now?" says a smug Knowles.

"I think you just did that for me, Counselor. Get on with it," says Judge Barnett, directing one of his sternest looks at the defense attorney.

"With pleasure," says Knowles. "In fact, I'm just getting warmed up..."

Chapter 111

KNOWLES TURNS BACK TO ME, edging closer. So close I can smell his designer cologne. Eau de Pompous, perhaps? I never liked this man, not even when he was at Peter's and my wedding reception. Hard to imagine it now. Peter's buddy cross-examining me in court at a murder trial?

"Do you know the very last words recorded by the Coast Guard when Jake radioed them during the storm?" he asks.

"No, I don't."

"I do—it's right here," he says, strutting back to the crowded defense table. He picks up a yellow legal pad and adjusts his glasses. "Right before the radio went dead, Jake Dunne screamed, 'No, Katherine, don't!' "

Knowles folds his arms and stares at me. "Don't *what,* Dr. Dunne?"

I look at him blankly. I'm trying to remember—there was so much going on during the storm.

Finally, it comes to me. *The bin.*

"I think I was opening—"

He cuts me off. "You *think?* What is that supposed to mean? Do you remember it or not?"

"Objection, Your Honor," says Heath, rising from the prosecution table. "He's badgering the witness. Dr. Dunne isn't being given a chance to answer the question."

"I'll retract the question," says Knowles.

Of course he will, the tricky bastard—it's already done its damage. No wonder Peter likes this obnoxious creep so much.

He continues: "Dr. Dunne, how much money did you inherit when your first husband died?"

"I don't know the exact amount."

"Would it be safe to assume that it was over a hundred million dollars?"

"Yes," I say.

"You were the last person to see your first husband alive on his boat, were you not?"

"Actually, no—"

"Objection!" shouts Heath. "This is outrageous. Relevancy!"

Knowles quickly turns to the bench. "Your Honor, the death of Stuart Dunne was ruled to be accidental. I'm simply trying to point out that accidents happen on boats, just like anywhere else."

"I'll allow it," declares Judge Barnett.

Knowles pivots back to me. "In fact, Dr. Dunne, as you mentioned in an earlier deposition, your boat had suffered mechanical difficulties—*accidents,* if you will—prior to the storm, correct?"

"Yes. We had a ruptured through-hull line."

"For those nonsailors among us, that's basically a hose that channels in seawater from outside the boat to cool the engine, right?"

"I didn't know that myself until Jake explained it to me."

"Indeed, your former brother-in-law managed to fix the problem. As you mentioned in your deposition, how did he describe what he did?"

Even before Knowles finishes the question I realize how damaging my answer will sound.

"He cut out a piece of the fuel line and spliced it onto the engine-cooling water line," I say.

"I'm sorry, could you please speak up, Dr. Dunne? Did you say he cut the fuel line?"

"Yes."

"So he cut out a piece of the hosing that carries the flammable fuel to the engine and then he patched it back together? Is that right?"

"I don't know for sure. I wasn't with him when he did it."

"Ah. Which means you don't know how good a job he did, do you?"

This guy's like a human minefield. No, he's worse than that. He's Captain Knowles of the SS *Reasonable Doubt.*

And I'm starting to get a sick, sinking feeling in my stomach.

"Last question, Dr. Dunne, and I'll remind

you that you are still under oath," he announces over his shoulder. "Have you ever been in the employ of the U.S. Central Intelligence Agency?"

I can practically hear the neck of every person in the courtroom snap as they quickly look from Knowles to me. Where did *that* come from? What a bombshell of a question.

Same for the answer, I suppose.

The whole truth and nothing but, huh?

I lean forward to the microphone. Lord knows I don't want to have to say it twice.

"Yes, I worked with the CIA."

Chapter 112

PETER MET UP with Bailey again that night at the Alex Hotel. It had become their secret rendezvous point, at least until the trial was over. Their first night there had been highlighted by two bottles of Cristal, right before Peter left for the Bahamas. But ever since he had returned in handcuffs, no pricey bubbly had been flowing.

Soon, though, thought Peter.

He was feeling confident in the wake of the superb job Knowles did on Katherine with his cross-examination. It was a masterpiece, really. *Couldn't have done it better myself. Well, maybe a little more painful shredding of Kat.*

"Are you sure you still want to testify tomorrow?" asked Bailey, curled up next to Peter under the sheets. God, the girl had perfect breasts, even when he couldn't actually see them and had to tell just by touch.

"Forget what they're teaching you at NYU," he answered. "Defendants in murder trials should *always* testify. Besides, I've got absolutely nothing to hide. That's the best reason to testify."

Bailey fell silent for a moment. It was the kind of silence that spoke volumes as far as Peter was concerned. Something was troubling the lass.

"What is it?" he asked. "And please don't say it's nothing, Bailey."

"No, it's definitely something," she said. "There's something I need to know, Peter."

Ever since Peter was released on bail, he'd been anticipating this moment. He thought that Bailey, being Bailey, would ask him right away. Then again, he *had* done a brilliant job of gaining her trust. He should be flattered that it had taken her this long, months and months in fact, to pose the question.

He decided to beat her to the punch. “No, I did not try to kill Katherine and the kids.”

Bailey cupped his face in her hands and gently kissed his lips. “I had to hear you say it. Can you forgive me? I’m so sorry, Peter.”

“Don’t be. It’s just the lawyer in you. I respect that.”

“Do you *forgive* me?” she asked.

“More important, do you trust me?”

“I do,” she said. “I truly do.”

He returned her kisses, pulling her tight against him.

“Now, going against every primal and sexual urge in my body, I’ve got to get some sleep,” he said. “Tomorrow’s going to be an eventful day. *Trust me.*”

Chapter 113

I WATCH as Nolan Heath slowly walks toward the witness stand as if he were Gary Cooper in *High Noon.*

This is it, isn't it?

He knows it, I know it, the whole courtroom knows it—including the jury. *It's him against Peter.* One very determined prosecutor versus one very, *very* smart defendant. Whoever wins this ultimate showdown probably wins the trial.

"Mr. Carlyle, let's clear up one thing right at the start. Dr. Dunne herself told you that she had once done some work for the CIA, did she not?"

Peter nods easily. "Yes, she did."

Heath draws an imaginary gun, pointing his finger around the courtroom. He looks silly and gets a few chuckles from the gallery. Precisely his point.

"Did Dr. Dunne tell you that she was some sort of covert agent, traveling the world to assassinate dictators and help overthrow governments? A female version of James Bond?"

"No."

"That's right," says Heath. "In fact, what she told you was that she had helped organize a research study to measure the effects of different neurotoxins on the human heart, correct?"

"Yes."

"Not exactly cloak-and-dagger stuff, huh?"

Peter doesn't respond.

"But speaking of covert activity, Mr. Carlyle, I'm curious about your behavior in the Bahamas. Agent Pierce testified that she saw you walk out of a remote bar in Nassau with a man who minutes later tried to kill her. Do you deny that she saw you there?"

"I don't know if Agent Pierce saw me, but I was there."

"What were you doing at the bar?"

Peter shrugs. "Having a drink."

"Are you aware that there were seventeen bars in Nassau closer to your hotel?"

"I was trying to avoid the media. They had been relentless, in case you've forgotten. *They still are.* In case you haven't noticed them on your way in and out of the courthouse."

"Who was the man you were having a drink with?"

"I don't know. I wasn't having a drink with anyone."

"Wait, I'm confused," says Heath, turning to the jury. "You walked out together, correct?"

"If you mean did we leave the bar at the same time, yes," says Peter. "I'd never seen the man before, but he said he recognized me from the news. We talked briefly as I left. I didn't even get a name. I drove off one way, he drove off another."

"Yes, and when Agent Pierce followed this supposedly harmless stranger, he opened fire on her. Why do you think that is?"

"I don't know. As I said, I didn't know the man."

"Yes, you did say that, didn't you? You

don't know." Heath folds his arms, shakes his head incredulously. "I must say, Mr. Carlyle, although you're a very smart guy, there sure are a lot of things you don't know in this trial."

"I know I'm innocent," says Peter in a flash.

"Yes," says Heath without skipping a beat. "*Until proven guilty.*"

Chapter 114

WITH THAT, Heath really kicks it into high gear. His questions come rapid-fire, his tone more aggressive, if not bordering on angry. He's putting the *cross* in *cross-examination,* and I am on the edge of my seat. Literally.

"Mr. Carlyle, how does a military-grade explosive with the power to blow a large boat to smithereens end up on *The Family Dunne*?"

"I have no idea," says Peter.

"How about this: why did the boat's emergency radio beacon emit an erroneous signal that put the Coast Guard hundreds of miles off-course in its search?"

"I assume the beacon malfunctioned."

"Oh, really? When exactly did you assume that? Because when you began your one-man search, you somehow started with the islands closest to where the boat *really* went down. How is that?"

I watch as Peter smiles as if he's got it all under control. It's scary to think I used to love that smile very much. It used to make me feel safe and warm.

Ha!

"What you claim to be suspicious is really just common sense," Peter answers. "Why would I search the area where the Coast Guard was already searching?"

"So let me get this straight. Looking for your family where they *weren't* supposed to be—that was merely a hunch on your part?"

"More like hoping against hope, I guess. But I also made an assumption that if they were in an obvious place, they would already have been found."

"Well, you sure got lucky, didn't you?" says Heath sarcastically. He glances about the courtroom. "Then again, maybe not *that* lucky."

The bark to my left is Gordon Knowles

objecting. "Your Honor, he's badgering the witness."

Judge Barnett nods agreement. "Get to your next question, Mr. Heath."

"My apologies, Your Honor. It's just that there's something else I can't figure out, Mr. Carlyle. Both Dr. Dunne and her son Mark have testified that they first spotted you in your plane flying directly over them while it was still daylight. They were waving at you like crazy—they thought they were finally saved, for God's sake. Why didn't you stop?"

"That's just it," answers Peter with a relaxed shrug. "I saw them trying to signal me all right, but in light of what Agent Pierce told me about the drug traffickers, I was afraid that my family was actually trying to warn me. That's why I waited until the dark of night to return—and yes, with a gun. For all I knew, my family was being held hostage."

Nolan throws up his hands, incredulous. "Held *hostage?* Do you really expect this courtroom to believe that?"

Peter doesn't flinch, not even a blink. "Yes, I do. Just as I would expect that a federal agent like Ellen Pierce would be telling me the truth."

I shake my head. This is ridiculous! How can he sit there so calmly and lie through his teeth? What's even more ridiculous is that the jury seems to be taking him seriously. *Oh, Christ, did that old lady on the end of the first row just nod in agreement?*

No! No! No! Nolan's right, how could anyone really believe that we were being held hostage? The jury has to be seeing through all this, right? Whatever Agent Pierce told Peter, there's just too much other evidence—too many coincidences—stacking up against him. They have to realize it.

Hell, even Peter has to know he's truly up against the ropes.

But you wouldn't think so, looking at him. It's almost as if he knows something that no one else does. *What's he up to? I'm starting to get a really bad feeling.*

Then, in a heartbeat, the damnedest thing happens.

Chapter 115

HEATH FIRES OFF his next question, aimed squarely at motive. “Mr. Carlyle, do you know how much you stood to inherit if Dr. Dunne and her three children died while on their sailing trip?”

Peter fires back immediately. “I imagine it’s the same amount as if their plane had crashed when they all flew out to Aspen last winter and spent two weeks at the St. Regis.”

“What happened, did the bomb not go off on that flight?” asks Heath. “Or at the hotel?”

Gordon Knowles launches up from his

chair to object, only he's beaten to the punch.

By Peter.

"Now you listen, you son of a bitch!" Peter shouts, his cool veneer cracking like a cheap vase. "You don't know what it was like for me. I was stupid, cheating on my wife, whom I truly did love. Then I find out she's missing, along with the kids. Do you realize how guilty I felt? I was desperate to find them, do you hear me?"

Peter's face flushes red as he leans forward in the witness chair. The veins in his neck and forehead pop in unison as he yells even louder. "I'm not a monster! I've made mistakes, but I'm not a monster! I'm certainly no killer. How could you—"

Suddenly he stops. Peter clutches his arm.

Then his chest.

He staggers to his feet and stumbles off the witness stand. Directly in front of the jury box his body folds, collapsing to the floor with a horrific thud.

The elderly juror on the end of the first row lets go with a scream. The entire courtroom stands to see what just happened.

Peter's lying flat on his back, his face

contorted in extreme pain. His eyes are open, full of fear.

"Help . . . me . . . ," he sputters.

The first to reach him is the court clerk, followed by Gordon Knowles.

"He's having a heart attack!" Knowles shouts.

Everyone spills forward. Someone shouts, "Give him some air! He needs air!"

Knowles barks, "What he needs is a doctor!"

That's when I realize I haven't moved from the first row behind the prosecution table. I'm a statue, frozen. It's as if I've forgotten that I'm a cardiac surgeon.

But others around me haven't.

I look over at the jury in time to see heads turning from Peter on the ground to me still in my seat.

Peter looks helpless. Harmless.

I look cold. Heartless.

Like *I'm* the monster in this courtroom.

Even Nolan Heath finally calls out, "Katherine? Can you help?"

I can't. I know the Hippocratic oath by heart and still I don't move. All I can do is watch. Stare. I feel paralyzed from the neck down.

Until, through the sea of legs gathered around Peter, a space opens for a second, just long enough for our eyes to meet. It happens so fast I'm sure no one sees it—except the one person who's supposed to.

Me.

Peter winks.

Chapter 116

ELLEN PIERCE wasn't about to miss Peter Carlyle's big day in court, hopefully his total humiliation. She expected a spectacle but certainly not like this. One minute he's lying his ass off on the witness stand, the next he's lying on the floor.

A heart attack?

It certainly seemed that way, especially when the EMS guys showed up and took some quick vital signs. Within minutes they had Carlyle strapped to a gurney and were wheeling him out of the courthouse.

"What hospital will they take him to?" she asked a guard out in the hallway. She could barely hear her own voice above the commotion. Photographers were tripping over themselves to snap pictures. *Front page, anyone?*

"They'll probably take him to St. Mary's Hospital," answered the guard. "It's the closest."

He was right.

In less than eight minutes Ellen was stepping out of a taxi and into the hospital's crowded emergency room.

No one asked if she needed help. That was the beauty of New York City. Too many people to notice any one person.

Ellen looked around the bustling emergency room, a full three-sixty degrees. An ice pack here, a bandage there. The only grisly sight was a construction worker at the counter with blood dripping from his fingertips. His hand was wrapped, but from her angle Ellen could see the problem. Ouch! He'd been caught on the wrong side of a nail gun.

For good measure she spun around again, another three-sixty degrees. No sign of Peter Carlyle, though. Did they take him to a different hospital?

No.

The rush of air from the sliding doors opening behind her hit her in the back. She turned to see the EMS guys from the courtroom wheeling in Carlyle. Leave it to a New York City cabdriver to beat an ambulance, sirens and all.

Ellen quickly stepped to the side as two nurses met the EMS guys. The gurney never slowed down. In fact, as the nurses took over they began to jog. *No time to waste! Got to save this scumbag's life.*

Ellen trailed them down a corridor, spying as Peter was stripped of his clothes and Rolex while being prepped for an EKG. Then they all disappeared into a room and drew the curtains on the observation window.

What now?

The thought of following Carlyle again immediately took Ellen back to Nassau and Billy Rosa's bar. She would never forget how close to death she'd come when that mystery bastard opened fire on her on that dirt road. Even now she swore she could still taste the dust in her mouth.

It didn't matter what the verdict in the trial was, guilty or not guilty. She was going to find out how and why Carlyle was meeting up with that man. That was the key to everything; she was almost sure of it. Another one of her gut instincts.

But first things first. Carlyle. His health.

Ellen thought about waiting a bit before flashing her badge and pumping the closest doctor for some info. Was Carlyle truly having a heart attack? Was it something else? Or maybe it was nothing at all? A false alarm?

At this point she was putting nothing past the guy. But as eager as she was to find out, she knew that was a risky gambit. She'd just come off suspension, after all. No way she should approach a doctor in the ER.

Besides, suddenly she had a much better idea.

Chapter 117

I KEEP TELLING MYSELF: no regrets.

With Peter being held overnight for observation at St. Mary's Hospital, Nolan Heath spells out the options in his office this afternoon. It's his call, of course, and I can tell he's inclined to proceed with the trial. But he wants my input—my vote on this is important to him. As Nolan told me when we first met, "This may be my job, but it's your life. I never forget that."

So he makes it very clear that he could demand and probably get a mistrial.

"But we have to be careful what we ask for, Katherine. The odds for conviction go down considerably in a retrial," he says.

"And if you don't ask for a mistrial?"

"Then I'm sure the defense will rest. After closing statements, it will be in the hands of the jury. At this point it's irrelevant whether your ex-husband faked a heart attack or not—the jury won't be told either way. All they'll know is what they saw. Could it influence them? Sure. Could it make them ignore all the evidence? I would sincerely hope not."

Then he tosses in the monkey wrench, the *x* factor, and explains why he wants to make sure I fully understand all the ramifications of *my* decision.

Money.

"The risk of proceeding, of course, goes beyond Carlyle's being acquitted. He'll sue you for defamation of character, claiming irreparable harm to his law career. He'll probably win, too. The only question would be how much money he could extract from you."

Heath looks at me from behind his tidy desk. He works as he dresses: neatly. I can tell he's expecting me to ask questions, really mull things over.

Screw that, though.

Screw Peter.

"I'm alive. Try as he certainly did, that's the one thing Peter couldn't *extract* from me," I say. "As far as another trial goes, there's not enough money in the world to make me go through this again. In other words, whatever I might have to pay Peter, it would be a bargain. I don't care about the money."

"Are you sure, Katherine?" asks Heath. "Sometimes in the heat of things people make snap decisions they later regret."

I don't hesitate. Not for a moment. "Yes, I'm sure. *No regrets.*"

Chapter 118

THE JURY DELIBERATED for three long days, and the wait was nearly impossible for our family. On Friday afternoon at a quarter to five, the foreman informed Judge Barnett with a folded note that they had reached a unanimous verdict. Apparently justice had weekend plans.

"What do you think, Mom?" asks Ernie on our way to the courthouse. I'd told him that the only way he could attend the verdict was if it somehow occurred after school.

Sure enough . . .

"I think I have no idea, that's what I think," I tell him in the back of our speeding cab.

I'm serious—I really don't know what to expect. I've got no gut feeling about the outcome and whether it will have any connection to justice as I see it.

Neither does Nolan Heath. "It makes me laugh when those pundits on TV predict a verdict based on how long the jury was out," he tells me on the phone. "Truth is, they don't know squat, and neither do I."

Ernie and I take our seats up front in the courtroom. I'm amazed at the buzz in the air. It's electric.

Only when Judge Barnett appears do things settle down. Assuming his perch on the bench, he grabs his favorite gavel and bangs the gallery into silence.

With the slightest of nods he instructs the court clerk to let in the jury.

As they shuffle to their assigned seats, I do something I haven't done the entire trial. I steal a glance over at Peter. He was conveniently absent during the closing arguments, the implication being that he was recuperating from his apparent heart attack.

Surprise, surprise—he's well enough to be on hand *after* the jury's made its decision.

There's a part of all this that still feels like an out-of-body experience to me. I mean, how did it happen? How did I get here?

How could I have been so stupid as to fall in love with handsome and charming and very evil Peter Carlyle? He's a murderer, for God's sake.

One of these days I'm sure I'll stop beating myself up over it. Nothing that a few dozen sessions in Mona's office can't fix, right?

"Has the jury reached a verdict?" asks Judge Barnett. Talk about the ultimate rhetorical question.

The jury foreman stands up slowly. Should that tell me anything? "Yes, we have, Your Honor."

The court clerk delivers the verdict to Judge Barnett. The man must be one hell of a poker player, because his face gives absolutely nothing away as he reads it to himself.

Then he nods at the foreman—a CPA, I'm told. He looks nervous. Not as nervous as I am, though. Not as nervous as Peter, I hope.

I take Ernie's hand and squeeze it hard. *Here we go. Get him — take down Peter!*

"In the case of the State of New York versus Peter James Carlyle..."

Chapter 119

JUDGE BARNETT'S COURTROOM explodes with one giant gasp and Nolan Heath reaches out for me. Meanwhile, I'm hugging Ernie—for all the wrong reasons.

Gordon Knowles is pumping fists with the rest of his defense team, then he turns to Peter and plasters him with a hug. Just watching the two of them makes me sick. I'm also numb.

"I'm sorry, Mom," says Ernie. "It's not right. He tried to kill us."

I barely hear him. All I want to do is keep holding him tightly.

So this is it? This is how it ends? Peter gets away with it. He killed Jake, and he tried to kill the rest of us.

That's all I can think.

Meanwhile, Ernie lets go of me.

Sidestepping out into the aisle, he walks straight up to Peter. He taps him on the back. What is he doing? As Peter turns around, little Ernie winds up his right leg and kicks him hard in the groin. Good!

And just like that, I'm no longer numb. I feel everything. But most of all . . . *I feel fine.* Better, anyway. I almost start to laugh.

Maybe it's watching Peter buckle over, the look of intense pain rippling across his face. Or maybe it's Ernie's look of satisfaction as he turns back to me.

All I know is that compared to what we've been through, today is a drop in the ocean.

This *isn't* it.

This *isn't* how it ends.

Haven't I learned anything?

The boat trip was about a family that needed to come together again. *My* family. And that's just what happened, in ways we never could have imagined.

Nothing will ever change that. The Dunnes are going to be okay. We're a family again, and we've never been stronger, tougher, more together.

Chapter 120

IT TOOK TWO HOURS before the ache from Ernie's kick to the crotch finally subsided. A small price, Peter figured. Especially with the big payday to come.

It came.

Much faster than he thought, too.

In less than a month, Peter went from being an almost-free man with money to being an almost-free man with oodles of money. Once he filed his civil suit, he fully expected an out-of-court settlement. What he didn't expect was that Katherine would roll over so easily—and for so much. Big whoop that he didn't get her entire fortune.

Sixteen million still bought a lot of champagne.

It was time to celebrate.

"C'mon, let's go out and hit the town," said Peter, sitting up in Bailey's bed. The days and nights at the Alex Hotel were over. "I'll take you to any restaurant you want. I can't wait to be out on the town with you."

Bailey snapped the elastic on his boxers, his only stitch of clothing. "I already ordered Chinese, silly. I want my moo shu pork."

Peter shot her a dubious look. "You're still hung up on our being seen together, aren't you? I keep telling you, it's not a problem anymore. I'm innocent. I'm free as a bird. Justice was done in that courtroom, thank God."

"I know, I know. Just give me a little more time with that, okay? I'm not quite ready yet to see my picture splashed on Page Six of the *Post.*"

"I am," said Peter. "Then everyone will know how incredibly beautiful you are—and how lucky I am." He leaned over, stroking her cheek. "Hey, why don't we get out of the city, take a vacation somewhere?

We could leave tomorrow. Dare I suggest the Caribbean?"

"You're forgetting something," said Bailey. "My classes."

"Skip 'em."

"Easy for you to say, Mr. Sixteen- Million-Dollar Man."

"What good is all that money if I have no one to spend it on? Think about it."

"Oooh, I like the sound of that. Maybe a trip is a good idea."

Bailey pressed her naked body tight against Peter. She was about to kiss him when the intercom buzzed. "Moo shu pork!" she declared with a giddy smile, practically leaping up from the sheets.

Bailey wrapped herself in a plush white robe that had been draped over the leather chair by the window. As Peter looked on, he couldn't help reminiscing about the time he had sat in that chair back when Katherine had just left for her trip. How could he ever forget that little dance Bailey had performed for him? And what happened next.

"Do you want to eat in bed?" asked Bailey.

"Sure," said Peter. "And then some."

She walked out of the bedroom grinning

and disappeared around the corner into the living room.

When she returned moments later, however, there was no moo shu pork in her hands.

Instead there was a gun at Bailey's head.

Chapter 121

"GEE, I'M SORRY to barge in like this," said Devoux, his voice dripping with sarcasm. "I hope I'm not interrupting anything."

He nudged the lovely Bailey toward the edge of the bed, the long barrel of his gun's silencer pressed tightly against her right temple. The harder he pressed, the more she cowered in fear and submitted to whatever he wanted.

"For Christ's sake, *what are you doing?*" demanded Peter.

"You and I have some unfinished business, Counselor," said Devoux.

The words trembled out of Bailey's mouth. "Peter, what's going on? Who is this?"

Devoux chuckled. "You mean you haven't told her?"

Peter wanted to play dumb. *Deny! Deny! Deny!* But there was no chance of that now. Devoux wasn't fucking around.

"Honey, I'll explain everything," said Peter, trying to calm Bailey.

"You bet you will," said Devoux. "You can begin by telling me where my money is."

Peter's head snapped back in disbelief. "*Your* money?"

"The back end, Counselor. You should've wired it by now, don't you think? Where is it?"

"What, are you crazy? You're lucky you're getting to keep the down payment. In case you haven't been reading the papers, things didn't go exactly as planned."

With a quick shove, Devoux sent Bailey flying onto the bed. His gun had a new target now—the space right between Peter's eyes. "Yes, and in case you're blind, this really isn't a negotiation," he said. "I'm here for my money."

Peter raised his palms in the air. "Okay,

okay. You can have your money." He nodded at Bailey's laptop, a black MacBook on the desk in the corner. "I can wire it right now."

"Good answer," said Devoux with a satisfied grin. "There's just one little twist. You're going to be wiring a little bit more than what we agreed to."

Peter blinked hard. He couldn't stand feeling this helpless. Or taken. "How much?" he asked.

"Well, let's see—what was that number I read in the papers? Was it sixteen million?"

"Now I know you're crazy," said Peter. "I'd sooner die than give you all the money."

Devoux's grin widened. "I actually believe you, Counselor. That was a risk all along, wasn't it?" He cocked his gun. "That's why it's always good to have a Plan B."

Slowly he swung his arm over to Bailey.

"Oh, please God, no," she begged, retreating to the headboard and hugging it.

"I'm with you, pretty lady," said Devoux.

He turned to Peter. "So how about it, Counselor? A change of heart, perhaps? Or does the pretty girlfriend die?"

Peter looked over at Bailey, the sheer terror in her eyes. *Why had he had to meet her? Why did he have to feel something for her?*

She was trembling, a mess. All because of him.

Fuck!

The jig was up. Absolutely. He had no choice, none whatsoever.

Or did he?

Getting up from the bed, he walked to Bailey's computer. "Easy come, easy go," he said.

He logged onto his bank in the Caymans, entering the code and password for his numbered account. With a few more keystrokes he prepared a transfer of $16 million. Every zero he typed was like a punch to the gut.

He turned around to Devoux. "Okay, where's it going?"

Devoux grabbed Bailey from the bed and practically dragged her to the middle of the room. "Stand right here with her," he told Peter. "You two can fool around if you want to."

With his gun trained on both of them, Devoux chuckled as he went to the desk and started typing. One eye on the screen, the other on Peter and Bailey.

As discreetly as possible, Peter glanced at his platinum Rolex. In his head he was practically counting down the seconds.

Five. Four. Three. Two . . .

Bailey's computer suddenly blared with a loud ringing that startled the hell out of Devoux. Peter had set the alarm on the built-in clock.

Now!

Peter lunged for the gun and knocked it to the floor. Throwing all his weight, he tackled Devoux into the wall. He landed one punch, then another.

Down went Devoux.

But not out.

The two of them had similar builds but not the same training. With a sweep of Peter's legs, Devoux got the upper hand again. Pummeling away at Peter's face, he made the beating outside the Plaza look like two kids tussling in a sandbox. Forget the gun—he was going to kill Peter the old-fashioned way.

Then, out of nowhere, Bailey's voice filled the room, bringing everything to a stop.

"Freeze!" she yelled.

Chapter 122

PETER SIGHED SO DEEPLY that he felt light-headed. Or was that just the lingering sting of Devoux's punches?

Who cares?

All that mattered was that Bailey had the gun now. *Think fast,* he told himself. It wasn't as if they could call the police. He needed a plan in a hurry.

But Devoux already had one. "What are you going to do, sweetheart, shoot me?" he asked, taking a step toward Bailey.

"Yes, that's exactly what she'll do," said Peter.

"No she won't." Devoux took another

step. He was only about six feet away from her, and that was too close.

"Bailey, if he comes any closer, you shoot him. *Just pull that trigger.*"

"She won't do it," said Devoux. "She's not a killer, like you. Are you, Bailey?"

"Don't take another step, do you hear me!" barked Peter.

But that's exactly what Devoux did.

"Do it!" yelled Peter. "SHOOT THE BASTARD NOW!"

Bailey squeezed the trigger hard, her hand as steady as she could manage.

Pffft! came the sound of the bullet through the silencer. It was so quiet Peter almost didn't hear it.

But he felt it.

What the . . . ?

Peter looked down at the small hole in his stomach, the bright blood oozing down over his striped blue boxers. He staggered backward, his legs feeling like rubber. He was trying to keep himself standing.

He was trying to figure out what had just happened. *Had it really happened?*

"Bailey?" he said, gasping for air.

She shook her head, and then she started

to . . . *smile?* "You know, for a good-looking guy, Peter, you sure were a lousy lay."

Devoux slipped his hand inside her robe and reached around her. "Don't give me that shit," he said, grabbing her ass and pulling her close. "I know you enjoyed it with him. Don't beat him up when he's down like that."

Peter watched incredulously as the two of them kissed. It was no peck on the cheek, either. More like tongue-on-tongue tonsil hockey.

Oh God, no. Devoux and Bailey?

Then Peter collapsed to the floor, clutching his stomach, which was starting to ache. The blood was spurting through his fingers. He could barely breathe, and his vision was collapsing at the edges.

Devoux pulled back from Bailey and turned to look at Peter with a wink.

"The things we do for money, huh, Counselor?" said Devoux, all of the irony intended.

"But I—I kept you out of jail. We had a deal."

"Stupid lawyer. You didn't do it for me. It was just another payday for you, just like this is for me. You're a loose end, Peter.

Besides, you deserve to die—you were going to kill all those kids. And your loving wife."

With that, he returned to the computer and completed the transfer of the $16 million. "Ya know, I've never felt better about a job, not once. This is the perfect ending."

All Peter could do was watch and think about dying. His life was draining out of him; he was turning weaker by the second. Soon his body would go into shock.

His mind was already there, wasn't it? *How could this be happening*?

Devoux fucking him over—that he could almost understand. But a girl like Bailey? A law student? She *was* a law student, right?

"Who . . . who are you?" asked Peter, every word a struggle now.

Devoux folded shut the computer. He stood, walked over to Bailey, and took the gun from her hand.

"She's my Plan B," he said. "Every good magician has an assistant, no?"

There was no wink this time, not even a half-smile. Instead he took two steps toward Peter, raising the gun.

"Go to hell!" snarled Peter.

"You first," said Devoux.

He squeezed off two more shots. *Pffft! Pffft!* The first exploded through the center of Peter's forehead, the second went straight through his cold heart. *Pure precision.*

Kneeling down, Devoux grabbed Peter's wrist and felt for a pulse. Not because he thought the lawyer might somehow manage to survive three bullet wounds, but because he wanted to feel him die. Or already dead.

"Hey, nice watch," said Devoux, eyeing Peter's Rolex. He promptly slipped it off the lawyer's wrist and put it in his pocket. *Finders keepers, right?*

"C'mon, baby, we've got a plane to catch," said Bailey.

Devoux stood and blew her a kiss. "I'm afraid you're only half right, sweetheart."

Pffft! Pffft!

And then there were no loose ends at all.

Chapter 123

LESS THAN THIRTY-SIX HOURS LATER, Devoux was strolling along the Champs-Elysées, and everything was sweetness and light, couldn't have been better. The late afternoon sun was beginning to dip from the sky, its light engulfing the Arc de Triomphe with a majestic orange glow. God, he loved Paris.

He breathed it all in, closing his eyes finally. The crisp October air was laced with the smell of fresh bread and coffee from the outdoor cafés. It was positively intoxicating and as familiar as an old friend.

"America is my country but Paris is my

hometown," said Gertrude Stein, famously.

He knew exactly what the old broad meant.

With the money he'd made off Peter Carlyle, he could afford an extended European vacation—to put it mildly—and that's precisely what he had in mind. Besides, too much killing wasn't good for the soul.

Suddenly the voice of a passerby made him stop.

"Est-ce que vous avez l'heure, s'il vous plaît?" she asked.

Yes, as a matter of fact, he knew exactly what time it was. *Always.*

As Devoux pulled back the sleeve on his Prada waxed cotton duster, he barely glanced at the woman who had stopped him. Instead his eyes were trained on his newly acquired platinum Rolex.

I'll give you this, Carlyle, you at least had taste. You knew how to spend a buck.

Devoux finally looked up, about to tell this stranger in his best French that the time was twenty minutes after five.

That's when his mouth froze.

This was no stranger.

"Don't move an inch!" said Agent Ellen Pierce, taking two steps back, with her Glock .40-caliber drawn. "I swear to God I'll shoot you right here and now!"

Of all things, Devoux smiled. "I should've killed you when I had the chance," he said.

"Yeah, life's just full of regrets, huh?" came back Ellen. "And little surprises. Now put your hands behind your head and drop down to your knees. Do it now."

By now passersby were gasping in horror at the sight of Ellen's gun. They were drawing back in hordes, hiding behind trees and cars.

Meanwhile, Devoux wasn't budging.

"I said, *put your hands behind your head and drop to your knees!*" ordered Ellen.

Instead Devoux took a step toward her.

Ellen jabbed her Glock straight at his chest. "LAST WARNING!" she yelled. "TAKE ONE MORE STEP AND YOU'RE DEAD!"

It wasn't just one step that Devoux took. Behind a death-wish laugh, he suddenly lunged for Ellen, his arms extended for her gun.

BLAM!

Ellen pumped a shot into his chest. The crowd of onlookers screamed with fear. Several of them began to run away.

Devoux staggered backward, his legs buckling. But they didn't quite fold.

He should have been flat on his back, dead as disco. Instead the son of a bitch was still standing! *Worse, he was coming for her again! He had a switchblade knife from somewhere.*

BLAM! BLAM!

This time the Mystery Man went down, and he stayed there for good.

Ellen knelt on the pavement and pulled back the left sleeve on his coat. It was amazing what flashing a badge at a hospital nurse could get you.

Namely, Peter Carlyle's watch for a few hours, just enough time to outfit it with a transmitter.

"If at first you don't succeed," Ellen said to herself, "try, try again."

She could hear police sirens in the background. The next few hours would be filled with super-irritating questions from and reports by the French gendarmerie. Then she would probably get suspended by Ian again. Whatever the cost, Ellen knew it was worth it.

When all was said and done, she had indeed "caught a bad guy." A very bad guy, for sure. After that day he tried to kill her in the Bahamas, she'd made a promise to herself. No matter what, she'd get the Mystery Man.

"Don't ever try and kill me, you bastard," she said to the dead man before her.

Epilogue

A PROMISE IS A PROMISE

Chapter 124

OF COURSE, everyone's first thought was that I pulled the trigger on Peter and his supposed girlfriend. I don't know whether I should be insulted or flattered.

It didn't take long for the NYPD to rule me out as a suspect, though. Notwithstanding the fact that I was giving a lecture on heart disease at the 92nd Street Y while the murders took place, the detectives on the scene could tell this was no crime of passion. It was too clean, too neat; the shots were too precise. Whoever did this had killed before, they said. Probably numerous times.

It took two days for the bodies of Peter and the girl to be discovered. It probably would've taken longer if a neighbor had not complained to the super about some alarm clock in the apartment. It had been buzzing nonstop.

When I heard the news, I pretty much felt the same way I did when I first heard the verdict in the courtroom. Numb. No real surprise. I quickly stopped feeling anything for Peter Carlyle. He became dead to me. Now he's dead to everybody.

I guess the only thing I'm still thinking about is the girl. The police told me they found a Nevada driver's license in a bedroom drawer. Her name was Lucy Holt and she'd been arrested twice for prostitution in Las Vegas—not the street corner variety, though. Apparently she was a very high-priced call girl, the kind that fetched top dollar. So what was she doing in New York, living in such a modest apartment? And what was she to Peter?

No one knows, including the apartment's owner, who was illegally subletting it. All he knew was that he was getting paid in cash. Undoubtedly by Peter.

I even called Agent Pierce over at her

DEA office, hoping maybe she had some thoughts. She wasn't there, though. Her assistant mentioned that she was taking a couple of vacation days, something about a trip to Paris. Good for her. After the verdict she had looked pretty ballistic.

Anyway, the police investigation continues, but as far as I'm concerned this whole ordeal is over.

And that means one thing, and one thing only: a promise I made to a few kids, who happen to be mine.

Chapter 125

"I'LL HAVE THE STEAK FOR ONE, medium rare," says Mark to the waiter at Flames Steakhouse near our country house in Chappaqua, one of our favorite places to eat.

"I'll have the same," says Ernie.

"What about the soufflés?" asks Carrie after ordering a filet mignon. "I distinctly recall your promising soufflés, Mom."

"Of course," I say. A promise is a promise.

I order the chicken parm, my personal favorite here. Then I look around the table, happy to have my family together. Before last summer, you couldn't pay Mark and Carrie to come down from school for the weekend. But this was *their* idea, and I know it wasn't just for the steaks.

The waiter leaves and Mark raises his Diet Coke. "Here's to Uncle Jake," he says.

The rest of us raise our glasses.

"To Uncle Jake," I repeat with Carrie.

"To Uncle Jake," says Ernie.

As we all clink glasses, Ernie catches my eye and shoots me a wink. He asked that we keep our secret just that. *Our* secret. I have no problem with it. Carrie and Mark don't need to know, at least not now. I suspect one day when he's older—maybe even after I die—he'll tell them.

"So I've got only one question," I say as we settle back into our comfortable chairs.

The kids all look at me.

"What are we going to do next summer?" I ask. "Any ideas for a good family vacation? Anybody up for a sail?"

About the Authors

JAMES PATTERSON published his first thriller in 1976 and since then has become one of the best-known and best-selling writers of all time, with more than 140 million copies of his books sold worldwide. He is the author of the two most popular detective series of the past decade, featuring Alex Cross and the Women's Murder Club, and he has written numerous other number-one bestsellers. He has won an Edgar Award—the mystery world's highest honor—and his novels *Kiss the Girls* and *Along Came a Spider* were made into feature films starring Morgan Freeman.

His charity, the James Patterson Page-Turner Awards, has given hundreds of thousands of dollars to individuals and groups that promote the excitement of books and reading. He lives in Florida.

HOWARD ROUGHAN is the author of *The Up and Comer, The Promise of a Lie,* and most recently the coauthor, with James Patterson, of *You've Been Warned.* He lives in Connecticut with his wife and son.

THE NOVELS OF JAMES PATTERSON

Featuring Alex Cross

Double Cross
Cross
Mary, Mary
London Bridges
The Big Bad Wolf
Four Blind Mice
Violets Are Blue
Roses Are Red
Pop Goes the Weasel
Cat & Mouse
Jack & Jill
Kiss the Girls
Along Came a Spider

The Women's Murder Club

7th Heaven (with Maxine Paetro)
The 6th Target (with Maxine Paetro)
The 5th Horseman (with Maxine Paetro)
4th of July (with Maxine Paetro)
3rd Degree (with Andrew Gross)
2nd Chance (with Andrew Gross)
1st to Die

The James Patterson Pageturners

The Dangerous Days of Daniel X (with Michael Ledwidge)

The Final Warning: A Maximum Ride Novel

Maximum Ride: Saving the World and Other Extreme Sports

Maximum Ride: School's Out—Forever

Maximum Ride: The Angel Experiment

Other Books

Sail (with Howard Roughan)

Sundays at Tiffany's

You've Been Warned (with Howard Roughan)

The Quickie (with Michael Ledwidge)

Step on a Crack (with Michael Ledwidge)

Judge & Jury (with Andrew Gross)

Beach Road (with Peter de Jonge)

Lifeguard (with Andrew Gross)

Honeymoon (with Howard Roughan)

santaKid

Sam's Letters to Jennifer

The Lake House

The Jester (with Andrew Gross)

The Beach House (with Peter de Jonge)

Suzanne's Diary for Nicholas
Cradle and All
When the Wind Blows
Miracle on the 17th Green (with Peter de Jonge)
Hide & Seek
The Midnight Club
Black Friday (originally published as *Black Market*)
See How They Run (originally published as *The Jericho Commandment*)
Season of the Machete
The Thomas Berryman Number

For more information about James Patterson and his books, visit www.jamespatterson.com.